THE WIDOWS' GUIDE TO FOUL PLAY

AMANDA ASHBY

Storm
PUBLISHING

Ebook ISBN: 978-1-83700-445-4
Paperback ISBN: 978-1-83700-446-1

Cover design: Versha Jones
Cover images: Shutterstock

Published by Storm Publishing.
For further information, visit:
www.stormpublishing.co

ALSO BY AMANDA ASHBY

The Widows' Guide to Murder

The Widows' Guide to Backstabbing

The Widows' Guide to Skulduggery

The Widows' Guide to Last Orders

Domestic thrillers

The Stepmother

The Ex-Wife

I Will Find You

Remember Me?

Romance – adult

Once in a Blue Moon

What Were You Thinking, Paige Taylor?

Falling for the Best Man

Dating the Wrong Mr. Right

You Had Me at Halo

Romance – young adult

How to Kiss Your Enemy

How to Kiss Your Crush

How to Kiss a Bad Boy

The Heartbreak Cure

The Wedding Planner's Baby

Middle Grade – paranormal adventures

Midnight Reynolds and the Phantom Circus

Midnight Reynolds and the Agency of Spectral Protection

Midnight Reynolds and the Spectral Transformer

Wishful Thinking

Under a Spell

Out of Sight

Young Adult – paranormal adventures

Demonosity

Fairy Bad Day

Zombie Queen of Newbury High

ONE

SUNDAY DECEMBER 7

On a good day, Little Shaw was the most picturesque of Lancashire villages, with a narrow canal winding through the centre, straddled by a stone bridge that spilled out onto a charming high street. However, as Ginny Cole hurried along said high street, clutching a bag of half-finished costumes, she had to admit that today had *not* been a good day.

A December breeze cut through her new winter coat and turned her fingers to ice. The weather was almost as frigid as her sister-in-law's voice during their recent phone call. Ginny increased her pace, hurrying past the shop windows full of Christmas displays, but even the seasonal cheer couldn't distract her from Nancy's remonstrations.

What would Eric think about me arguing with his only sibling?

It was a rhetorical question, of course. Not only had Ginny's beloved husband died almost two years ago, but he'd never been a fan of the extravagant Christmases his sister adored so much. This year it was a trip to Reykjavik to see the Northern Lights. Ginny probably would've agreed to go, despite being horrified at the expense, but she'd already signed up to help at the pantomime produced by the local theatre, so had—respectfully—declined.

The news hadn't gone down well, and Nancy had accused Ginny of caring more about helping behind the scenes of *Mother Goose* than spending time with her own family.

It wasn't true. Ginny loved Nancy and her tribe, but she also loved her new life in Little Shaw and had quickly discovered that when it came to village activities, participation was not optional, which explained the principal boy's cape and doublet she'd spent the previous night bedazzling.

She tightened her grip on the bag as the Little Shaw Playhouse came into view.

It was a Georgian two-storey, made from the same local stone seen throughout the area. The building had once belonged to a mill owner before being sold off and broken up into flats. Then in the sixties it was gifted to the village as a theatre and a governance trust was formed to run it.

Light-boxes flanked the doors, displaying the bright posters advertising that *Mother Goose* was coming soon. And there, in font larger than the name of the pantomime itself, was the announcement that the celebrity star was none other than Monica Larkwell, a well-known English actress and host of a famous nineties dating show called *First Kiss*. Well, famous to everyone but Ginny, who had clearly been living under a rock back then.

Ever since the announcement, the good-natured locals had tried to jog her memory by helpfully repeating a selection of catchphrases that Monica was synonymous with. Unfortunately, no matter how many times they said: *Be still, my beating heart* or *Tell Monica all about it,* Ginny was none the wiser. All she knew was that Monica had first appeared in a Little Shaw pantomime thirty years ago, before her career really took off, and was now back for a repeat performance and to celebrate the anniversary.

It had caused a lot of press attention in the local and regional newspapers, which Ginny supposed was the whole point. She turned away from the posters and walked down the side of the building.

The stage door was barely visible, hidden behind a jostling crowd of people. Several of them were wearing floral jackets, which Ginny had learned was Monica's iconic look, while others waved their phones high in the air, waiting to snap a photograph.

Confusion marred her brow. What were they doing there at six pm on a cold Sunday evening? It was like she'd stumbled onto a pop-up nightclub. A tall, familiar figure stood at the door, with a black beret slanted on her silver hair.

At seventy-one, JM was one of the three women who had befriended Ginny when she moved to Little Shaw, lost in the fog of Eric's death. It had been a huge comfort to know that JM, Tuppence and Hen—who were also widows—had found a way to carry on and create new lives for themselves.

'Ah, there's Ginny. You lot, move aside so she can get through.' JM, who was volunteering as stage manager, waved a clipboard in the air. It worked much like a police badge and the crowd moved back. Ginny resisted the urge to smile. On the outside JM was formidable but to her friends and those she cared about she was fiercely protective and incredibly kind.

'It's all right for some. Why can't we come in as well? It's bloody freezing out here,' a man wearing a 'Tell Monica' T-shirt yelled.

'Then go home and come back when we open. Tickets are available on the website and all the money goes to upgrading our backstage area,' JM said. Several people grumbled, but the crowd obediently thinned out as Ginny reached the door.

'What are they doing here?' she asked as JM handed her a sign-in book.

'Trying to sneak in to watch Monica rehearse instead of waiting for our run to begin,' JM retorted in a booming voice directed at the crowd. 'What they don't understand is that most of the cast and crew are volunteers and that the whole reason the board booked Monica to star in the pantomime is so we can raise money. Which means if they want to see her perform, they can come back on Boxing Day for opening night.'

'But that's sold out,' someone complained. 'And the tickets are far too expensive. Why should I pay all that money when I only want to see Monica?'

'That's a question only you and your conscience can answer,' JM said.

'Thanks for nothing,' another woman muttered and slunk away as a man in his mid-thirties stepped forward clutching a basket, his movements fluid like a panther. There was no Monica T-shirt or floral coat. He was dressed in a flamboyant burnt-orange suit with heeled black shoes, and possessed the kind of confidence Ginny could only dream of having.

JM raised a questioning eyebrow. 'Yes?'

'Hello, my queens. This is for Monica. It's her favourite chocolates, champagne, throat lozenges and bath salts. I give them to her before every new show as a good luck charm. I'm Andrew, by the way.'

'I'm sorry, Andrew, you'll need to come back once the show has started.'

Instead of being repelled like the other fans, Andrew raised a shoulder and returned JM's glare, a bemused smile twitching at his lips. 'You're very sweet, but I don't think you understand. This is part of her ritual,' he countered and thrust the basket forward. 'Please be a doll and help me get it to her.'

Ginny's eyes widened, but if JM took offence to being called a *doll* she didn't show it.

'I can try but I'm not making any promises. She's been in her dressing room for most of the day and the few times she has come out, she's been followed by that plaguey documentary crew. As if I don't have enough things to manage. Do you know, I caught them filming my feet at lunchtime?'

At the mention of the documentary crew, Andrew struck a dramatic pose that reminded Ginny of a movie poster. 'Put in a good word for me, will you? I've been following Monica for years and worship the ground she walks on. I'm the perfect person to represent her Larks, as I've been telling the director. If you need to get in touch with me, I'm staying at Holly Farm Bed and Breakfast.'

'I'll pass on the message,' JM said and gave him a dismissive flick of her head.

'You're an angel. Ta-ta, bye.' Andrew blew them both a kiss and waggled the tops of his fingertips in lieu of a wave, then disappeared towards the front of the building.

JM turned to Ginny. 'It's been like this all afternoon. They call themselves the Larks, but I think it should be the Barks because they're all barking mad. One chap drove from Hull to see her *and* he brought flowers. Even I know that's bad luck, and so I told him.'

'The Larks?' Ginny frowned. 'Is that short for Larkwell?'

'Yes, that's it. They're Monica's superfans,' JM clarified.

'Oh.' Ginny blinked. She supposed it made sense. 'Is it true that opening night has already sold out?'

'Yes, isn't it marvellous? And we've had to add on more meet and greets. At this rate the revenue they'll earn will be enough to pay for the maintenance they've planned.'

Ginny was pleased, and it made her feel better about her decision to stay and help rather than join Nancy for Christmas. Perhaps her sister-in-law would relent when she knew how much money the pantomime had raised?

The stage door opened and a short man with wispy brown hair brushed across his scalp stepped out. He was in his sixties and was wearing a brown shirt and trousers. It was Arnold Connell.

Ginny wrinkled her nose, unsure how to greet him.

They'd never been officially introduced but she'd often seen him walking a black poodle outside the small library that Ginny managed, while waiting for his wife Cleo to finish her volunteer shifts there. It had always surprised Ginny that her very chatty volunteer hardly ever referred to her husband—even when he was just yards away with the dog—apart from mentioning his habit of tracking dirt and mud into the house after she had vacuumed.

Yet, she could hardly ignore him. His own face grimaced and she wondered if he was caught in the same conundrum. Silence wove around them and Ginny realised it was up to her to break the invisible barrier that would move them from familiar strangers to casual acquaintances.

'Hello, Arnold.' She offered him up a bright smile. He gave an awkward nod, suggesting he struggled in social situations. It would explain why he never came inside the library.

'Mrs Cole,' he said and turned to JM. 'Cleo sent me to mind the door. She's worried you'll miss the rehearsal.'

'Cleo would do well to worry more about learning her lines and less about me,' JM said in a stern voice and glanced at her watch. Then she studied Arnold. 'Are you sure you're up to the job? Some of them are cunning. I've managed to get rid of the crowd, but there might be more. The only people allowed through are on this list. And they must sign in and out. Are we clear?'

'No unauthorised people will get through on my watch,' he replied stoically as his life partner appeared beside him, her brow knitted in annoyance.

'Arnold, did you give JM my message? Why is she out here?' Cleo snapped.

She was the same height as her husband, but her stance was more imposing, as was the mulish set of her jaw. It appeared Cleo was the driving force in the relationship. Then again, judging by the loving way Arnold was looking at his wife, this seemed to suit him very well.

'*She* has been dealing with the fans,' JM retorted with a chilling emphasis on the first word. 'And I'm giving Arnold some last-minute instructions.'

'I don't want Monica to think we're lacking in manners,' Cleo retorted, her interest switching to the bag by Ginny's feet.

'Oh, hello. Do you have my queen outfit ready? I hope Hen isn't going to use calico instead of silk.'

'She has some lovely fabric selected and should start cutting it out tomorrow,' Ginny assured her.

'Tomorrow?' Cleo scowled. 'Isn't that leaving it a bit late?'

'It'll be ready in time for the dress rehearsal.' JM handed the clipboard to Arnold and readjusted the gift basket in her hands. 'Come on, then. Let's go, Cleo.'

Once they were gone, Arnold gave Ginny an apologetic smile. 'Cleo's very excited to be playing the Queen of Gooseland. She's a huge Monica Larkwell fan. She has ten lines of dialogue with her.'

'It's a wonderful opportunity,' Ginny said supportively, well-used to how Cleo acted when she was excited, upset or distracted. 'Are you sure you'll be okay out here?'

'Oh yes.' Arnold tightened his grip on the clipboard. 'Don't you worry about me. I won't hold you up from making the costumes. Sign here, and then you can go in.'

Ginny, who was starting to lose circulation in her toes thanks to the weather, wrote down her name and the time then stepped inside. Still, it was nice to finally be on nodding terms with Cleo's elusive husband.

The backstage area was in a state of disrepair, and she walked past the wing of dressing rooms down a gloomy corridor cluttered with years of unwanted props.

No wonder the board of trustees were so desperate to raise the money to maintain it.

The dark passages were empty of actors and volunteers alike. Ginny could only assume that they were either on the stage taking part in the rehearsal or they had slipped away to watch it.

After one last turn, she reached the costume room. Racks of clothing ran down one side while industrial sewing machines, rolls of fabric and a cutting table took up the rest of the space.

Hen was seated at a machine, almost hidden behind a cloud of purple feathers. When Ginny had left her yesterday, she had been working on Prissy's goose costume, and it clearly wasn't finished.

'I hope you didn't stay here too late last night,' Ginny said by way of greeting.

'Not *too* late.' Hen got to her feet and blew several feathers out of her mouth. She was of a medium height with wide brown eyes and a preference for florals and amazing handknitted cardigans. 'Maybe I was a bit ambitious to redo the entire costume when there was a perfectly good one already here, but we wanted to create a proper headpiece instead of merely using a fake beak. What do you think?'

She pointed to a large goose head on the workbench. At that moment Tuppence appeared, grasping a hot glue gun. As usual she was wearing a pair of comfortable overalls and a brightly coloured jumper underneath, while her wild grey curls sprang out in all directions. 'It's a beauty, isn't it? I used papier mâché to build the base and then we glued all the feathers on. There are eyeholes and everything.'

'It's lovely.' Ginny admired it before taking out the garments she'd been working on. 'I hope these are okay. I can change them if you want me to.'

The regular volunteer wardrobe master, Ants Mancini, had been called away on a family emergency, and asked Hen to step into the role, which had left her friend both terrified and excited. Ginny couldn't blame her and was determined to help.

Hen studied them carefully and gave Ginny a grateful smile. 'They're fabulous. Thank you so much. Do you mind working on the cape lining tonight?'

'Of course. Whatever you need,' Ginny said then glanced at the several mocked-up toiles that were hanging against the wall. Hen had spent the last week working on them and had planned to measure Monica today. 'But if you want help on the dresses, let me know.'

Hen's smile faded. 'Monica was due for a fitting at lunchtime but never showed. The documentary crew didn't like the lighting, so advised her to wait until later tonight when they could set it up properly.'

'That's show business for you—' Tuppence was cut off by a blood-curdling scream that rang out from the front of the playhouse. It was followed by a cacophony of agitated voices.

Were people arguing?

'Do you think that's part of the rehearsal?' Hen's brow wrinkled.

'I don't remember seeing it in the script,' Tuppence said. 'Should we go out there?'

Ginny couldn't recall there being any scene that would necessitate this level of noise. Her skin prickled as the screaming increased.

'Yes, I think we'd better find out what's going on.'

TWO

SUNDAY DECEMBER 7

It wasn't hard for Ginny and her friends to navigate the corridors through to the main stage. All they had to do was follow the noise, which hit fever pitch as they reached the heavy velvet curtains that hid the backstage and technical areas from the audience. The curtains twitched and a distraught Cleo stumbled through the velvet, her face pale as a ghost. She was closely followed by Andrea, another library volunteer, and Cleo's regular sidekick.

At the sight of the tears streaming down Cleo's face, Ginny's jaw dropped. 'What's happened? Is everything okay?'

'Okay? I'm never going to be okay again. She's sexist, heightist... and queen-ist. I wish she'd never come to Little Shaw,' Cleo wailed and ran down the corridor.

'She's had devastating news.' Andrea pointed to the heavy curtains that were adding to the gloom backstage. 'Thanks to *that* woman.'

'What woman?' Ginny stared at the burgundy velvet fabric that fell in a puddle onto the floor, then thought through Cleo's words. 'You don't mean Monica Larkwell, do you?'

'That's exactly who I mean. However, to stand by Cleo through this dreadful ordeal, I have taken a solemn vow to never mention *her* name again,' Andrea said in a dramatic voice then peered down at her T-shirt which said, *Hail, Queen Monica.* Andrea quickly put her hand across the damning slogan in solidarity.

'What happened?' Hen asked.

'I bet I know what it is,' Tuppence interjected. 'Did Cleo forget her lines? It's easy enough to get stage fright. Or celebrity paralysis, but I'm sure she'll be fine. She needs to breathe through it. Or picture everyone naked.'

'I don't think she should picture Reverend Audrey naked. He's always part of the ensemble cast, but is very traditional and quite a stickler for good manners,' Hen countered. 'Though I suppose once you turn eighty, you've earned the right to stickle-ness.'

'That's a good point.' Tuppence nodded, as if much struck. 'He very well might find it unseemly. In that case I advise Cleo to picture everyone *but* Reverend Audrey naked. It's sure to do the trick.'

'Do the trick?' Andrea gave them an astonished glare. 'This has nothing to do with stage fright *or* naked clergy-people. It's about poor Cleo being demoted.'

Demoted?

'You mean she's no longer playing the Queen of Gooseland? But how is that possible? She auditioned for it and won the part.' Ginny's brows drew together. Over the last two weeks Cleo had re-enacted her entire audition daily to any library patrons who fell into her orbit.

'That's correct. Hazel said it would be an honour to direct someone with Cleo's talents. But then'—again Andrea's gaze fell on the heavy velvet curtain and what lay beyond—'*she* decided Cleo was too short for the role and insisted that Malcolm Mathers take the part. She said it was more fitting to the panto tradition to have a man playing the queen. Now poor Cleo is forced to play a—a goblin.' The last words were choked out.

'But surely Monica can't do that,' Tuppence spluttered.

'Oh, can't she just? Tell that to Cleo... and to Tyrone Barry who is now playing a tree—though in Tyrone's case, there's no denying it makes sense. His delivery was very wooden,' Andrea said before collecting herself. 'I need to support Cleo in her hour of need.' She gave them an anguished look and hurried away, her arm still clamped across her T-shirt.

Ginny rubbed her chin, Hen blinked and Tuppence made a low whistling noise as angry voices once again rose from the other side of the heavy curtain.

Whatever was happening wasn't over.

Tuppence and Hen stepped closer, and Ginny could feel herself being pushed forward. She gulped and fumbled with the curtain until she found the break. Then she stepped through.

Centre stage, standing on a green cross, was a tall woman wearing white silk trousers and a matching blouse, along with bright red lipstick. Her complexion was flawless though her expression was tight, as if she couldn't easily move her brows. Still, Ginny recognised her from the posters plastered around town.

Monica Larkwell.

But while seeing her made sense, not much else did. Circled around her was a group of actors all trying to speak at once. Monica stood unflinching, as if bored by their conversation. To add to the strange scenario, a man with a camera mounted on his shoulder was running around them, stepping closer and then jumping back. A second man with a nose ring and baggy trousers was busy talking into his phone.

He was Asian and his black hair had been dyed blond, while a large pair of headphones hung around his neck. As he spoke, he used his spare hand to urgently gesture at the cameraman, pointing at various spots around the stage.

It had to be the documentary maker, and his gleaming eyes suggested he was delighted with the drama.

Volunteer crew members were scattered throughout the

stalls, all looking on with keen interest. Some of them had their phones held up to film it.

'Whatever could be happening?' Hen said in a fretful voice, her fingers clutching together, no doubt missing the knitting needles that were usually close to hand. 'Why is that cameraman filming?'

'I wonder if they've purposely created chaos to make their documentary more exciting?' Tuppence frowned. 'I've heard that's a thing on reality TV. How interesting to get to see it first-hand. I'd like to know what they've been whispering into everyone's ears.'

Ginny scanned the stage. 'Where's JM? I can't imagine her letting anyone argue.'

'There she is.' Hen pointed to the far side where JM was stepping out from behind the curtain, her commanding presence filling the stage.

'She does *not* look happy. This is about to get interesting,' Tuppence added as JM put her fingers into her mouth and a sharp whistle rang out.

It had the immediate effect of silencing everyone. JM lost no time in using her arms to break the circle and disperse the various actors away from Monica. They scattered, except for a woman in her sixties with a dynamic purple buzz cut, who stepped closer to the famous actress.

It was Hazel Holdsworth, the director.

Ginny had met her at enough local events to know the director loved large smock dresses that hung around her like a tent, and also sported a collection of colourfully framed glasses. Today the orange and pink fabric of the dress perfectly matched the spots on her frames. However, the bright colours were at odds with the pained expression on Hazel's face.

'Monica, can we have a word backstage, please?' Hazel said.

Monica's stony expression didn't change. 'Why? I've got nothing to hide.'

Hazel grimaced, as if trying to get her emotions under control. 'As you please. Can you explain what the problem is?'

'I'll tell you what the problem is. I seem to have stumbled into amateur hour,' the actress replied. Her voice was deep, rich, and very commanding. Suddenly Ginny could understand why she'd had such a long and varied career. 'I find some of the casting unacceptable.'

'That's not your place,' Hazel protested.

Monica shrugged. 'You brought me here for a reason. But if you want to keep a local happy rather than someone with over thirty years of experience, then that's on you. As for this ridiculous dance... I will *not* be performing it.'

Hazel's jaw muscles flickered, but before she could answer, a lovely-looking woman somewhere in her early forties stepped forward, clutching at a sheaf of notes. She had ebony skin, thick hair, and moved with the grace of a dancer.

'It's *not* ridiculous,' the woman protested. 'It's a TikTok dance called the Griddy and our audience will love it. Once you try it for yourself, you'll see what I mean. There's a good chance we can go viral.'

'That's Desiree Northam. She's helped with the choreography and is an understudy for a couple of roles,' Tuppence whispered.

'Go viral?' Monica raised one arched eyebrow, her voice glacially cold. 'My dear, I hardly need to rely on a stupid dance to capture attention.'

Ginny couldn't help but agree with Monica. She herself had struggled through too many exercise classes to know the dread of learning any kind of dance routine.

'I did *not* sign up to be treated like this.' Monica made a huffing noise and threw her script onto the floor, much to the delight of the cameraman who scuttled forward. 'I will be taking the rest of the evening off, and I hope that tomorrow you'll have come to your senses.'

Then without another word she flounced away, ignoring the

man with the phone's pleas to face the camera so they could get another angle of her face.

As soon as Monica swept through the curtains, the cast and crew surrounded Hazel, all speaking at once while JM pulled her phone out of her pocket and held it up to her ear.

'Oh no. What a disaster,' Hen said. 'Poor JM. I wonder if she's calling the board.'

'I should think so. It was their decision to bring Monica in,' Tuppence said and glanced at her watch. 'I suppose we should leave them to it and get back to work. I have to finish Prissy's neck feathers.'

'And I can get the cape lined,' Ginny said, looking at the green cross on the stage where Monica had been standing. 'Somehow I don't think she'll be coming in for her fitting tonight.'

'No, I suppose not,' Hen said then let out a pained sigh. 'And if Cleo's no longer the Queen of Gooseland it means she'll need a goblin costume. Should we wait for JM?'

But at that moment their friend made several complicated hand-signals which Ginny took to mean she would join them in the costume room.

'Let's go,' Ginny said in a soft voice, pleased to leave the chaos of the stage behind. As the arguing continued, she could almost feel sorry for everyone's shattered illusions. Then she thought of the fans lined up at the stage door, so eager to meet Monica Larkwell. It proved that no good could come from meeting your idols.

Especially when your idols were in show business.

THREE

SUNDAY DECEMBER 7

It was some time before JM could join them, but, finally, she walked into the costume room, carrying a tray with four mugs and a large teapot. Ginny couldn't help but be pleased. She'd tried to go into the kitchen an hour ago with the hope of making hot drinks, but Hazel had been having a private conversation with several of the distraught actors, and Ginny hadn't wanted to intrude.

'How's it going?' Hen abandoned the striped pantaloons she had been working on. 'We've been ever so worried about everyone.'

'Monica definitely caused chaos. I thought I was the only one ruffling feathers.' Tuppence plucked another purple feather out of her curls. She'd finished the goose costume and Hen had moved it through to a separate room so it wouldn't get damaged, but she continued to find the feathers everywhere.

'I wish that were true.' JM sighed, her usual unflagging spirits quite missing. 'Two of the board members arrived and spoke with Hazel, before leaving again. The rest of the cast and crew have also gone home.'

'What do you think the outcome will be? Will the board ask Monica to leave?'

'That's what Hazel wants. Apparently, she was against the decision to bring Monica on, but the ticket sales have been so good, and they don't want to jeopardise them, so I suspect the board will concede to Monica's wishes and we'll muddle on as best we can,' JM said then grimaced. 'Muddle is not a word I've ever identified with.'

'Perhaps once Monica's had a good night's sleep things will get better? For all we know she might have been tired from her trip,' Ginny said.

'What trip?' Tuppence raised an eyebrow. 'She lives in Cheshire, so she isn't even staying in Little Shaw. It's a one-hour drive at the most.'

'Oh, well, sometimes the traffic can be bad,' Hen, who never liked to think the worst of people, offered.

'And sometimes it can be excellent,' JM retorted and sat down in a chair. 'I wish the board had listened to Hazel.'

'Is there a reason Hazel didn't want Monica to do the show?' Ginny asked out of curiosity as she poured out four cups, added milk and passed them around.

'Oh yes.' Tuppence nodded her head. 'According to some of the cast, when Monica was here thirty years ago, she didn't just play the principal girl... she also *did* the principal boy.'

'An affair?' Ginny's brow shot up.

'That's right,' Hen agreed. 'Though it was never proved. But it was a terrible thing. You see, the role of Jack was being played by Hazel's husband, Alan. They broke up not long after and Alan died ten years ago, so I suppose it's water under the bridge. But it must be strange for Hazel to have to work with the woman who ruined her marriage.'

'It's unfair to blame it purely on Monica,' JM said in a stern voice, before relenting. 'However, I do acknowledge the extra tension isn't helping matters. I had no idea theatre folks were so temperamental.'

'You haven't seen anything yet,' Tuppence said. 'I've volunteered on loads of productions doing scenery, and actors are very mercurial. I once painted a peacock into a garden scene and the leading lady had such a tantrum over it. Apparently, the feathers are considered bad luck because the pattern looks like an eye. An *evil* eye. I had to redo it as a waterfowl.'

'Oh, I remember that. Such a pity. It was a jolly good peacock.' Hen let out a sigh and took a sip of tea. Then she looked at the clock on the wall. 'My, it's almost ten-thirty and poor Ginny has to work tomorrow.'

'At least I'm familiar with the ebb and flow of the library, but in the theatre one never knows what's going to happen next,' Ginny said.

'You can say that again.' JM drained her tea and got to her feet. 'Let's call it a night. I have the keys.'

Tuppence swallowed a yawn and shrugged on her winter coat. Ginny quickly gathered up the teacups, tidied her workspace and followed her friends through the twisting corridors.

'If you three go out, I'll set the security alarms and turn everything off,' JM announced and waited for Ginny and her friends to step into the night. The weather hadn't improved and the moon was concealed by dull clouds, while icy gusts swept past them.

An exterior light glowed from the side wall as a shadowy figure stepped forward.

Ginny jumped back, almost crashing into her friends.

'Sorry, I didn't mean to startle you.' The voice was familiar. It was Monica Larkwell's fan, Andrew. His orange suit was half buried under a dramatic faux fur coat and a camera bag was hanging from his shoulder.

'Goodness, what are you doing out here?' Hen said, clearly worried about anyone standing in such nasty weather.

'Don't tell me this is about the basket?' JM said from the doorway. 'Because I left it in Monica's dressing room, and if you've waited all night to discover that, then more fool you.'

'I never doubted you,' Andrew said with a wink, though some of the lightness had left his smile. Not that Ginny could blame him. If he'd been there all evening, he must be freezing. 'I'm here to walk Monica to her car.'

'Monica?' Tuppence frowned and shook her head. 'She left hours ago.'

'What?' His shoulders stiffened under the enormous coat. 'I knew I shouldn't have deserted my post to go to the toilet. What a nuisance.'

'If that's what you want to call it,' JM retorted, clearly still exasperated at the actress's earlier tantrum. Then she flicked off the lights and closed the door.

Andrew's face drained of colour. 'What the hell are you doing?'

'Excuse me?' JM demanded, eyes flashing even in the gloom.

'I will not,' Andrew retorted, his attitude returning in full. 'Why did you turn off the lights?'

'Why wouldn't I?' JM challenged.

'Because it's bad luck.' He clicked his fingers. 'You need to leave a ghost light on, or something dreadful will happen.'

'Is that so?' JM's tone was frosty. 'Well, considering the chaos your beloved Monica has caused, I think "something dreadful" has already happened.'

'Monica's unwavering in her demands for excellence,' Andrew said simply, not showing surprise to hear his idol spoken about in such a way. 'But I can assure you that if you want to keep her happy, you *will* need to leave on a light.'

'Who says I want to keep her happy?' JM replied as another gust of chilly wind ran down the alley.

Hen coughed tentatively. 'What if we put the corridor light on?'

'It's a master switch, which means the entire place will light up. It's a complete waste of electricity.' JM's brow puckered in a frown. 'I have no time for ghost lights, or any other superstitions.'

'That's what they said in Cardiff before the fated production of *Moby Dick*,' Andrew retorted.

'What happened?' Hen's eyes filled with worry. 'I hope it wasn't anything dreadful.'

'I suppose that depends on what your definition of dreadful is.' Andrew inspected his nails with a dismissive shrug before grinning and leaning forward. 'I heard that they refused to leave a ghost light on and then on opening night, the entire stage was besieged by rats. They spilled out of a huge wooden barrel, which had been filled with fish. Apparently, they brought them in to make it appear realistic.'

'It certainly sounds realistic.' Hen shuddered.

'I'm still not clear what it was that they brought in? Was it the fish or the rats?' Tuppence frowned.

'The fish,' Andrew clarified. 'I think it was herrings. Anyway, the rats must have got into the barrel overnight, and by the time the play started, they'd slept off their feast and were ready for round two.'

Tuppence whistled. 'All because they didn't leave a ghost light on?'

'Exactly,' Andrew agreed.

Ginny stepped towards the door. 'What if I pop into the nearest dressing room and turn a single light on. Is that enough?'

'Yes, that's acceptable,' Andrew agreed and peered at JM, clearly understanding that she held the final decision.

She let out an irritated sigh. 'Oh, fine. Though I don't hold with it. However, the sooner this night is over, the better. I'm all out of patience with the theatre.' She deftly unlocked the doors and tapped in the security code. She flicked on the lights and stared at the closest door, which said: *Monica Larkwell*. 'I have a good mind to wash my hands of the whole production.'

'Oh no. You can't do that. It's been a long night, that's all,' Hen fretted, coming to JM's side and giving her a hug. 'You'll see, everything will be better tomorrow.'

'Thank you,' JM relented in a gruff voice. 'We'll leave Monica's light on. And while I don't believe she'll thank you for it, if you're right, at least she'll know the tradition has been maintained, and we can forget about this nonsense once and for all.'

'Wonderful.' Andrew clapped his hands together and moved towards the door, clearly eager to get a little bit closer to his idol, even if it was vicariously through a dressing room. 'This is a dream come true.'

Ginny wished she could share his excitement, but all she wanted to do was go home and sleep. She purposefully twisted the door handle. Part of her expected it to be locked and was already mentally planning to try the next dressing room along, but the handle turned easily and she stepped inside, feeling around for the light switch.

The main light didn't come on, but the fluorescent bulbs around the makeup mirror flickered to life, illuminating the room.

Ginny gasped as the floor transformed into a sea of tiny gleaming lights, much like the Christmas displays she had passed earlier. *No. Wait.*

They weren't lights, but, rather, scattered fragments of cut glass.

Lying in the middle of the floor were the remains of an ornamental chandelier. Underneath them was a crumpled figure in white silk trousers and matching blouse.

Monica Larkwell.

FOUR

SUNDAY DECEMBER 7

'No, no, no.' Andrew let out a piercing scream and rushed forward—a blur in orange and faux fur. Ginny quickly put up her arm to hold him back. 'What are you doing? We have to help.'

'I agree.' Ginny focused on Monica's limp body. 'But if she's alive, we need to be careful how we move her. It's impossible to see what's happened.'

Tuppence switched on two freestanding lights in the corner, that the documentary crew had most likely left, and the room brightened.

Andrew tried to step forward again, but this time it was JM who stopped him. 'Ginny's right, you need to stay back,' she said in a stern voice, which seemed to break through his panic. She softened her tone. 'We might not know much about ghost lights, but we know plenty about mysterious goings-on.'

'That we do,' Tuppence agreed, surveying the scene. 'And this is most definitely mysterious.'

'I'll call the ambulance,' Hen said. 'I do hope she's okay.'

So do I. Ginny swallowed and stepped closer to the half-hidden body. Broken glass crunched under her feet as she tentatively lowered herself to inspect Monica's slender arm. The bluish-purple tinge was not promising.

Unfortunately, JM was right when it came to how much they knew about mysterious goings-on. And while Ginny wasn't sure how it had happened, ever since she'd moved to Little Shaw she and her friends had managed to get muddled up in far too many murders.

Please don't let this be another one.

She pressed her fingers onto Monica's wrist to search for any signs of life, trying to ignore how cold the skin was. Swallowing, Ginny desperately waited for the familiar thump of a pulse, but after a minute of silence she put Monica's limp wrist back down.

There was nothing.

She couldn't help but think of Monica's catchphrase. *Be still, my beating heart.*

A shiver went through her as she stared at the unmoving body. Was Monica really dead? But how? It was too dreadful that such a terrible accident would befall the woman, regardless of how rudely she had acted earlier.

'I-Is she okay?' Hen asked in a cautious voice.

'I can't find a pulse,' Ginny admitted. She'd had enough experience with emergency situations, thanks to managing Eric's surgery for thirty years, but it didn't make this any easier. A heaviness filled the room and Ginny turned to her friends. JM stood statue still, the only sign of shock the shudder that went through her rigid body. Next to her, Tuppence's endless energy seemed to desert her as she stared at the unmoving Monica. Ginny could almost imagine her friend, a talented artist, was trying to capture the last image of the actress. While Hen began to shake, tears streaming down her face.

The collective silence was broken by Andrew. He let out a sob and turned wildly to JM. 'You said this place needed maintenance, but you didn't mention it was a death trap. This is your fault.'

It snapped JM from her trance but before she could reply,

Tuppence turned on him. 'Well, just hang on there a moment. You can't blame JM. How's she meant to stop a chandelier from falling onto someone?'

'It's a health and safety issue.' Andrew continued to cry. 'And Monica's paid the price.'

Hen brushed away her tears and turned to him. 'You don't mean that.'

'Yes, I do. I warned you what would happen if you didn't leave a ghost light on.'

Ginny swallowed down her own shock and pointed to Monica's mottled blue skin. 'This happened at least an hour ago. See how livor mortis is setting in?'

'An hour ago? We were in the costume room, then,' Hen said. 'With the lights on.'

'So, you have no right to blame JM.' Tuppence bristled.

'It's okay. I know he's upset.' JM's face was drained of colour. 'And he does have a point.'

'What do you mean?' Hen frowned.

'This place does have health and safety issues.'

Ginny's skin prickled. Of course it wasn't JM's fault, but if it was an accident, then who was liable? The theatre? The trustees? The maintenance workers?

What a terrible tragedy. Out of habit, she peered around the room, somehow hoping she could get some answers.

Below the makeup mirror was a long dressing table. There were several bathroom bags, but none of the usual detritus one might expect to see. Was that because Monica had only just arrived, or because she'd been packing up? At the far end of the table was the basket that Andrew had given JM. A small bottle of champagne had been opened, and next to it was an empty crystal flute. A large, ornate floor-length mirror leaned against the other wall, and by the door was a clothing rack with what looked like a real fur coat hanging from it.

Ginny swallowed her distaste at the body and the coat, and studied the ceiling. However, instead of ripped electrical cords, to suggest the chandelier had fallen, she saw that the cable had been neatly sliced through.

Oh dear.

So much for thinking it was an accident. For whatever reason, it looked as though someone had cut the cable holding the chandelier, so that it had landed on Monica and—Ginny had to assume—killed her.

'Ginny's mouth is an O-shape. I think she's figured something out,' Tuppence declared.

'Do tell us,' Hen urged.

'I could be wrong,' Ginny said, self-consciously flexing her jaw into another position. 'But look at the ceiling. I'm sure that cable has been cut.'

'Cut?' Andrew abruptly stopped crying. 'What are you saying?'

'I'm sorry, Andrew, but I think that Monica's death might not have been an accident. It looks like she's met with foul play.' Ginny frowned.

'That's dreadful.' Hen's hand flew to her mouth.

Yes, it is.

Ginny swallowed. She'd need to let Detective Inspector James Wallace know. He was also her next-door neighbour and after getting off to a rocky start, she now considered him a friend. Though how long that would last once he knew that Ginny had stumbled onto yet another dead body, was anyone's guess. Still, that was a worry for another day.

She retrieved her phone. There was no answer so she followed it up with a short text message—after recently learning that grammatically correct texts were wasted on him. There was no reply but two little ticks let her know he'd received it. A wave of nerves hit her. His silence was even worse than his temper.

'Who did you message?' Andrew demanded. 'I hope you're not contacting the press.'

'The press? Ginny would never do that,' Hen assured him. 'I think she was calling Wallace. He's a detective and ever so good.'

'That's right. Sorry to give you a fright,' Ginny said and then peered around the room to where they were all standing, the broken shards of crystal now trampled on, and moved from their original positions. Wincing, she turned back to them. 'We should probably wait for them in another room.'

'And leave Monica alone?' Andrew shuddered.

'Just to keep the crime scene safe,' Tuppence explained. 'Ginny's right. It's very important we don't disturb it more than we already have. So the police can find out who did this to her.'

Andrew let out another wail. 'I can't believe Mother is dead.'

'Mother?' Hen gave him a confused look then hurried over and put her arm around him, trying to support his grief.

'Mother.' He dabbed at his tear-streaked face. 'Monica cared deeply about her fans and encouraged us to think of her as family. She loved us... *and we loved her.*'

'Of course she did,' JM said in a surprisingly patient voice. 'I saw how many of them travelled just for a chance to be near her. But we all need to wait somewhere else until the police get here. It's for the best.'

'JM's right,' Tuppence agreed and took Andrew's other arm. 'Here, let us help you.'

'Okay.' He allowed himself to be led out of the dressing room.

Ginny gave her friends a grateful look as they all left the room and huddled in the corridor. By the door was the clipboard with the list of everyone who'd come into the theatre, including the times they arrived and departed.

Did that mean the killer's name was there?

Her throat tightened at the idea a killer had simply walked in and out through the stage door. Was it someone they knew? More importantly, was it someone Monica knew? Was she scared when it had happened?

The questions crowded Ginny's mind as she turned once more to stare at the unmoving body. It was too awful.

'Andrew, can you think of anyone who would do this?' Hen asked.

'No,' he said then winced. 'Well, there were plenty of online trolls, but they usually stay behind their computers. Don't they?'

'I'm not sure.' Ginny shuddered as the whirr of sirens filled the air. JM hurried to the stage door to open it up as an ambulance pulled up, followed closely by a marked police car.

It was going to be a very long night.

FIVE

MONDAY DECEMBER 8

The following morning, Ginny locked her car and made her way to the Little Shaw library. With its red bricks and high windows, it had once been a Victorian parish school before becoming the heart of the small village. The sight of it usually made her smile, but the combination of the early morning fog and gloom, and the events of last night, made it harder for her to feel happy. If she'd had her way she would've stayed at home with her cat, but knew all too well how quickly the library would fill up with locals wanting to talk about what had happened, along with journalists, curious out-of-towners, and, of course, the regular library patrons who didn't see why their routines should change because someone had been killed.

She'd been shocked the first time it happened, but now she understood the power of people grieving collectively, and if the library could provide that safe space, then it was her job to make sure they were welcome—regardless of how distressing she might find it. As she fumbled with her key, she wasn't surprised to see the lights already on. Connor rented a room in Hen's cottage so she would have told him the news.

'Thought you might need a hand today.' Connor brought the book trolley he'd been pushing to a halt as Ginny stepped through the front door and locked it again. 'You know how this place gets after there's a murder.'

'We don't know it's a murder yet,' Ginny reminded him and tried to push away the terrible memory of Monica's dead body, crushed beneath the chandelier. 'But thank you for coming in. It's very thoughtful.'

'No big deal.' He shrugged.

When she first started at the small but vibrant library, Connor had been on the verge of getting in trouble with the law, communicating in monosyllables, and keeping most of his face hidden behind a tangle of dark hair. But now, along with a haircut and speaking in full sentences, he had gone from a volunteer to becoming the second in charge. And despite him being twenty to her sixty-one, she also considered him a friend.

'Thoughtful? He's as keen as I am to know what really happened,' a second voice said as a skinny man with a wide belly appeared from behind the magazine racks. Like Connor, Slim had gone from being a volunteer to a part-time paid staff member. He was also a reformed thief, but his natural liveliness made him a favourite with everyone.

Unfortunately, it didn't mean Ginny wanted to talk about what she'd seen.

'Speak for yourself,' Connor retorted, giving Slim a sharp glare. 'Mrs C has better things to do than be hounded by us. Besides, she's going to get harassed as soon as the doors open.'

'Yes, it'll become a veritable hotbed of gossip. But don't worry, me and Connor have your back,' Slim said, then gave her a roguish smile. 'So, is it true the Detective Club found the body?'

Ginny sighed and put her bag down on the counter.

She no longer bothered to correct Slim or Connor when they used the silly name, since it only encouraged them. Instead, she went through what had happened, only leaving out the part about the chandelier's electrical cord being cut. She already regretted speculating on it in front of Andrew, and if Detective

Inspector James Wallace wanted it known, he'd go public with the information. Well, she assumed he would, but since he hadn't been forthcoming, it was hard to say.

In fact, when he'd walked into the dressing room last night, Wallace's expression had gone from bewilderment to anger in less than a second, and Ginny had taken an involuntary step back. Swiftly, he'd directed a couple of young PCs to cordon off the area, and instructed Detective Constable Anita Singh to take the official statements while he shrugged on white coveralls over a pair of smart grey trousers and a white ironed shirt.

It had made Ginny wonder if he'd been in the middle of a date.

Her suspicions were confirmed several minutes later when Wallace's lovely girlfriend, Imogen Smith, who was a forensic pathologist, appeared. Her outfit was hidden behind white coveralls, but the makeup and sparkling earrings told their own story.

Ginny didn't see them again as she and her friends gave their statements and were eventually sent home, along with a reminder not to talk to anyone about what had happened. Not that she had any desire to do that: her tiredness was courtesy of the flashbacks that came on every time she'd closed her eyes—of Monica Larkwell's crushed body, the coldness of her blueish-purple skin and the complete lack of a pulse.

Horrible.

'I'm sure we'll find out more today.' Slim picked up several of the national papers that had been delivered. 'Can you believe there's nothing in here?'

'Hasn't stopped people from finding out about it,' Connor said.

'I expect the police will release something today,' Ginny said.

'If they've got time. I heard that the police have called in everyone who was at the playhouse last night to give statements,' Slim said.

'Yeah, about that. Cleo and Andrea texted to say that they won't be in, because they need to go to the station. Which was the other reason I figured I'd better come in, since we'd be down on helpers,' Connor admitted.

Part of his new role was to manage the volunteer library staff, and he received a flurry of text messages and phone calls each day as a result. Not to mention photos of grandchildren, updates on if the doctor thought the cream was working and random pocket dials. But he took it in his stride.

'I thought the police would need to see them,' she agreed, remembering Cleo's hysterical reaction to the news she'd been demoted to a goblin. But Ginny pushed away the thought. She might've been dragged into several murder cases, but this was one that she was happy to leave alone.

She'd learned there was a fine line between helping and hindering, and the last thing she wanted to do was jeopardise anything. And it wasn't officially a murder investigation yet, she reminded herself.

'Since I'm in, I'll finish getting ready for the next Savvy Senior Skills session,' Connor said. 'Last week William managed to switch the language on the computer and turned everything Japanese.'

'He has a talent for trouble, that one. Can't wait to see what apps he manages to download,' Slim retorted. 'I think you'll have your hands full. There are already ten sign-ups for the next course. It's almost as popular as my Dungeons and Dragons club.'

'It's not a competition,' Connor said, quoting Ginny.

'That's right.' She managed a faint smile. She loved how much enthusiasm and energy Connor and Slim brought to the library. They chatted for a few minutes then she took off her coat and made a start.

By the time the three of them had finished setting up the chairs for a book group, it was opening time and Ginny had unlocked the front door when her phone buzzed with an incoming call. These days she carried it in her pocket whenever she could, and she quickly checked the screen.

It was Nancy.

Ginny swallowed, and, dredging up all her courage, declined the call. She'd already spoken to her sister-in-law several times before she'd even finished breakfast and wasn't up to another conversation. Instead, she sent Nancy a quick text to say they'd talk later.

Nancy answered with a photograph of the stunning Northern Lights and several fingers-crossed emojis. Ginny sighed and put the phone back.

The library was as busy as Connor and Slim had predicted, and by lunchtime the police had released a press statement, which had resulted in a deluge of online articles about Monica's unexpected death. There weren't any details in the statement, but it hadn't stopped the headlines, and it was obvious the press were only getting started.

The lights finally go out for National Treasure, Monica Larkwell.

Monica Larkwell's comeback is no more.

From First Kiss to Mother Goose. How the mighty fall.

But though the headlines differed, the stories were identical.

Monica Larkwell was a fifty-five-year-old actress who helped others find love but had never married. She went to drama school in London and performed in minor roles afterwards, including a pantomime thirty years ago at a small regional theatre in Little Shaw. Her career really took off after being selected to host *First Kiss*, which she worked on until it was cancelled twenty years before. She then participated as a contestant on a reality television show set in the Welsh mountains, and not only won it, but was dubbed a national treasure for going makeup-free on screen. Ironically, her second chance with fame was marred by controversies surrounding plastic surgery, which she vehemently denied. However, Harley Street doctors were unanimous in pointing out various work. Last, Monica had recently announced her comeback.

That would explain the documentary crew that had been following her around at the theatre.

The newspapers also hadn't missed the fact that Little Shaw had become a notorious location for murders over the past few years, and there was already intense speculation in the press.

Ginny cringed. Poor Wallace. There was no mention of cause of death or anything to imply it was a murder, but it seemed people were putting two and two together and getting killer. Especially when it came to Little Shaw. And while Ginny hadn't given out any information, it was hard to imagine, after seeing the cut chandelier and the blood, that Monica had died of natural causes.

She switched off her computer monitor and rubbed her eyes.

Monica's life had been diffused down to a few paragraphs that revolved around her career. But who was she beneath that?

What did she like? What was she passionate about? What were her hopes and dreams?

And what about her family? There was no mention of children or a partner, but there must be people out there grieving for her.

Ginny's throat tightened at the dreadful pain they would now be experiencing. It was something she knew all too well.

She was prevented from going down a dark path by the ding of the issue counter's bell, calling her back out to the floor. The rest of the afternoon was busy, and several journalists had appeared during the day hoping to get an interview with anyone involved in the production, but Connor and Slim had refused to let them get near Ginny, which she appreciated.

The locals weren't so easily put off, but Ginny kept her answers short and to the point and people had moved on. Plus, with so many of the villagers at the rehearsal the previous evening, there were enough other firsthand accounts to go around.

Finally, the last of the patrons left the library and Ginny finished her tasks and returned to Slim and Connor. She'd half expected to see her friends during the day, but JM had texted to say the theatre board had asked them to support the cast and crew as they dealt with the fallout of Monica's death.

'Thank goodness today's over.' Slim stretched his arms up towards the ceiling then slung his coat on. 'I'm knackered. Think I'll head off unless you need me for anything else.'

'No, I have to go as well before my cat thinks he's become an orphan. Would you and Connor like a lift home?'

'Thanks, Mrs C, but I've got my nan's car. She wants me to take her to bingo,' Connor explained as they walked to the door, stopping only to lock it on the way out.

'And my mate's collecting me,' Slim said as headlights came to a halt. 'Here he is.'

'Well, have a lovely evening.' Ginny bid them both farewell and gratefully climbed into her small silver car, pleased she hadn't decided to walk in the bitterly cold weather.

Several minutes later she pulled into Middle Cottage, her misnamed semi-detached house with a pink door and a small front garden. Out of habit, she peered to Wallace's side of the fence, but there was no sign of his EV, or his father's practical white van. It wasn't a surprise. Wallace would be putting in long hours now, what with Monica's death, and Ted—his father—had started working part-time at the local pub since he made the permanent move to Little Shaw. While Ginny could go for days without seeing either of them, she was finding it increasingly comfortable to know she had neighbours she could turn to if she needed help.

She let herself into the house and was greeted by a small black cat, perched halfway up the stairs, staring at the wall to fully make his point that his dinner was late. Edgar had been a rescue cat but was now living the lifestyle of one born with a silver spoon between his claws.

'No doubt you've contacted the Complaints and Grievances

line at the Feline Protection League to let them know about the wrongs you have suffered.' Ginny joined him on the stairs, where he ignored her attempts to pat him. 'If I had my way, I would've spent the day at home with you. We've been so busy.'

'Meow,' he replied, not looking at her.

Ginny sighed and got to her feet. 'I see this is going to take several of your extra special treats.'

'Meow.' The cat relented and followed her into the kitchen, managing to weave through her legs as she walked. It improved his mood and she chatted to him while she boiled the kettle and shook out several of the eye-wateringly expensive cat snacks.

Outside, a car pulled up and an engine switched off. Since Wallace's vehicle was silent, she supposed it was Ted, so was surprised to get a knock on the door.

'What if she's not at home?' Tuppence's voice rang out.

'Of course she's at home. Look, her car's there,' JM countered in an imperious tone.

Ginny smiled as she made her way down the hall and opened the door. 'Come in. I've just boiled the kettle.'

'There's no time for that,' JM announced.

'What's wrong?' Ginny's spine stiffened, noticing that Hen was absent. 'Has something happened?'

'You could say that,' Tuppence agreed.

'Hen's down at the police station being interviewed,' JM said in a flat voice that made Ginny's stomach tighten.

'Interviewed?' she repeated, aware of how inane it was, but also unable to stop the words from coming out. 'But why? We've already given our statements last night.'

'Yes, but that was before the police looked at the camera footage. They caught the killer on tape.'

Killer?

So, it was true. Monica had really been murdered. Ginny's mouth went dry and she gripped at the stair railing for support.

'I don't understand what that has to do with Hen?' she said.

'The killer used Prissy's costume to hide their identity,'

Tuppence said with a shake of her head. 'I've never been more shocked in my life.'

Ginny's jaw went slack. There was no way they would joke about something that concerned their friend. Which meant it must be true:

The killer had worn a giant purple-feathered goose costume.

The costume that Hen had made.

SIX

MONDAY DECEMBER 8

JM honked the horn of her small silver car and the crowd outside the police station grudgingly parted, allowing her to park. None of them spoke as Ginny, JM and Tuppence climbed out and hurried towards the single-storey bungalow, with a wheelchair ramp running up one side. It was a depressing building at the best of times, but the cool evening air gave it a frigid appearance that did nothing to take away the nerves Ginny always felt when she was forced to interact with the police. And no matter how many times she went to the station, it never got easier.

So much for exposure theory.

Part of her knew that the police would only be interviewing Hen about the costume and getting the measurements, but there was no way Ginny, JM or Tuppence could wait at home for her. Since meeting her friends, they had become a family and that meant turning up.

'Oh, have you had news? Has Hen McArthur confessed to the crime?' someone called out, which earned them a chilling glare from JM.

'She's not a suspect, you ninny,' Tuppence growled, sounding angrier than Ginny had ever heard. Though it made sense. While Ginny and JM were newer arrivals to Little Shaw,

Tuppence and Hen had both grown up together in the village and had always been there for each other, including through the loss of their husbands.

'Ignore them.' Ginny tucked an arm through Tuppence's elbow and gave her hand a reassuring squeeze. 'She'll be okay.'

'Of course she will,' JM said, though her usual stoicism wasn't there. 'This whole thing is nonsense. They should be out there trying to find the real killer.'

'You're right, but I'm sure that Hen's statement will help them do that,' Ginny consoled her as they made their way to the police station proper. The inside was as gloomy as the exterior, though unlike other times Ginny had visited, tonight the waiting room was even more crowded than outside.

She recognised numerous faces from the pantomime, including the director, Hazel. There was a pinched expression on her mouth, but she didn't appear upset.

The hairs on Ginny's arms prickled as she recalled what Tuppence had said about Monica's affair with Hazel's husband Alan, and how it had ruined the marriage.

Next to her was Desiree Northam, the choreographer and understudy who'd argued with Monica. Her thick hair stood out from her lovely face, though her ebony skin was tinged with red, and her lips were chafed, as if she'd been chewing them. On the other side of the room, several of the pantomime's extras were having an animated conversation.

'Why, no, officer, I did *not* interact with the deceased last night,' the first extra said.

'Hmmm, you're almost there, but if you could project your voice louder and focus on your articulation...' the second advised.

'Perhaps use your hands more. To make it feel authentic. Let's do it again, from the top,' the third chimed in.

Ginny blinked, momentarily distracted from Hen's plight. She turned to her friends. 'Since when do people rehearse to give a witness statement?'

'They're very dramatic.' JM frowned.

'It's called hamming it up,' Tuppence whispered. 'And it makes me realise we should have gone over our stories last night. To make sure we got everything straight. What if we've accidentally got Hen into trouble?'

'Nonsense. There was nothing to get straight. It's always better to tell the truth,' JM said as they reached the bland reception desk half covered by a Perspex screen. 'Unless, of course, the truth is stupid.'

'None of us have done anything wrong, Hen included,' Ginny said, reverently hoping that JM hadn't felt the need to fabricate part of her statement last night. 'I'm sure they're getting information about the costume.'

'That had better be all it is.' JM leaned forward to attract the PC's attention. 'Excuse me, can you tell us when Hen McArthur will be released? As her legal counsel I require an update, and to request that any statements she's given be expunged from the records until she has consulted with me. Well... don't just stand there.'

JM wasn't precisely a lawyer; she had done half a law degree in the seventies and still volunteered for a local solicitor. Her words had an instant effect on the young PC, who blanched, as if frozen to the spot. She was stopped from answering as the door next to the reception counter swung open and Hen appeared, followed by Detective Constable Anita Singh.

At the sight of her friends, Hen's face lit up and her eyes misted. 'You're here."

'Of course we are,' JM said staunchly, though a relieved smile tugged at her lips.

'We've been worried about you.' Tuppence drew her into a hug.

'Are you okay?' Ginny rubbed Hen's arm while JM patted her shoulder.

'Oh yes. Anita's been ever so kind. They even made me a cup of tea,' Hen managed to say as they all untangled from each other.

'Thank you for your help, and I'm sorry for keeping you so long,' Anita said in her familiar Scottish accent. She was petite with dark hair and an ambition to one day become a detective inspector like Wallace.

'That's okay. I wish I knew more. I feel so guilty. If only I hadn't changed the costume, this never would have happened. Why did I suggest we make a full headpiece?' Hen gave a helpless shrug, worry filling her eyes. 'That's how they hid their identity. It's all my fault.'

'Nonsense. Whoever was behind this could as easily have dressed up in any number of costumes,' JM reassured her.

'That's right,' Tuppence agreed. 'You should take it as a compliment that they went for Prissy instead of that moth-eaten bear costume from last year's *Goldilocks*.'

'The important thing is that we have the measurements, because it will make it easier to narrow down the suspects.' Anita winced, as if worried Wallace might have overheard her. 'Forget I said that, and please don't mention it to anyone else.'

Ginny grimaced.

Was Anita worried that they might start investigating? Because if so, she had nothing to fear.

Her friends nodded their agreement and after promising Anita they'd call if they thought of anything else, they bundled Hen up and took her out of the station and home, to where her lovely Labrador, Brandon, was waiting.

It was a cosy cottage filled with squishy sofas, floral prints and well-loved wooden furniture. Hen's knitting was in a large basket and she made a beeline to it, as if knowing it would bring her comfort. In one corner was a living Christmas tree in a bright red pot. Two old-fashioned hatboxes were nearby, and handmade decorations were spilling out of them.

There was no sign of Connor, who'd become Hen's flatmate eight months ago, then Ginny remembered he'd taken his grandmother to bingo.

They had been quiet on the trip back, but once Tuppence

returned from the kitchen with a large pot of tea and four cups, JM broke the silence.

'What else did Anita tell you? Did she give you any idea if the police have finished at the theatre?'

Hen cast on her knitting and some of the colour returned to her face. 'She didn't mention that. All she said was that Danny Ling, the documentary maker, had put a small camera in Monica's dressing room, and that's where they got the footage from.'

'Did he just?' JM's brow lifted. 'I hope Monica knew about it, otherwise that is pretty underhanded.'

'According to Anita, Monica had consented,' Hen said. 'Though I got the feeling Danny didn't tell the police about it straight away. I think SOCO discovered the camera while they were looking for clues.'

'I wonder if Danny would've passed it over, if the police hadn't asked for it?' Tuppence said. 'I think we need to consider him a suspect.'

Suspect?

Ginny opened her mouth to protest, but before she could JM shook her head.

'Sorry, Tuppence, but we need to sit this case out.'

'We do?' Hen's eyes went wide.

'Why?' Tuppence folded her arms. 'What if the police get it wrong?'

'What if they don't? As far as I can tell, they have the matter well in hand,' JM returned. 'Besides, we can't be in two places at once and we need to be ready to get back to work when the board of trustees make their decision. Well... that's assuming that they vote to go ahead with it.'

'Decision?' Hen finally stopped her knitting. 'What do you mean? Are you saying that they might cancel the pantomime altogether?'

'It's a possibility. Some of them think it might be bad luck to continue without Monica, but I'd be surprised if they vote no. The best way to honour her legacy is by carrying on,' JM said and they were all silent. Clearly Ginny wasn't the only one still picturing Monica Larkwell's dead body.

'I hadn't considered that,' Tuppence finally spoke. 'Even if they go ahead, it will put us well behind our schedule with the scenery.'

'And the costumes.' Hen began knitting again, her agitation sounding out in the click, click, click of her needles. 'I doubt the police will give us back Prissy.'

'It's lucky Monica didn't come in for her fitting, so we can make them directly for the understudy,' Ginny said, in reassurance.

'Desiree will be playing the Dame. How lovely. She's ever so talented,' Hen said.

'And that means she can do her special TikTok dance,' Tuppence added brightly.

'Which would be a very good motive for murder,' JM said then frowned. 'Please ignore that statement.'

'Consider it ignored,' Hen told her warmly. 'It's going to take time to get used to the idea of sitting it out.'

'Except we *haven't* properly decided. If we really want to honour Monica's legacy, shouldn't we be trying to get to the bottom of this?' Tuppence clearly wasn't convinced. 'What do you think, Ginny?'

Ginny blanched under the gaze of her three friends. 'I agree that the best way to acknowledge Monica's passing is for her killer to be brought to justice, but the fact the police have camera footage and the killer's measurements suggests they have the matter well in hand. I think they're the best people to do the job. And if the pantomime does go ahead, we would still be honouring her.'

Tuppence slowly nodded. 'Okay, so it's agreed that we leave the murder to Wallace.'

'We leave the murder to Wallace,' Hen seconded and held up her knitting needles as if in a toast.

'We leave it to Wallace,' JM confirmed.

'I think we're making the right decision,' Ginny said, trying to push aside the fact that Monica Larkwell was murdered and that they'd been the ones to find the body. The police knew what they were doing.

And with that she took another sip of her tea, feeling better already.

SEVEN

WEDNESDAY DECEMBER 10

Ginny shifted in her seat, while Hen reached into her knitting bag, but instead of retrieving her needles and wool, she brought out a red bodice and a length of boning that she'd been hand sewing into place. There had been no official word about the fate of the pantomime, but the board of trustees had requested the cast and crew attend a meeting at the Little Shaw Playhouse, which was why Ginny and her friends were currently sitting in the front row, staring up at an empty stage. The only update they'd had was police were now officially calling it a murder.

There hadn't been any mention of suspects or lines of enquiry, but it had caused chaos in the press and the village was flooded with journalists and Monica Larkwell fans alike.

The meeting was meant to start at six o'clock, but it was already ten minutes past the hour and while the front stalls were filled with the actors and behind the scenes volunteers, there was no sign of any activity. Ginny, who had come straight from the library, tried not to think of her dinner.

'Did I see the curtain rustle?' Tuppence leaned forward, her gaze fixed on the heavy velvet curtains that hung down to the well-trodden floorboards.

'I hope so. This is a tad dramatic for my liking. If they'd

involved me in this business, I would've ensured they kept to the schedule,' JM retorted as the lights dimmed and the curtains shifted apart.

'Finally,' someone from behind them muttered as the curtains continued to slowly draw back to reveal six chairs on the right-hand side of the stage, and a podium in the centre. A spotlight swept across the stage then settled onto five people, who entered from the wings and walked towards the chairs, their steps punctuated like soldiers on parade. One by one, they sat down.

The spotlight settled onto the middle chair, which was empty but for a floral jacket and a bottle of champagne. The sight of it caused a roar from everyone in the stalls and Ginny blinked as people around them got to their feet and started to clap.

'The empty chair is for Monica,' Tuppence observed. 'It's another one of those theatre traditions.'

'Isn't it lovely?' Hen sighed.

'It's very thoughtful.' Ginny nodded and stood up. She hadn't known Monica but after reading article after article about her public image, with almost no mention of who she was as a person, Ginny had felt inordinately sad that someone was only being remembered because of their celebrity.

The applause went on for several more minutes as Hazel Holdsworth crossed over to the podium. She wore a black wool dress that floated out around her like a storm cloud, while her glasses were snow white against her short hair, which had been dyed black.

It was definitely a statement.

Hazel paused to adjust the microphone then held a hand up to her heart. 'Thank you for joining us today. As a family, I'd like to acknowledge what a difficult time this is and how deep the loss is being felt for our leading lady, Monica Larkwell. Not only is Monica loved by the entire world, but she's always held a special place in our hearts due to her long association with this theatre.

The board and I have been working closely with the police and will continue to do so to ensure justice is served.'

At the mention of the police, the spotlight abruptly swung towards the side stage, where DI Wallace was standing, arms folded as he surveyed the audience. His scowl darkened at the sudden attention and he muttered something under his breath. Ginny didn't need to be a lip reader to guess that what he said wasn't polite. The light quickly returned to Hazel in the centre of the stage.

But Ginny's gaze remained on Wallace, his dark figure visible against the folds of the curtain. The theatre was no longer cordoned off, so why was he there? Was he going to give an update of the case, observe everyone's reaction? Or... was it to see who was missing?

Ginny shifted in the seat again and followed his gaze as he scanned the crowd. There were several cast members who hadn't turned up, including Cleo and Andrea. Both women had given statements on Monday, but neither had come into the library since. Ginny had left several messages for each of them, and while Andrea let her know she had a cold, Cleo had yet to reply.

She had hoped it was merely because she wanted to avoid the library patrons who might ask too many questions, but it was hard to imagine why Cleo wasn't at tonight's meeting... unless it *was* to do with the case. But surely Wallace didn't think Cleo was a suspect? Or her husband, Arnold? A fresh wave of concern filled her and she fumbled for her phone and sent another text message, asking Cleo if everything was okay.

'We have several pieces of news to give you,' Hazel continued, and Ginny quickly slid her phone back into her handbag. She'd have to remember to check for a reply once she was at home. 'And to do that, I'd like to invite up our chairperson, Suzette Ryan.'

On cue, a well-dressed woman in her fifties waved and made her way to the podium while Ginny studied the remaining board members. She was surprised to recognise Desiree Northam, who had been arguing with Monica about the TikTok dance. Like Hazel, Desiree was dressed all in black and her hair had been threaded into intricate plaited rows.

Next to Desiree was a man with a narrow face, a pencil moustache and bald head. He was wearing a bland brown suit that seemed like something Arnold Connell would own, and to his right was a taller man with classic good looks, dark blue eyes and a mahogany tan. Ginny didn't recognise either of them.

'The one with the moustache is Suzette's husband, Ian. They're both accountants and have their own business,' Hen explained.

'And at the end is Paul Atkins.' Tuppence leaned over. 'He runs several tanning salons. In case you couldn't tell.'

Suzette finally reached the podium and Hazel gave her a supportive pat on the arm. 'Thank you. As Hazel said, this is a terrible time but we wanted you to know that after many discussions, and in consultation with DI Wallace'—the spotlight darted across the stage to him, before darting away, as if worried he would somehow reach out and snatch it—'we've decided that the show must go on, and that it's our best way to honour Monica Larkwell's legacy.'

The announcement caused another round of applause to break out in the stalls. Suzette held up her arm again, much like a politician working a crowd. After several minutes, she tapped the microphone to get everyone's attention.

'We're delighted you feel as strongly about it as we do. Now, for our second announcement. Unfortunately, it's difficult to say when the official funeral will be, so Ian and I are throwing open our doors on Monday evening to celebrate Monica's achievements. The theme is floral extravagance and the martinis and nibbles are on us. There's nothing Monica liked more than a naughty school-night tipple, so we feel that this is what she would have wanted.'

'She probably wanted to not be clocked on the head by a falling chandelier,' someone behind them said.

'It's clear they're trying to spin the narrative. Look at Hazel Holdsworth, she can barely contain her smile. And no wonder. It's a win/win. She gets rid of the woman who screwed up her marriage, and the board gets the publicity for the show without having to shell out two thousand quid on a dried-up television star.'

Dried-up television star?

Ginny's spine stiffened at the way Monica was being described. Yes, her behaviour hadn't been wonderful, but everyone had a bad day. Or a bad year. And none of that made her passing any less tragic. To insinuate her death was a good way to save money was chilling. And two thousand pounds was very cheap. Unless Monica had another reason for wanting to come back to Little Shaw.

She turned to where the two women were talking. They ignored her outraged stare and moved on to discussing some of the other cast members.

'I'm sure they don't mean it.' Hen leaned closer. 'It's just their grief talking.'

'I hope that's true.' Ginny turned back to face the stage, trying to shake the callous conversation from her mind.

'I hope so, too. But it does make me wonder about Hazel. They were right that she has a motive to kill Monica,' Hen said then grimaced. 'Oh dear. I keep forgetting that we're not investigating the case. I think it's because I feel so guilty about designing Prissy's costume. If police could have seen the killer's face, then poor Wallace wouldn't be standing up on the stage looking so grumpy.'

Tuppence patted Hen's arm. 'You can't help that when it comes to design, you excel. And I was the one who actually made the mask and put the feathers on it. I'm as much to blame as you. That's probably why yesterday, after I remembered what Andrew said about how many trolls there were on Monica's message boards, I was going to suggest we research it.'

'I *did* start researching them. There are a lot of nasty people out there. Some of the things they were saying about Monica were vile. I won't give them credence by repeating them,' JM admitted, a little sheepishly. 'Then I wondered whether I should lean on Wallace to find out the cause of death. I got as far as the end of my driveway before remembering that we're not involved.'

Ginny pressed her lips together. She, too, had found her thoughts drifting back to Monica's lifeless body. 'I know it's difficult, but we're doing the right thing.'

'Yes, and I'm sure the police have it all under control. It's probably why Wallace is here. And now the panto's back on, we're going to be busy,' Hen said, resuming her hand-stitching. 'To think, we still have so much to do and five days fewer than we'd planned.'

On the stage, Suzette gave Hazel a concerned look as the chatter in the stalls rose, but it was Paul Atkins who got to his feet and crossed over to the podium. He was about fifty and at least six feet tall, and his gait swayed and bobbed as if a soundtrack was playing in his mind. He paused halfway to roll his hands in a dance move that Ginny hadn't seen since the seventies. It had the desired effect on the audience and a few people began to clap a beat, which Paul rewarded with another shimmy of his hips.

Finally, he reached the podium and bent down to the microphone and smiled a dazzling set of teeth. 'Hey, folks. Thank you for the support. It means. The. World. To. Us.' He thumped his chest with each word then gave them another smile. 'But we won't keep you any longer since we're sure you're keen to get home... or to the pub. So, enjoy your last night of freedom, because tomorrow rehearsals will pick up again and we're going to need all hands on deck. But...' He paused and held out his arms like a preacher. 'Together we can move mountains. Together we can honour Monica's memory and put on the best pantomime ever.'

The crowd roared and he dropped one arm and kept the other up in the air, making a V for victory sign with his fingers.

Ginny winced, not sure if she was watching a motivational speech or a cult leader, but it had the desired effect and there was another round of applause before the curtains came down and the lights turned on.

Still, regardless of the over-the-top speech making, Paul Atkins had a point. If the pantomime was going to be ready for Boxing Day, there wouldn't be much time for anything else.

EIGHT

THURSDAY DECEMBER 11

'Damn, I wish Cleo was here,' Slim said the following evening after he finally convinced a couple of Monica's Larks to pack up their laptops and leave. It was twenty minutes after the library's regular closing time, and the Larks had refused to stop the livestreaming they'd been doing for their social media account. In the end, Slim had simply put his hand in front of the lens until they responded to his request.

'That makes two of us. I don't think I've fully appreciated her skills in the past,' Connor admitted as they locked the door. 'Cleo would've had them outside before they could say, "subscribe to my channel."'

'And probably scared off the rest of that mob.' Slim nodded over to the people milling around outside the library, visible under the Christmas lights strung up around the nearby trees. The crowds had increased since Monday as journalists, tourists and the growing contingent of Larks flooded into the village to pay their respects to Monica, while waiting for the next update from the police.

Unfortunately, the longer the update was taking, the more people continued to arrive, and while many based themselves at

The Lost Goat pub and the several coffee shops in the village, the majority opted for the free wi-fi and heating of the library. It didn't help that the latest newspaper headlines shouted to the world that a killer was on the loose thanks to the bumbling efforts of the local Keystone Cops. Not even the news that the pantomime was going ahead had eased the growing tensions.

'So, you off to the theatre?' Connor asked as they walked towards the crowd.

'Yes, there's so much sewing to catch up on. Though, first, I'm going to drop off a care package to Andrea, then visit Cleo,' Ginny admitted.

Andrea's cold hadn't improved and Cleo still wasn't answering any messages. And while, as volunteers, they weren't obliged to come in, Ginny was concerned about their continued absence.

'You need back-up?' Connor asked in a cautious voice, clearly not relishing the task.

'Or someone to run interference?' Slim said, sounding even less certain.

'It's probably best that I go alone.' Ginny bit back her smile as the pair of them wiped their brows. 'But thank you for offering. And for all the help over the last week. I'm not sure what I would've done without the two of you.'

'Teamwork makes the dream work,' Slim said as William, one of the library regulars, broke away from the throng of people outside and ambled over. 'Hey, old fella. Why aren't you at home?'

'Thought I'd hang around and see what leads Ginny is going to follow up first,' William announced and tugged a deerstalker further down around his face. 'It's more exciting than going home to watch my recorded episodes of *Strictly*. It's not the same now that nice television copper got kicked off for messing up her samba.'

Ginny's chest tightened. All week, patrons had been coming

up to her, asking how the case was going or wanting to share bits of theatre gossip that might relate to the murder. And all week, she'd been trying her best to shut it down. She was saved from answering by Slim.

He patted William on the arm. 'Sorry, bud, but like I've already explained, Mrs Cole and the team are sitting this one out.'

William slowly rubbed a mittened hand across his chin. 'I thought that was a joke. To throw us off the scent.'

'Why would she joke about it?' Connor stepped up, arms folded.

'Yeah. If the Detective Club wants to sit this one out and leave it to the police, that's perfectly valid.' Slim mirrored Connor's posture.

She gave them a grateful smile. 'William, I'm sure the police have it well in hand. Now, I'm about to visit Cleo but would you like a lift home? I'm going past your place.'

William's shoulders dropped in disappointment. 'That's very kind, Ginny, but I'd best go to the pub and pray that the police get their act together. It's been woefully disappointing so far. Can you believe there's been no press conference since yesterday? What's the world coming to?'

Ginny winced, but once again reminded herself that it wasn't her job to defend the police.

She said goodnight to everyone and headed for her car to deliver Andrea's care package. It was a quaint terrace house on one of the cobbled streets that ran up the side of the hill. Andrea was at the window, blanket around her shoulders and a very red nose. She waved to Ginny through the window but gestured for her not to come in because she didn't want to pass on the cold. Smiling, Ginny left the care package at the door and headed to Cleo's house.

The volunteer lived outside Little Shaw, and after navigating the heightened traffic in the village, Ginny was soon pulling up outside a neat brick bungalow with several manicured hedges dotted around the lawn. Most of the neighbours had Christmas lights that illuminated the night, but there was no sign of any festive cheer from Cleo's yard, though, as Ginny walked up the path, she was greeted by a collection of ornamental rabbits that were clustered to either side of the low step.

A faint light peeked out from behind the curtains and Ginny was relieved when the door opened not long after she knocked. Arnold was wearing another brown outfit, complete with brown tartan slippers. His face was pale, as if he hadn't slept much. A black poodle poked its head around Arnold's legs.

A rush of guilt went through her: was she imposing? 'I'm so sorry to disturb you, but I was hoping to speak to Cleo... to make sure she's okay.'

'Y-you want to speak to Cleo?' he said in alarm, as if she'd asked him a trick question.

Ginny's guilt turned to confusion as a shuffling noise came from somewhere behind him. 'Er, yes. I've been worried about her.'

'You want to speak to Cleo because you've been worried about her?' Arnold repeated, his voice getting louder as he went. The shuffling noise increased and Ginny pressed her lips together and met his gaze. She didn't consider herself the bravest of people, and while JM or Tuppence would've happily marched inside, she couldn't bring herself to. However, it was clear something was going on.

'Arnold, can I please come in?' she asked.

Indecision danced in Arnold's hazel eyes, but he finally stepped aside. 'Fine.'

'Thank you.' Ginny followed him and the dog through to a neat living room with two black leather sofas that sat at right angles. A small Christmas tree was in one corner and more rabbit ornaments were scattered across the low unit that sat underneath the wall-mounted television; the only pictures were also of rabbits. Ginny had never realised her volunteer had such a fondness for them.

The room was empty, but a swish of fabric caused Ginny to turn around and study a Cleo-sized bump in the curtains.

'Er, the thing is, I'm not sure where she is,' Arnold said, in a heroic voice. A *tskking* noise came from behind the curtains, and Cleo finally stepped out. Her normally neat, bobbed hair was ruffled and full of static and she was wearing a hand-knitted jumper with a rabbit on the front of it.

'There's no point saying it now that you've let her in the house,' Cleo grumbled and joined Ginny in the middle of the room. 'I suppose it was only a matter of time before *he* sent you here.'

'He?' Ginny wrinkled her nose. It was clear Cleo didn't have Andrea's cold, but it was also clear that *something* was going on. If only Ginny knew what that something was.

'Wallace.' Arnold took his wife's hand and gave it a tight squeeze. 'He's been sniffing around here all week trying to crack Cleo, but she's held strong.'

'And you can tell him from me that I don't appreciate him sending his lackeys to do his job.' Cleo pushed her chin defiantly into the air.

Ginny's jaw began to ache as she studied the pair of them. It wasn't a surprise that Wallace might want more information, considering Cleo had had a run-in with Monica, and Arnold had been manning the stage door when the murder took place. Which meant they were both very much involved in the lead-up to Monica's death.

It wasn't even a surprise that Cleo and Arnold might think Ginny was involved in the case, given her history. However, she wasn't sure why Cleo, who wasn't much over five foot high, seemed to think she was a suspect.

'I'm only here in my capacity as the library manager,' Ginny told them both gently. 'We've been worried and I wanted to make sure everything is okay.'

'A likely story.' Cleo sniffed, though she did lower her chin.

'I promise that I've not spoken to Wallace since Sunday night.' Ginny raised her hands to prove her innocence.

Arnold loosened his grip on his wife's hand. 'So, you're not investigating this case?'

'Not even a little bit,' Ginny assured them. 'It's been ever so busy at the library without you and Andrea. I'm popping in purely to see if you need anything.'

'Why should we believe you?' Cleo said.

Ginny pressed her lips together. She wasn't in the habit of lying. Especially to her friends and colleagues. 'Cleo, I'm not sure what happened since you've given your statement, but I can assure you that you're not a suspect.'

'A-ha.' Arnold pointed a finger at her and the dog barked. 'So, you *are* involved in the case, otherwise how would you know that?'

Too late, Ginny remembered what William said about the lack of press conference. That meant people didn't know the killer had worn Prissy's goose costume. Surely it wouldn't be long until it was announced, and if it meant that Cleo and Arnold would no longer be keeping themselves locked in their cottage, too scared to talk with anyone, it had to be worth telling them.

'The documentary crew had a hidden camera in Monica's dressing room. Unfortunately, the killer was wearing Prissy's costume, which is why police haven't made an arrest yet.'

'What?' Cleo's mouth fell open. She closed it again and dropped into one of the black sofas. She waved Ginny to do the same. 'Are you sure?'

'I am.' Ginny nodded as Arnold gazed at them both in consternation.

'What's going on, love? What does this mean?'

'It means that I couldn't have killed Monica, despite my obvious motive.' Cleo patted his hand, though it was hard to see if she was relieved or disappointed. 'You see, Arnold, Prissy's costume was made to fit Kaleb Shepard.'

'Kaleb? But he's at least six feet tall,' Arnold said as his gaze swept over his diminutive wife. Then, understanding hit him. 'Which means Cleo couldn't have done it.'

'It appears so.' Cleo straightened her shoulders and blinked, as if coming out of a daze. 'I've neglected my library shifts for the week... and my sewing class. Oh dear, now I feel quite silly.'

'You have nothing to feel silly about,' Ginny assured her. 'Though we have missed you at the library. It took us twenty minutes to convince the last of the patrons to leave tonight. It was a couple of Monica's Larks who wouldn't stop livestreaming.'

'Twenty minutes?' Cleo's eyes flashed, making her look much more like her usual self. 'Unacceptable. As for livestreaming after closing time? No. No. No. I've told Slim and Connor enough times that they're far too soft, but will they listen?'

Ginny bit back a smile. 'Like I said, we've missed you. And Andrea. The poor thing has a cold.'

Another flash of worry crossed Cleo's face. 'I haven't even made her my famous chicken soup. Or offered you a cup of tea.' She suddenly jumped to her feet and disappeared into the kitchen, leaving Ginny, Arnold and the dog alone.

'Your visit has done her the world of good. I think we both panicked a little bit,' Arnold confessed.

'It can happen to the best of us,' Ginny said and peered around, once again taking in the rabbits. There were certainly a lot of them.

Arnold must have read her expression. 'Cleo's mad for them, though these days I'm the one who finds them.'

'Every year without fail Arnold gets me a new one.' Cleo reappeared, clutching at a loaded tray. 'Though we haven't even put the Christmas ones out yet. It shows how upside down we've been.'

'Well, now we can get the place decorated and things can go back to normal,' Arnold declared as he poured out three cups of tea from a large pot.

'I feel silly. What if people tease me at the library?' Cleo said, chewing her lip. 'Or, worse, if Hazel gives my role away again? She called last night and left a message about the play and begged me to come back.'

'I'm not surprised. You were born to play the Queen,' Ginny said. 'And everyone loves you at the library.'

Cleo swallowed and dabbed at her eyes. 'Thank you, Ginny. That's very kind of you to say so.'

'Not at all. I can't imagine how worried you've both been, but hopefully you can now see that you've done nothing wrong.'

'Yes, I suppose you're right,' Cleo said uncertainly, then gave her husband a concerned look. Arnold swallowed and studied his tartan slippers.

Ginny's skin prickled. 'Is there a problem?'

'Not a problem, exactly.' Cleo gave Arnold a sharp nod of her head.

'When I gave my statement, I told the police I was at the stage door until ten o'clock, when most of the cast and crew left, but that wasn't quite true,' he said.

'W-what do you mean?' Ginny studied the married couple. 'Are you saying that you lied to the police?'

'I didn't lie, exactly,' Arnold said, eyes downcast with misery. 'Well, maybe a little bit. You see, Cleo was so upset after the argument that I wanted to comfort her, so we went into the props room. I made her a nice cup of tea and we had a good chat.'

'How long were you in there for?' Ginny asked, brows knitting together.

'Only thirty minutes. Between nine-ten and nine-forty,' he said, a defensive note in his voice. 'I didn't want to tell the police in case it looked like Cleo and I were conspiring before the murder. I know I shouldn't have left my post... I feel like it's my fault. What if the murderer snuck in when I wasn't there?'

'You can't blame yourself,' Cleo said staunchly, though colour flooded her round cheeks. Ginny winced. If Arnold had lied, it meant that Cleo had as well. Was that the other reason she hadn't left the house?

'You need to tell the police the truth,' Ginny said, feeling sorry for Wallace as she thought of his shadowy figure on the edge of the stage. Judging by the worry lines around his mouth, he and the team were still looking for leads.

And, all the time, Arnold had lied about being at the door. The information might be the break they needed.

'If Wallace is any good, he'll figure it out on his own,' Cleo defended her husband.

'That's not how it works—and this is important evidence. I'm sure you want the police to find whoever is responsible.'

'Of course we do,' Cleo said and clutched at Arnold's hand. 'Despite what happened, we've both been huge Monica fans and it's dreadful she's now dead.'

'We just didn't want to accidentally get in any trouble,' Arnold admitted. 'But you're right. The police need to know.'

'Would you mind telling him on our behalf? I'm sure he'll take it better coming from you.' Cleo swallowed and peered at Ginny from between her lashes.

'Sorry.' Ginny shook her head. 'I'm really not involved in this case. Besides, you don't have anything to fear. Wallace isn't an ogre.'

'Tell that to Andrea,' Cleo said, shoulders going back. 'After she gave her statement, Wallace had the cheek to tell her she was exaggerating. Just because she got a bit muddled about where her stage left was... and she accidentally said Monica was holding a knife to my throat while delivering the horrific news about my demotion. And really, when you think about it, she *did* put a knife to my throat. Albeit a metaphorical one.'

'R-right.' Ginny pressed down on her lips and got to her feet. 'All the same, you should contact Wallace yourselves. It will be much better coming from you both, then if he has any follow-up questions, you can answer them at the same time.'

'I suppose you're right,' Cleo agreed grudgingly. She gave a shy dip of her head and picked up the phone to make the call as Ginny slipped out into the night. She had no idea that staying out of a case was as exhausting as being involved in one.

Still, she had stuck to her word, and, for that, she was proud.

NINE

FRIDAY DECEMBER 12

A sharp whirring sound filled the bedroom and dragged Ginny from her sleep. She opened her eyes with a start and checked the time. It was seven in the morning.

Usually she woke up much earlier, but she'd struggled to fall asleep, her slumber disturbed by the vision of Monica's crumpled body underneath the fallen chandelier as a figure in a purple-feathered goose costume rushed from the dressing room.

Edgar, who was curled in a ball near her feet, didn't move, and Ginny wriggled her legs to get past, lest she disturb him. The poor thing had probably only had fifteen hours' sleep. Her smile faded as the whirring sound started again. It was coming from next door's back garden.

She trudged to the window and peered out into the frosty morning. It was still dark, with the winter solstice nine days away. But the inky sky was illuminated by freestanding work lamps in the garden next door, and, in their glow was a man in his sixties with salt and pepper hair and a short silver beard and moustache.

Ted Wallace.

Of course it was. Why was she even surprised? Ted had moved to Little Shaw four weeks ago and was staying with his son while he searched for a house of his own. Despite having a part-time job in the local pub, he tended to keep to himself. However, while he appeared to be reticent by nature, he made up for it with his love of power tools and DIY projects.

Sawdust flew as the incessant whirring noise continued despite the pitch-black skies. The darkness was further punctured by a nearby bedroom light flicking on. A second house lit up and a window cracked open.

Oh dear.

At this rate the entire neighbourhood would be awake, and while for Ginny, getting up at seven was almost a lie-in, for others, it probably wasn't the Friday morning they'd been hoping for.

'I'd better tell him,' Ginny announced to the sleeping cat. Edgar didn't move as she got changed quickly and made her way downstairs, stopping only to put on the old wool coat she used for gardening. Her silver hair was cut into a bob and most days she tried to style it into submission, but it was too early and the whirring sound made it difficult to concentrate, so she covered it with a bright blue beanie hat that Hen had knitted.

A tall fence divided the two properties and cut into the back fence was a gate leading out to the field behind the houses. She unlocked it and went through. The once wild growth that ran along the verge had been tamed and she hurried over to Wallace's back gate. It was unlocked, no doubt thanks to Ted, who tended to go walking in the fields behind the houses most mornings.

The darkness was matched by the frigid air, which nipped at her cheeks as she stepped into Wallace's garden.

Ted, who had been hovering over a piece of wood propped up on two work horses straightened. He pushed back the safety goggles, leaving large clear circles around his eyes. A faint layer of sawdust covered the rest of him.

'Sorry, did I wake you?' Ted's breath came out in a column of steam.

'I think you've woken the whole street.' Ginny nodded to the row of houses around them, which now had their lights on, glowing like malevolent eyes against the dark sky.

'I don't sleep that well,' he admitted and put down the power tool in his hand. 'So, I thought I'd keep working on the stage props. I suppose I should have waited a bit longer.'

'At least until daylight,' another voice retorted and Wallace emerged from his house nursing a cup of coffee. He was fully dressed and shaved with a leather jacket to ward off the cold, but it was clear he wasn't happy to be awake. Considering he had probably been up late working on the case, Ginny couldn't blame him.

'It's daylight somewhere in the world,' Ted said in defence and held up his hands. 'It won't happen again.'

'That's what I told the four angry phone calls I've already fielded since getting out of the shower. Perhaps we should add "no-neighbours" to your list of requirements while we're house hunting,' Wallace said, taking a slug of coffee. Ginny knew that Ted had already looked at several properties to buy but hadn't found anything suitable. Or, considering how much he liked to build things, maybe he was wanting something *un*suitable to fix up?

'It's okay,' she said, not wanting to hurt Ted's feelings.

Wallace sighed. 'I blame myself for encouraging him to volunteer at the theatre. I thought it would be a good chance to meet people.'

'I work in the pub three times a week. I meet plenty of people,' Ted protested.

'Yes, and you refuse to make conversation with them,' Wallace retorted.

'I only refuse to take part in idle chit-chat,' Ted said, unmoved as he walked over to a nearby hard case and packed away the power tools he'd been using. He gave his son an impatient glare. 'Why don't you invite Ginny into the house and make us both a coffee? I'll be in there as soon as I've put everything away.'

Wallace's jaw tightened, and Ginny didn't know whether to be surprised or relieved that his frustration wasn't aimed at her. However, the distraction also stopped her from explaining that she didn't need a coffee, *or* to go inside, and too late she found herself being led by Wallace through the lovely double doors and into what was a brand-new kitchen.

Despite being neighbours, Ginny had only been inside Wallace's house a handful of times and never to the kitchen. So, while she had no idea what it had looked like before, she had to admire the pale olive paintwork, the thick wooden countertops and the butler's sink.

Was it all Ted's work?

'Oh, this is lovely,' she said as Wallace guided her to a scrubbed pine table.

'I suppose the old man does have his uses,' Wallace agreed, pride in his eyes. It soon faded as he carried a French press, half full of coffee, over to the table. 'It's still warm. Unless you'd like a cup of tea.'

'Coffee's fine, thank you,' Ginny said, not sure why she was here. To apologise for Ted's noise? It was possible, but apologies weren't really Wallace's style.

Nerves skittered along her skin. Was he annoyed that she and her friends had turned up at the station? She couldn't blame him since they'd managed to insert themselves in several of his murder investigations, much to his irritation. Did he think that's what they'd been doing?

Or, had Cleo and Arnold mentioned her name when they'd made their phone call last night?

Ginny silently groaned. Why hadn't she left Ted to his own fate? He was perfectly capable of dealing with angry neighbours. Well, not so much capable, as oblivious, and his usual method was to slip away until the shouting had stopped. Either way, Ted was a grown man and she should have let him face the consequences of his insomnia and need to make things. Instead, now she was stuck in Wallace's kitchen wearing an old winter coat and a bright blue beanie.

'Milk?' Wallace poured her a cup and pointed at a milk carton. She nodded and took the coffee, once he had added a splash.

'Thank you.' She swallowed. Wallace's gaze was unreadable. 'I-Is this about the police station? Because we were only there to collect Hen. So... if you're worried we were snooping, don't be. As for Cleo and Arnold—I was visiting as a friend and manager. It had nothing to do with your investigation. Between the production going ahead, and of course Christmas, we'll be flat out managing our obligations, so we agreed to sit this one out.' The words came out in a rush, but instead of looking happy, Wallace's scowl remained in place.

'You agreed to sit this one out?' he repeated as if she had said something scandalous.

'Yes.' She cautiously nodded, not sure why he was looking so unhappy. 'I thought you'd be pleased.'

Silence filled the room as he took a long slug of coffee then let out a pained sigh. 'I can't depend on anything.'

Depend on anything? What did that mean? Ginny's heart hammered. 'James, is something wrong?'

'You mean apart from this damn village?'

'You don't like Little Shaw?' she said, shocked.

Some of his anger dissipated. 'Not the village, the people. Or perhaps it's the time of year? Whatever it is, I can't get a straight answer out of anyone. I've had far too many "he's behind you" and "oh no she didn't's" thrown at me since Sunday night.'

'There is a bit of panto-mania going around,' Ginny admitted, thinking of the group of actors who had been rehearsing in the police station, and the ongoing dramatics of the Larks descending on the library. Even the showmanship of the theatre board at the meeting had suggested that giving a good performance was more important than telling the truth.

'You think?' he growled then rolled his shoulders. 'Sorry, I've had five days of nonsense only to discover that Arnold Connell wasn't in fact at the stage door when the murder happened, which means we've wasted a lot of time. Now we need to go back over everything from scratch.'

Ginny closed her eyes. Even though it wasn't her fault, she couldn't help but feel guilty. Perhaps if she'd visited Cleo and Arnold sooner, Wallace's leads wouldn't have gone so cold. 'They were scared. And I'm sorry for mentioning the goose costume.'

'At this point, I'm pleased you did. Otherwise, I can only imagine how long it would've taken them to tell me what really happened.' He leaned back and raked a hand through his short hair.

'At least you know now,' she said, trying to lift his mood. 'Hopefully it will lead to more clues.'

'Or it could lead to more drivel. You wouldn't believe the superstitions I keep being given.'

'I do understand. Though in all fairness, the ghost light was the reason we went back inside on Sunday night,' she admitted, wondering what would have happened if they'd ignored Andrew's pleas for them to honour the tradition. Not that it would have changed anything, only that someone else would have discovered Monica's body the following day.

'That's not the only one.' Wallace retrieved his notebook and flicked through it. 'Let's see, I've had that Scottish play, break a leg, don't whistle, and always give the director a graveyard bouquet. The list goes on.'

He closed the notebook and leaned back in his chair. Dark shadows hung below his eyes and his jaw was tight. It was clear he was struggling to keep his temper in check with some of the villagers.

'I'm sure they're not doing it on purpose. Perhaps it's better if DC Singh or PC Bent do the interviewing,' she diplomatically ventured, knowing how blunt the DI could be when he was pushed.

'I wish. Yesterday Liam was convinced that the deceased had been killed because she opened a compact mirror on the stage. Seems that's another no-no.'

Ginny swallowed. She'd heard that it was a no-no, too, but suspected it was more from a practical need to avoid the lights refracting off it. 'I'm sure people will settle down soon.'

'Meanwhile I have a murderer in hiding, while the trail gets colder. My gut tells me that it's someone inside the playhouse, but I have a huge caseload, no money for overtime and the national press sniffing around wondering why we have so many murders in this village. I need results fast on this one. Which is what I wanted to talk to you about. I'd like your help.'

TEN

FRIDAY DECEMBER 12

Ginny's jaw went slack. Was Wallace really asking for help? Somewhere outside the house, the sound of Ted's boots on the frost-tipped ground echoed, but inside the kitchen there was absolute silence.

Wallace wasn't known for talking about his active cases with civilians. They had recently reached an understanding while trying to solve two linked murder cases, but she hadn't expected it to be something that was repeated.

'Are you feeling okay?' she finally asked.

A flicker went through his dark eyes. 'Am I feeling okay about someone else murdered in Little Shaw? No, I'm not. And I'm definitely not okay that we haven't made an arrest.'

'Isn't it a bit early to be making an arrest?'

'It's *never* too early. Especially with the media interest and the guv breathing down my neck.'

Despite all of the murders she'd helped investigate, Ginny still didn't know the full inner workings of the police force, but she suspected that the detective chief inspector was always aware of how Wallace conducted his cases. And even with Arnold's omission about manning the stage door, it didn't seem like Wallace to be so worried.

'What's this really about?'

Their eyes met and he let out a pained laugh. 'I have a feeling that if you'd joined the force when you were younger, *you'd* be the guv breathing down my neck. You really don't miss much, do you?' He retrieved a small jeweller's box from his leather jacket and flipped it open to reveal a simple gold band embedded with a large solitaire diamond.

Oh. Ginny let out a soft gasp as she recalled Wallace's outfit from Sunday evening and his infuriated glare. She'd suspected the call must have come while he and Imogen were on a date, but it hadn't occurred to her that he'd been about to *propose*.

'How wonderful—not about the murder—but about Imogen. I wish you both all the happiness,' Ginny said, but she couldn't help but look down at her own simple gold wedding band. She and Eric never bothered with an engagement ring, deciding it was better to focus on using the money to build their future together. A lump formed in her throat at the memories, and she pushed her hand back under the table.

'She hasn't said yes,' Wallace reminded her then closed his eyes. 'I didn't even get a chance to ask her. I suppose I should be lucky I hadn't got down on one knee when the call came through. I might not believe in theatre superstitions, but I imagine that a murder isn't considered a good way to start an engagement. And now, trying to solve a case with the national press lurking around, well—' He snapped the ring box shut and pocketed it.

Ginny swallowed back her sadness and smiled at him. 'She will say yes, I'm sure. But I see your point. You can't very well propose in the middle of a murder investigation.'

'And I can't run the investigation properly until people trust me. Someone there knows something and I need to find out what it is.'

'You want us to go undercover?'

'No, but you, JM, Tuppence and Hen are already in there. I just need you to do what you usually do. Ask questions, pay attention to the details and keep me posted,' he said. When Ginny didn't answer he rubbed his chin. 'I know that Cleo and Arnold weren't the only ones holding back. Since the cast and crew won't talk to me, perhaps they'll talk to you.'

Dipping her head, Ginny closed her eyes. While she wanted to assure him that wasn't true, she had a sneaking suspicion that it was. The locals of Little Shaw were nothing if not eccentric and having witnessed several village rivalries, Ginny had no problem understanding how challenging Wallace and his team were finding making them open up. It was made worse by the knowledge that the longer it took, the colder any potential leads would go.

'I'll talk to the others but I'm sure they'll agree to help. What can you tell me?'

'I have theories but nothing solid. At this point everyone who had access to the theatre that night is a suspect.'

'So, everyone on the sign-in sheet,' Ginny clarified, then considered it. 'Was there any other way in or out?'

He shook his head. 'No. The front doors have a chain and padlock around them, and a CCTV camera on the street let us see that no one went in or out. There are three fire doors, but they were all alarmed, so it's only the stage door.'

'And what about alibis? Does everyone have one?'

'One? I wish. Most of them have several, which is what's been hampering the case. My resources are limited but we're obliged to follow leads that are taking us nowhere,' he said, frustration marring his brow. She opened her mouth, but he gave a curt shake of his head. 'Unfortunately, there's nothing else I can share at this point. However, we will be having a press conference later today and will be releasing information about the costume and the video. Can I ask you to not mention it until then?'

Ginny nodded. It wasn't the first conversation they'd had about police procedure and following protocol, and most of the time she did her best to do as Wallace asked. 'I understand and would never want to jeopardise any case you were building.'

'Thank you,' he said in a gruff voice. 'Just go about your business, listen to what people are saying, and keep me up to date. I suspect the locals won't clam up around you... and you're sensible enough to work out the difference between fact and fiction.'

Sensible? For most of her life, Ginny would have agreed with this definition of herself, but since moving to Little Shaw she was feeling less and less sensible every week that passed. And what if she and her friends didn't find anything?

But then the image of Monica's lifeless body flashed back into her mind. Someone had killed her. Ginny might not have even known who the actress was two weeks ago, but she still deserved the truth.

'We'll try our best,' she said as the sound of power tools once again rang out.

Wallace's phone buzzed and he scowled. 'What the hell happened to packing up?'

Ginny followed him from the house and gave father and son a quick goodbye.

Her mind whirled as she made her way back next door.

So much for their promise to stay out of the investigation. But at least now they wouldn't be sneaking around behind Wallace's back.

By the time she stepped into the kitchen, her phone was buzzing with a call from Nancy. Ginny ignored it. Wallace might've changed his tune about her habit of getting involved in murder cases, but she doubted her sister-in-law would be pleased to hear that there was another reason for Ginny not to join her on holiday. Besides, she needed to call her friends with the news.

'You definitely told him that we planned to sit this one out?' JM demanded as soon as Ginny turned down the side of the theatre and joined her three friends who were waiting in the narrow alley, along with Brandon, Hen's dog, who was pressing into her legs. They were all wearing heavy coats and scarves—apart from Brandon—but despite the cool morning damp, none of them appeared put out by Ginny's request to meet.

If anything, they seemed excited. JM's eyes gleamed, Hen grinned and Tuppence radiated with enthusiasm. Ginny couldn't blame them. A small part of her had kept wanting to make notes and discuss theories ever since the murder happened, and now, thanks to Wallace, that's exactly what they could do.

'I did,' Ginny said as JM marched up to the stage door and thrust a key into the lock.

'And that we voted on it?' Hen double-checked, rubbing her mitten-covered hands together for warmth.

'Yes, I was very clear,' Ginny assured her.

'Well, I for one am not surprised. I knew it was only a matter of time before he officially welcomed us onto the team,' Tuppence said, her breath coming out in a column of mist.

'That's a good point.' JM, who had been in the process of opening the door, stopped and pivoted. 'Did he mention compensation? It's not unusual for police to hire specialists when necessary.'

'Compensation? Oh no. Surely not.' Hen's hands dropped down. 'Why, only last week I saw Anita painting the wall around the side of the police station, which had been covered in graffiti. I don't think they have a very big budget. Plus, we've never asked them for money. It wouldn't be right.'

'He doesn't have any budget, and we're not doing anything official,' Ginny quickly said. 'Wallace can't share any details with us. But he did let me know that the only way the killer could have got in and out was via the stage door, and that everyone on the sign-in sheet had an alibi. Or several. It's been costing them a lot of time and resources to follow them all up.'

'Which is where we come in,' Hen said in understanding.

'Exactly. Everyone they've interviewed has been evasive with their answers. Or regaled him with theatre superstitions.'

'I knew he wouldn't be pleased about that. And to discover that Arnold and Cleo had been holding out on the police. Very disappointing.' JM pursed her lips together. 'You're right about payment. We might find it restricts us on what we can and can't do. And it's bound to involve paperwork.'

'Paperwork? Count me out. I have enough of that at tax time.' Tuppence shuddered. 'Plus, Wallace might find some of our methods a little... unorthodox.'

This was most definitely true. So far, he'd caught them digging up a grave, breaking into a house and (accidentally) confronting more than one killer. No wonder Ginny's friends were processing his request carefully.

She had called them with the news, and would have arranged for them to come around to her house, but Ted had continued to make all kinds of hammering noises next door and Ginny thought it might be easier to discuss the case in a quieter environment.

'Let's go inside,' she suggested and JM pushed open the door and turned off the security system. Despite rehearsals starting again yesterday, crime scene tape hung limply down the door frame of Monica Larkwell's dressing room, and grey powder covered the door handle and light switches. Further along the narrow corridor, props were strewn around and small photography markers were lying abandoned on the floor.

Brandon barked and Ginny shivered at the stark reminder that a murder had taken place here. Despite the gossip and sensational stories in the newspaper, a woman—not much younger than Ginny herself—had died and whoever had done it was still out there. It was a sobering thought.

Ginny turned to her friends. JM was frowning, Tuppence was chewing her lower lip and Hen was swallowing, eyes filled with tears. Clearly, they were thinking the same thing. They would help the police, not because they'd been asked, but because it was the right thing to do.

Silently they made their way towards the costume room. It was time to get to work.

ELEVEN

FRIDAY DECEMBER 12

'What do we know?' Hen poured out four cups of tea and passed them around. The costume room had been thoroughly searched, but it hadn't taken them long to get everything back into place and to brew a pot of tea to go with the fruit cake that Hen had brought along with her.

'Did Wallace give us a time of death or the forensics report?' JM settled herself in front of an overlocker.

'No, he can't give us any information in case it compromises the investigation.'

'Oh yes, he's very big on the protocol,' Hen said before wrinkling her nose. 'I'm still not clear what the protocol is, but it makes sense that he has to do everything by the book.'

'Tosh,' JM growled. 'It makes no sense at all. But if he wants to stick with his protocol and procedures then we'll stick with ours. I suggest we work this case in our usual manner. I for one am not interested in having random conversations with people for no particular reason. If we do this, we do it properly. We owe it to Monica.'

'I'll second that. Plus, why fix something if it isn't broken? Our methods have worked so far.' Tuppence clapped her hands and peered around the room. 'Which means we need a murder board. Do we still have a whiteboard?'

'It's in my attic,' JM admitted. 'They might be useful but they're not aesthetically pleasing and I got sick of looking at it.'

'Plus, I think it might hinder our creative process,' Tuppence agreed.

'What about Flora?' Hen looked up.

'Flora?' JM peered around the room.

'It's the nickname for the dress form.' Ginny bit back a smile and pointed to a row of moulded upper bodies attached to metal stands. One at the end was half-covered in a floor-length crushed velvet cape, along with several pattern pieces attached to the shoulder.

'I forgot you hadn't met Flora yet.' Hen walked over and swept away the cape, to reveal the hessian-covered upper body of the form. 'Flora's been part of this workroom for as long as I can remember and is so old that we mainly keep her around for sentimental reasons. And while we're not meant to have favourites, I must admit I like Flora the best. I'm sure Ants Mancini wouldn't mind if she became our murder board.'

JM joined Hen in front of the mannequin and gave her a thoughtful poke with her finger to make sure she didn't fall over. Satisfied, she nodded her head. 'Yes, Flora's acceptable. We could pin things to her, then cover it with the cape.'

'Excellent.' Tuppence reached across a cluttered desk for a roll of wide tape and a permanent marker, as well as a bundle of thick paper tags. 'We use these to label the costumes while we're working on them. Let's start with the time of death. Do we know what it is?'

'No.' Ginny shook her head. 'But we know when Hen put the goose costume into the storage room, and what time it was when we went back inside. And that the body was already exhibiting signs of livor mortis. Oh, what am I saying? Wallace told me that Arnold left his post at the stage door at the time of death, which means it happened between nine-ten and nine-forty.'

'Excellent. This is a promising start.' Tuppence jotted everything down on the tape and then pressed it above where Flora's ribcage would be. She then took a second label and began to sketch. Her strokes were fast and fluid and when she finished, she held it up to show a stunning line sketch of Monica wearing a floral suit jacket. A speech bubble hung over the sketch with the words *Ask Monica* written in it.

'Oh, that's lovely,' Hen said as Tuppence attached it to Flora's chest.

'You've really captured her,' JM agreed, crossing the room to study it in more detail. 'Though why the quote?'

'I think it's so we remember to put ourselves in Monica's shoes,' Ginny said, giving Tuppence a smile. It was an excellent visual reminder that they weren't trying to simply solve a puzzle or do a crossword. A woman had been killed and the more they could find out what kind of person Monica Larkwell was, the more chance they had of solving the murder.

'You're both so smart,' Hen said, eyes bright with awe. 'And I have something else to be added—we know the costume measurements.'

'That's true. Whoever wore Prissy's suit had to have been at least six foot. If they were too short, the headpiece would have obscured their vision,' Tuppence added. 'Speaking of which, I believe Kaleb Shepard must be our first suspect. After all, the costume was literally made for him.'

'But he's such a dear. I saw him at the police station when I was called in,' Hen protested. 'I'm sure they would have removed him from their suspect list.'

'Yes, except clearly the police didn't get very far with any of the statements otherwise they wouldn't have called us in,' JM said in a stern voice.

'Okay, yes. Write him down.' Hen wilted under JM's sharp gaze.

'Excellent.' Tuppence selected a paper tag, drew a figure of a man in a goose costume and then wrote Kaleb Shepard's name underneath. 'Now, what's our timeline?'

'We saw Monica leaving the stage at seven-thirty pm and I took the goose costume into the wardrobe at eight forty-five pm,' Hen said as Tuppence wrote it down on a long piece of tape.

'And that most people left the building at ten. But we were here until ten-thirty,' JM continued. 'Which means we found the body at around ten-forty.'

'So, our killer could've come and gone from the building before Arnold got back, or they could've walked out with the cast and crew.' Tuppence wrinkled her nose. 'What about cause of death?'

'We don't know for sure what it was,' Hen said. 'Just that the chandelier fell on top of her.'

'And that the chandelier's cord was cut,' Ginny said and recalled the open bottle of champagne and the empty flute next to it. 'Andrew's gift basket had a bottle of alcohol in it and it appears as if she drank a glass. Is it possible she was poisoned first and the chandelier was a distraction?'

'Oh, that's a jolly good point.' Hen's eyes widened. 'Though Andrew did seem genuinely upset.'

'Which could've been a deflection.' JM rubbed her chin. 'He did insist that I give her the basket, and the fact we caught him at the stage door might have been because he was trying to escape. Plus, he's tall enough to wear the Prissy costume.'

'Andrew, poisoned champagne and falling chandelier,' Tuppence repeated, then made a quick sketch of a figure wearing a faux fur coat. She wrote his name underneath and pinned it to the form. 'Right, who else do we have?'

'There are the rest of the Larks,' Ginny said, recalling the group of fans at the stage door. 'We also know that Monica received abuse from online trolls.'

'I suppose that's the problem with the internet these days. Not only can keyboard warriors make threats against people, but it's easy to know a celebrity's every move. After all, so many of them turned up at the stage door before Monica was killed.' JM prowled the room, pausing at a shelf of jars, each one filled with buttons. She picked one up and moved it closer to a similar shade.

'So, we need to add a nameless Lark to the list.' Tuppence continued to sketch. 'Or Larks. There may have been more than one.'

Ginny turned to Hen. 'You said that the documentary maker, Danny Ling, only handed over the footage after the police found a camera in Monica's dressing room?'

'Yes, but surely he wouldn't have recorded himself killing her?' Hen wrinkled her nose.

'Unless he wanted to use it as an alibi,' JM said. 'As I recall, he's not tall enough to fit into the costume but his cameraman is. His name is Nolan Archer.'

'Nolan Archer. Let's get you up on Flora.' Tuppence jotted down notes onto the tags. 'We can't forget Desiree Northam. Not only did Monica rant about that TikTok dance, but she was Monica's understudy.'

'She's also on the board which meant she might have been behind the decision to bring Monica to Little Shaw,' Hen added.

'And she's quite tall, but is she tall enough to wear the costume?' Tuppence pondered then stiffened. 'Unless she had an accomplice.'

'That could be true of anyone,' Hen said with a groan as they stared at the dress form, which now resembled a beige Christmas tree, with the tags hanging down like baubles.

'There's a bit to do.' Hen gulped. 'I'm not even sure where to start.'

'Wallace once told us he starts a case by spreading the net wide.' Ginny studied the numerous names written up. 'JM, who's coming into the theatre today? Will you have the whole cast and crew?'

'Correct. I need people to clean up the mess left behind by

the police, and Hazel's continuing rehearsals so I'll be able to talk to people as I come across them.' JM nodded.

'I'll be painting the scenery, so will listen out for gossip,' Tuppence declared.

'I'm not working at the library until eleven, so I could visit Andrew and see what I can find out. Then when I get to work, I'll do some research. Most of the newspaper articles have kept their information about Monica vague. I'd like to dig deeper,' Ginny offered.

'What about me?' Hen asked, gazing at the large pile of costumes stacked next to the sewing machine. 'Should I go with Ginny, or help research?'

Tuppence shook her head. 'I think you should keep working on the costumes. And as the actors come in for their fittings you can get them talking.'

'If they're being reticent, you can always stab them with a pin,' JM added. 'That should do the trick.'

Hen's face drained of colour.

'Let's hope it doesn't come to that.' Ginny gathered her bag and coat. 'I'd better find Andrew. He told us he was staying at Holly Farm.'

'Don't take any nonsense from him.' JM got to her feet and swept the crushed velvet cape around Flora's shoulders to hide the murder board from prying eyes. Then she grinned. 'I need to prepare myself for tackling the cast and crew. They might have hidden things from the police, but I doubt they'll be able to hide anything from me.'

TWELVE

FRIDAY DECEMBER 12

Holly Farm was, as its name suggested, a quaint collection of fields, flanked by hedges of holly. Sheep were grazing in the distance and winter crops were visible from the car.

Ginny hadn't called ahead to see if Andrew was there; she hoped it wasn't a wasted trip.

She continued along the private drive that was thick with mud and the heavy tyre treads of a tractor. At least there hadn't been ice overnight, but dew clung to the bare branches that flanked the way. The drive opened out at the end to reveal a modern farmhouse next to an old two-storey stone cottage. Smaller cottages were dotted around the fields and there was a large wooden sign that said *Holly Farm B&B*.

Ginny pulled up next to a battered old Land Rover and climbed out, wishing she'd taken more time with her appearance. Still, she did her best to smooth down her grey hair and wrap an air of confidence around herself.

The door to the B&B was ajar and she stepped into a quaint open area with a large log fire burning at one end. There was a harassed woman at a reception desk with soft flyaway hair and faded brown eyes set deep in a narrow face. She could have been anywhere between fifty and seventy, and Ginny got the feeling that life hadn't been kind.

Currently, the woman at reception was glaring at a man in his mid-thirties who wore a pair of sequined overalls and a black leather cap. Andrew.

'You booked the room for four more days, and I'm going to have to charge you,' the woman was saying.

'But that's ridiculous. Surely you can rent it out to someone else? This town is full of tourists.' Andrew's body was coiled, reminding Ginny of her cat before he jumped onto the kitchen counter.

'How can I say?' The woman was unmoved. 'Our website shows that we're booked out so I've had no enquiries.'

Andrew made a clicking noise with his tongue. 'Well, if you changed your website to show that a room *is* available, then could I avoid paying?'

'And if I had a computer that worked the way it was meant to, perhaps I could.' The woman clicked the mouse several times and tapped furiously on the keyboard. There was venom in her voice, but it was unclear who it was being directed at. The world in general? 'There... I've done as you requested, but if it isn't rebooked, you *will* be liable for it. We have your credit card details.'

'What a delight it's been talking with you.' Andrew spun around and sauntered towards a staircase at the side of the reception area.

Ginny's stomach tightened. It was clear Andrew wasn't in a good mood. But she'd come all this way, and now she was curious. Why was he leaving so abruptly? Did Wallace know about it?

'Can I help you?' the woman at reception snapped, dragging Ginny from her thoughts. It also caused Andrew to swirl around like a disco ball, sequins glittering despite the dull winter's day.

'I know you. Ginny, isn't it?' He raised a perfectly groomed eyebrow in her direction. 'You were there that night at the theatre. We're trauma bonded.'

'That's right,' she said, pleased he'd remembered her. Then she turned to the receptionist. 'I'm actually here to speak with Andrew... if that's okay?' The last part was directed back at the flamboyant Lark.

'Good luck. Apparently, he's got *urgent* business that means he's obliged to break his legally binding contract with us.' The woman returned to her computer screen, which beeped at her.

Andrew gave her a glacial stare. 'Thank you for reminding me *yet* again. Ginny, we can talk in my room.' He gestured her to follow him up the stairs into a lovely bedroom with simple furniture and a large wall radiator keeping it warm.

A suitcase was spread out on the unmade bed, and brightly coloured clothes lay in a pile on top, while a small rubbish bin was overflowing with stacks of old newspapers.

'So, what's this about? Why did you want to see me?' He nodded to a wooden chair next to a writing desk and he took the edge of the bed. Andrew crossed his legs and leaned forward, his curious gaze taking her in.

Ginny shrugged off her coat, wishing again that she'd been more prepared. She felt incredibly underdressed in her simple black trousers and striped jumper, compared to Andrew and his sequins. At least she'd remembered lipstick. She sat and neatly folded her coat in her lap.

She didn't consider herself a natural conversationalist, so she always found this part tricky. She could hardly lead with: *I'm an amateur sleuth sticking my nose into something that has baffled the police, yet, apparently, I think I can help. Care to answer some questions?*

Then, she noted the pallor of Andrew's skin and the hint of sadness in his eyes, and some of her panic dissipated. He had said they were trauma bonded. Under his glamorous swagger, Andrew was still very upset.

Her natural concern took over. 'I wanted to see how you were doing. The other night must've been very difficult.'

'It's been horrible. I want to get the hell out of here.' He frantically waved his arms around the room. There were several silver bracelets on his wrist and they chimed in agreement.

'It's understandable that you might want to go home. Assuming it's okay with the police,' Ginny added, cautiously.

His posture relaxed and he let out a soft bark of laughter. 'Oh, it's fine by them. I spoke to that good-looking detective yesterday afternoon. He wanted a link to my livestreaming from outside the theatre. I sent it through to them this morning and it was timestamped. Some Scottish woman called an hour ago and accepted I couldn't be in two places at once. It's only that one downstairs who is making it difficult.'

Livestreaming?

Andrew must have sent through the video after Ginny had spoken to Wallace and if Anita had called him with permission to leave the area, it meant the police must have been happy with his alibi. Though, she could also understand why a local business would worry about filling a room so close to Christmas. 'Would you like me to talk to the receptionist for you?'

He let out a sigh. 'You really are a doll, but don't bother. Regardless of what *that* dragon says, I'm sure another Lark will snap this room up.'

Ginny nodded, but didn't understand why he was leaving so suddenly. Was it grief? Or something else?

'If you don't mind me asking, why aren't you waiting for the memorial on Monday evening? You'd be welcome to attend.'

'Sorry, like I said, I really need to get home.' Andrew flinched and lowered his gaze, inspecting his very long fingernails, which had been painted a shimmering silver.

Ginny's curiosity grew. 'Of course. Grief hits us differently... but the offer's open if you do change your mind.'

'I won't,' he said in a tight voice then looked up. Instead of sadness, his eyes flashed with something else. *Annoyance?* But why? She'd seen his reaction when they'd discovered Monica's body, and he'd been distraught.

'Andrew, is everything okay?'

'Oh yes, everything's just fine and dandy.' He got to his feet and stalked around the sparse bedroom. 'It's been an absolute delight to discover the woman that I've idolised for twenty years was nothing but a bitter, angry excuse of a human being.'

Then he burst into tears.

Oh dear. Ginny hurried over to him, her winter coat falling onto the ground as she went. She put her arms around his shoulder as he sobbed. They stood there for several moments before he finally heaved a shuddering sigh and used his knuckles to dab at his eyes.

'Sorry about that,' he said and settled back down on the side of the bed.

'Don't apologise,' Ginny said, though she couldn't contain her curiosity. She hadn't been sure what to expect with this interview, but it hadn't been this. What had occurred between Sunday night and today to warrant such a vehement about-face? 'Has something happened... I mean, apart from the obvious?'

'Just reality catching up with me,' he said, retrieving a handkerchief to continue dabbing at his tear-streaked face. 'All these years, waiting outside stage doors and near rehearsal studios... She was happy to take my baskets and to have me escorting her to the car, but she never even remembered my name. I doubt she could've pick me out in a police lineup.'

'I'm sure that's not the case.' Ginny frowned.

He let out a bitter laugh. 'Oh, it is. Was. I've been in denial for a very long time.'

'What makes you say that?'

His lips twitched, as if considering whether to answer the question. Ginny caught her breath, torn between wanting to respect his privacy, and rampant curiosity.

He rolled his shoulders and straightened his spine. 'The night we found her body... when I was at the stage door waiting for Monica, it wasn't to walk her to the car. It was to confront her about the argument I'd overheard. It made me realise the truth about her. That she was a monster.'

THIRTEEN

FRIDAY DECEMBER 12

A monster?

The room fell silent as adrenaline hammered through Ginny's chest. It had never occurred to her to question Andrew's reason for being at the stage door on that Sunday night, and his grief had been genuine.

'Who was she arguing with?' Ginny asked.

'Danny Ling.' Andrew gnawed at his lower lip and rubbed his eyes.

'The documentary maker?' Ginny's brow furrowed, recalling the man on the stage and the glee in his eyes as chaos erupted. 'Are you sure?'

'Oh yes. He's staying here, in a small cottage down by the pond. Him and that cameraman of his are always coming and going. I've tried talking to him a couple of times to arrange an interview. But he kept snubbing me. I don't forget stuff like that. Anyway, on Sunday night I was walking around the playhouse, checking out the locations, when Monica came outside. I was about to go and say hello but then Danny and the cameraman appeared.'

'And they were arguing? What about?'

'About the documentary. Danny was annoyed that Monica

wouldn't cooperate with him. She was yelling at him: "Get that thing away from me. I don't owe you anything." Then he flipped out. He said: "Bollocks you don't. You stitched me up and dragged me around this stupid village and now you won't spill. This thing is costing me a fortune and I've got sod all to show for it."'

Ginny's heart thudded. Even in the retelling, she could hear the anger hanging in the air like a visceral thing. But it didn't fully explain Andrew's own distress. 'Did something else happen?'

He closed his eyes and used his fingers to fan his face then straightened his shoulders. 'Then Danny asked Monica if he could at least interview some of the Larks and she—' He broke off. '*She* said: "The last thing I want is for those morons sprouting their crap. The whole point of this is for people to know the real me... and trust me, those idiots don't know a thing."'

His face crumpled. Poor Andrew. It was clearly painful to discover his idol was mortal like the rest of them, and that she apparently hated her fans so much. And Ginny felt as bad for Monica, who seemed to be painted as the very pantomime villain she was so desperate to avoid being seen as. While Ginny wouldn't enjoy having people running around after her, wanting to know her every move, she supposed that having fans was the double-edged sword of fame.

'Maybe she was having a bad night? She was agitated during the rehearsal. Perhaps there was something else going on? Especially since...' Ginny trailed off, not wanting to remind him of the details of the murder. What if Monica was being threatened? Would that explain her outburst?

'I've heard her be rude to people. Including me. But for so long I thought it was part of her personality. You know, tough love and all of that. And to be fair... I can be a bit spiky myself at times. But this was *vicious*. It really shocked me. That's why I waited behind. I wanted to "tell Monica all about it." See if she'd really meant what she said about the Larks.'

Closing her eyes, Ginny went through what this meant. What was it that Danny Ling wanted Monica to 'spill'? How much of his own money had he invested in the documentary? Was it enough to commit murder for?

'What time did this fight take place?' Ginny asked, opening her eyes.

'It was before I started livestreaming. It must have been at eight o'clock.'

'Did you tell Wallace?' Ginny asked.

Andrew blinked. 'About my livestreaming? Yes. He knows it's my alibi, but I never asked him to follow me. Do you think I should? Now that I'm no longer invested in Monica, I might have to rebuild my audience and reposition myself, but I'm sure it will be fabulous.'

Ginny shook her head. 'No. Did you tell Wallace about the argument with Danny?'

'Oh.' Andrew bowed his head. 'Not exactly. I was in such a state of shock that I wasn't thinking straight.'

'I understand how difficult it might be, but you do need to talk to the police about it,' Ginny said, gently.

'I suppose you're right.' He sighed, then perked up. 'If I invited that dishy detective here to do the interview, it might make that dragon downstairs get a fright.'

Ginny wasn't sure what to do with any of that statement, so reached out and patted Andrew's arm instead. 'Promise you'll make the call. The police need to know. And... could you direct me to Danny's cottage?'

'It's on the other side of the farmhouse.' Andrew gestured to the window. 'But he's not there. I saw his white van head out half an hour ago.'

Oh. Ginny didn't know whether to be pleased or disappointed she couldn't speak to him. Before she could decide, there was a pounding thump on the door.

'It's Trish. From reception,' said a voice on the other side.

'Of course it is.' Andrew let out a dramatic sigh, stood up languidly and peered out. 'Yes?'

'I wanted to tell you that the room has been rebooked and therefore you're released from your obligations. You'll need to check out by ten-thirty am,' Trish said in a thoroughly formal voice that didn't have much effect on her guest.

'Gee, it's almost like I predicted that would happen. Don't expect a good review.' Andrew pouted.

'That goes both ways,' Trish retorted and clomped down the stairs.

Ginny looked at her watch. 'I won't keep you. Though, could you tell me the best place to find information on Monica? I'm curious about her career. Her obituary didn't contain any useful details.'

'Tell me about it. The media keep those things on file and then whip them out as soon as anyone dies.' Andrew shuddered. 'There's a lot of useful stuff on the Larks' main message board. Just look up Live, Lark, Love and you'll find it.'

'Thank you.'

'That's fine. Actually, if you do want to read about her, you're welcome to have my collection since I no longer require it.' Andrew pointed to the overflowing rubbish bin before staring out the window, as if hoping the ghost of Monica Larkwell was hovering close by and could hear the displeasure in his voice.

'Your collection?'

'That's right. Some of my Monica Larkwell memorabilia that isn't signed. I was hoping to get her to do it on opening night. It's mainly newspaper clippings, theatre programmes and a few other bits and bobs. Clearly that won't be happening now.'

No, it definitely won't be.

Another wave of sadness hit Ginny, and while she could understand Andrew's disillusionment, she couldn't help but think he might change his mind once he had processed his grief. It was one of the most useful pieces of advice she'd been given after Eric's death: *Don't make hasty decisions until a year has passed.*

However, Ginny had also moved to Little Shaw on her own, eight months later. She swallowed back a smile. Sometimes it was a case of: do as I say, not as I do. She crossed over to his side and put a hand on his arm.

'That's a generous offer but I think you should keep your collection. In case you change your mind. I would hate for you to regret giving it away.'

'I won't.' He gave an adamant shake of his head. 'It's dead to me now. But if you don't want it, I'll leave it here for the dragon to deal with.'

'If you really don't mind me taking it, I admit I'm curious to read more about her.' Ginny produced a reusable shopping bag from her coat pocket.

'Knock yourself out,' Andrew said with a flourish and then checked the time on his phone. 'I need to finish packing if I want to make my train home. I have a rental I must return. Let's hope that your sexy detective doesn't keep me too long. Hmm, on second thoughts...'

Ginny bit back a smile, not sure if Wallace would thank her for sending Andrew back to him, but she was certain he'd need to take the statement directly and would no doubt have more questions for him. And with that she bade Andrew a quick farewell and made the short drive back into Little Shaw, going through everything she had learned.

FOURTEEN

FRIDAY DECEMBER 12

'Aren't these marvellous?' Hen said later that afternoon as they sat in the theatre stalls, going through the memorabilia. The library had been too busy for Ginny to do much more than flip through the many newspaper articles and ephemera. 'Look, here's a handbill from when Monica was in that Willy Russell play in London ten years ago.'

'She was so glamorous.' Tuppence leaned over to study a stunning photograph of Monica wearing a floral suit jacket and fishnet tights as she lay half-draped over a table.

'OH NO SHE'S NOT,' someone boomed. Ginny jumped, heart thumping in her chest.

'Well, that's rude,' Hen protested as the three friends looked up to the stage, where one of the actors was hanging from the side of a ladder. 'Oh, gosh, he did a great job of projecting his voice. I thought he was talking to us.'

'It was very believable,' Tuppence agreed and clicked her fingers as if at a poetry reading.

It was a little *too* believable; Ginny put her hand on her chest to help herself relax, which was silly because they weren't doing anything wrong. Wallace had asked them to help, so why was she so jumpy? She took a deep breath and turned back to the stage as Hazel Holdsworth stormed up to the actor. She was wearing a coffee-coloured dress with black-framed glasses that enhanced the grimace on her lips.

'Cactus Number Three, your line is: "Leave my domain now before I am forced to meet you with violence,"' Hazel told the man.

'At which point I say: "Violence," and offer up a menacing glare,' another actor added.

'Yes, Reggie, thank you for that,' Hazel snapped. 'But I'd like to concentrate on Bert's line. Right, Bert, from the top.'

The dangling man rubbed his brow and blinked. 'Wait? Are you speaking to me or to Cactus Number Three?'

'You *are* Cactus Number Three, moron,' someone else muttered, which earned a snicker from several of the cast who were waiting in the wings.

Hazel checked her watch and held up her arm. 'Bert and Reggie, that's enough for now. Can I get everyone in the dance scene to come to the stage? We'll go through the igloo number in five minutes.'

She stalked away, shaking her head as she went, while Desiree Northam herded the dancers to the centre of the stage.

'Oh dear,' Hen said in a low voice. 'Poor Hazel. Everyone is on edge about Monica. Yesterday, two of the goblins tried to stand on the same mark and tripped over each other. I hope it's not a bad omen.'

'There's been so many bad omens, what's one more?' Tuppence said as JM descended on them, using her clipboard to clear her path. She sat down in the next row forward, and twisted in the chair to face them.

'Sorry I'm late.' JM's gaze landed on the memorabilia they'd been sorting. 'Have you found anything? More importantly, have you heard back from Wallace about Danny Ling?'

'Not yet,' Ginny admitted, though she wasn't really surprised. After leaving Holly Farm, she'd messaged him about her discovery in case Andrew decided to leave town without talking to the police first.

Or in case Danny left.

However, Ginny had experienced enough of Wallace's terse text messages to know he didn't respond to everything. Still, she'd done her part and while the library had been too busy for her to do any research, she had kept her eyes out for the documentary maker, but there had been no sign of him there.

'At least we have a definite suspect,' Tuppence said. 'I've already double underlined his name on Flora and have been asking around. None of the cast or crew had a good word to say about him. One even saw him put an empty milk carton back into the fridge.'

'Oh, I hate that.' Hen frowned. 'It's very rude.'

'What can you expect from a killer?' Tuppence replied.

'Suspected killer,' JM amended, then gave them a glittering smile. 'I have the cause of death.'

'How?' Tuppence demanded. 'The police haven't released that information, which if you ask me, is a mistake. I think that's why everyone's fluffing their lines in the rehearsal, because they're worried the killer might come for them next.'

'They might be right.' JM leaned forward and lowered her voice. 'I was in the props room discussing the castle scenery with Ted Wallace when Suzette Ryan walked in. She was on her phone and it sounded like she was talking to her husband. Remember, he's on the board? She told him that the police will be releasing a statement this evening about the cause of death.'

'I wonder what time it will be? I do hate waiting,' Tuppence said then studied JM's face. 'Oh, right, I take it you know what it is. Do share.'

'I will, if you'll let me,' JM responded with a quelling glare. 'Monica Larkwell was killed by blunt force trauma, using a heavy object. The murder weapon hasn't been recovered.'

'So why cut the cable on the chandelier?' Hen wondered. 'It

seems like an unnecessary risk. What if the person got caught while doing it? Was it to make it look like an accident?'

Ginny recalled the clean cut of the wire and the glass of champagne. Clearly, they had been a distraction. Hen was right, the killer wanted people to know it had been done on purpose. There had to be a reason for it.

Oh.

They staged the scene to make a statement.

Ginny turned to her friends. 'A chandelier is a light, which could represent a spotlight. What does that tell us?'

'That her time on the centre stage was over.' Tuppence clapped her hands together.

'There's more to it, though,' Ginny admitted. 'To get so close to Monica and hit her hard enough to kill her is very personal. Which makes me think they were emotionally involved.'

Hen shivered and wrapped her arms around her chest. 'If that's the case, they obviously wanted Monica to suffer. But who would do something like that?'

'Someone who really disliked her, and perhaps had done so for a long time,' JM said as Ginny's phone buzzed with a text message.

It was from Wallace.

> Just interviewed Andrew and will follow up with Ling. Cause of death is blunt force trauma. It will be announced in an hour, along with information about the goose costume. Thnx

Ginny's brow lifted as she showed her friends. 'Look.'

'At least he's keeping us in the loop,' Hen said as Hazel reappeared on the stage.

'Why am I waiting for the igloo dancers?' Hazel's voice carried around the auditorium. 'I want—'

She broke off as Suzette Ryan stepped out from behind the curtain that concealed the backstage and walked purposefully towards Hazel.

There was a hushed conversation that lasted for five minutes and when it was finished, Suzette disappeared again, leaving Hazel standing on the stage surrounded by dancers, who were striking a pose that Ginny could only assume was meant to represent an igloo.

Abruptly Hazel called Desiree over and whispered something in her ear.

Desiree clapped her hands and returned to the dancers. 'Right, let's start from the top. Can we please have the music? I'll count you in.'

Hazel didn't wait to watch the dancers. Instead, she retrieved a phone from the pocket of her voluminous dress and made a call. Her face was strained and pale as she walked off the stage towards the stalls.

'What's happening?' Tuppence whispered. 'Do you think Suzette told Hazel about the cause of death and the press statement?'

'Most likely. Seems like Suzette can't keep a secret to save her life,' JM retorted as Hazel swept past them, phone clamped to her ear.

'Yes... she told me it's about to come out. I can't believe this. And yet... I don't regret what I did. If I had to, I'd do it again,' Hazel said, in a voice devoid of emotion.

Hen's eyes bulged but none of them spoke until Hazel had swept past, in the direction of the foyer and ticket office. Ginny's mind whirled as she went over the director's words.

I don't regret what I did. If I had to, I'd do it again.

What had she done?

Was this about what happened thirty years ago when Monica slept with Hazel's husband and ruined her marriage? Multiple people had confirmed that Hazel had been against Monica starring in the pantomime, plus she'd been involved with the theatre for such a long time that she could've easily found Prissy's costume and Monica's dressing room without getting lost.

A lump formed in Ginny's throat as she watched Hazel's retreating figure. Then she thought of the night of Monica's death. Hazel had wanted to speak to Monica alone. Was it because she had been angry at the chaos the actress had caused? Had it added to Hazel's reasons for resenting Monica?

Ginny fumbled for her phone to text Wallace with an update, but her friends were already on their feet. It was clear they were thinking that Hazel Holdsworth was most definitely a suspect.

'There she is.' Tuppence pointed as a coffee-coloured dress disappeared down the other end of the foyer. 'That way leads to the bar upstairs. What if she wants a drink?'

'Then she will be out of luck. The bar's closed, which she well knows,' JM said as they followed in Hazel's wake. 'Now, what's our approach?'

'We don't want her to think we're giving her the third degree,' Ginny said in a soft voice. 'It's important we put her at ease.'

'Yes,' Hen agreed, 'I would hate for her to think we're accusing her of anything.'

'Except, she might be guilty and is about to flee the country because she knows that we're onto her,' Tuppence said.

'True, but she might also be innocent and chatting to a friend,' JM countered. 'Ginny's right. We need to do this subtly.'

The vintage red and gold carpet dulled the sound of their footsteps as they climbed the stairs. The upstairs bar ran against a wall with several tables and chairs clustered near a mezzanine balcony that looked back down to the foyer below.

Hazel was at the far end, her back to them as she continued her phone call. It was unclear if she'd heard them approach, but JM made several hand gestures, which Ginny took to mean that they should stand in front of the stairs so that Hazel couldn't pass them.

'Okay.' Tuppence lowered herself into a position that reminded Ginny of a rugby player going into a scrum as Hazel finished her phone call and spun.

'JM, is there a production problem?' A frown rippled her brow.

'There are multiple problems,' JM answered coolly. 'However, this isn't my first rodeo when it comes to management, and I have them under control. We need to speak to you about something else.'

'Oh, really?' Hazel's eyes narrowed from behind her glasses.

'Yes, we want to know about your relationship with Monica Larkwell,' Tuppence interjected. 'And who you were speaking to on the phone. Are you organising a getaway?'

'A getaway?' Hazel's knuckles went white as she gripped her phone. Was she getting ready to speed dial someone? Oh dear. So much for putting Hazel at her ease.

'Yes,' Tuppence agreed. 'Er, I mean that you *might* be organising a getaway, however we're prepared to offer you the benefit of the doubt.'

JM stepped forward and gestured to a chair at one of the round tables. 'Why don't you tell us about Monica Larkwell? It wasn't a secret that you didn't want her to join the production.'

Hazel took her black-framed glasses off and studied JM through pale blue eyes. Sighing, she took the proffered chair. 'I take it you think I killed her.'

'Exactly,' Tuppence agreed. 'The plan was to put you at your ease first, but that takes up so much time and small talk. I prefer to dive straight in.'

Hazel's lips twitched and she broke into a smile. 'You're so right. I find the older I get, the less time I have for beating around the bush. Since you're interested, let me tell you what I told the police. It's no secret that I never liked Monica Larkwell. I wasn't involved in the production thirty years ago, but my husband at the time was. And the few times I met her, she was very rude. In the spirit of straight-talking, why are you so interested?'

'Does there have to be a reason?' Hen bluffed.

'When it comes to murder investigations, I would say yes... there really does,' Hazel retorted as an amused smile spread across her face. 'Which means everything I've read about you must be true.'

'What things?' JM growled. 'Could you be more specific?'

'That you like investigating murders,' Hazel replied in a calm voice. If it shocked her, she hid it well. 'I never believe half of what our local paper prints, but I'm starting to think they were right. So, what is your theory? That I killed Monica because she and Alan were rumoured to have had an affair back then?'

'Exactly,' Tuppence readily agreed before frowning. 'Though... as you mentioned, it is a theory. Sorry, maybe we should have started with more small talk. This conversation went better in my head.'

'Nonsense. I think it's going quite well,' Hazel assured them all, her shoulders relaxing. 'At the time everyone was gossiping about Alan and Monica, though he never confirmed or denied it.'

'Why wouldn't he deny it if it wasn't true?' Hen leaned forward, confusion marring her brow.

'Let's be fair. Even before *First Kiss*, Monica was building a career and had been in a couple of soaps. I think it suited his ego for people to talk about them sleeping together. And perhaps they did? I suppose we'll never know since they're both dead.'

'Is that why your marriage ended? Because Alan wouldn't admit the truth?' Ginny asked carefully, not sure what to make of Hazel's calm demeanour and willingness to answer their questions.

'Not at all. My marriage ended because I met someone else.' Hazel paused and fiddled with her phone and brought up a photograph of two women. One was Hazel looking radiant in a white over-sized dress, while a second woman stood next to her, also wearing a white dress. 'This is Ruby. She was visiting family in Little Shaw and came to see the pantomime, all those years ago. It was love at first sight and we've been together ever since.

We are very private people so we don't advertise our relationship —nor do we hide it.'

'I should hope not,' JM said as she studied the photograph and then bowed her head. 'We owe you an apology. I pride myself on not judging anyone, and we were swayed by gossip. I'm sorry.'

'We all are.' Hen dabbed her eyes as she smiled at the beautiful photograph.

'I'm pleased you found your person,' Ginny added.

'Thank you. Maybe Rubes and I would have been more open if we've been surrounded with friends like you.' Hazel smiled at them.

'I'd hope in this day and age you would be,' Tuppence said then wrinkled her nose. 'Though I'm not sure I understand why you were so against Monica coming back to Little Shaw, if you didn't resent her.'

'Yes, shouldn't you be supporting older women?' JM demanded.

At that Hazel laughed. 'I suppose you're right. But thirty years ago, I got to see firsthand what a diva Monica was. And when the board asked me to direct the pantomime, I had Desiree Northam in mind for the role. She's been waiting for her big break and would've been perfect. So, yes, I didn't want Monica Larkwell to come to Little Shaw.'

'Why *did* Monica want to come back to Little Shaw?' Ginny asked, recalling the conversation she'd overheard the other day. That the board had only paid Monica two thousand pounds. It seemed a modest amount considering the actress's fame. Surely there were other places to launch a comeback. Unless she wanted the nostalgia that went along with being recognised by the small theatre that had been her stepping stone to fame.

'No idea. I must admit I half expected her to refuse, considering how limited our funds were, but for whatever reason she agreed. Lucky me.' Hazel sighed, before collecting herself. 'I might not have liked her, but I didn't kill her.'

'Of course you didn't,' Hen said quickly.

'Can you think of anyone else who would have a good reason to murder her?' Ginny asked.

'No.' Hazel shook her head. 'However, as you witnessed the other night. Monica didn't go out of her way to make friends. I think she thought her fame would protect her.'

The shattered chandelier and its thousands of tiny crystals, sprang into Ginny's mind. If the fallen chandelier was a symbol that her time in the spotlight was now over, it meant that whatever Monica's fame had done for her, it had come at a terrible cost.

Closing her eyes, Ginny leaned back.

The more they discovered, the sadder this case was becoming.

FIFTEEN

SATURDAY DECEMBER 13

'Look at them fighting,' Slim said the following morning from the issue counter, as several of the regular patrons snatched at the national newspapers Connor had just put out. 'Though they really shouldn't use their walking sticks.' He broke off and whistled. 'You lot... we have pub rules here. No kicking, scratching or kneecapping. Am I making myself clear?'

There was some muttering as the group broke up, clutching at the papers as they made their way back to the various reading spots around the library.

'Thank you, Slim.' Ginny put down the reservations list she'd been studying. 'I suppose I should start ordering in extra papers until this case is over.'

'It might save some bloodshed. Not that there's much in the papers. Just fantastical headlines about how they suspect it's her plastic surgeon who topped her off. Apparently, he wasn't happy with the work he'd done on her. Though why a plastic surgeon would want to dress up as a goose is beyond me.'

Ginny shuddered. She'd avoided reading the sensationalist headlines that the case was attracting. Poor Monica. Her life reduced to her appearance. And the pressure on Wallace and his team mounted, with the release of the news that the killer had worn Prissy's purple-feathered suit.

She swallowed a yawn from another late night. After their encounter with Hazel, the friends had agreed that the director was telling the truth. Hazel had also gone on to elaborate that the phone call they'd heard just before their conversation was a discussion with a friend about one of the cast members that she'd suggested sing in a lower register because their high notes kept breaking.

It had been a humbling experience, though they had parted as friends and Hazel had even invited them around for drinks once the pantomime was over.

The rest of the evening had been spent reading the police statement that had been released, though it didn't tell them anything they didn't already know. Then they'd sorted out the piles of memorabilia Andrew had given them. Ginny, worried Andrew might want them back one day, entered everything into a spreadsheet so she had a record of it all.

There were some interesting insights into Monica's life in the stack of papers, but in general, the information contained there was more about things like Monica's preference to summer in the South of France and to never fly economy. Unfortunately, none of the press clippings Andrew had so diligently collected over the years had ever gone in-depth. It was the same with the collection of show programmes, which had helped them chart Monica's working life, but not much else.

However, they hadn't finished going through everything, so Ginny had brought the collection into the library with her.

'Your posse is here, Ginny.' Cleo appeared, pushing an empty book trolley. 'And a reminder that I can only work for another hour. I have rehearsal. I would've gone directly there but everything's such a mess here. I have no idea what Connor and Slim do with themselves all day.' Then without another word she disappeared into the returns room.

Slim grinned. 'I feel like order has been restored to the universe now she's back. I think even Connor missed her.'

'Yes, it was difficult getting through each day without being belittled,' Connor retorted, deadpan, from where he was processing new magazines. But his eyes were twinkling and Ginny bit back a smile. Despite Cleo's abrasive personality, she was as much a part of the team as anyone.

'I hope you can survive without me for half an hour? I need to do something private.' Ginny picked up the box of memorabilia.

'Fine by me, since it means our young Connor owes me a tenner.' Slim beamed. 'I knew you and the Detective Club would crumble and get involved. About time, if you ask me. Police are clearly getting nowhere on their own.'

'We *didn't* ask you,' Connor retorted then gave her an apologetic grimace.

Ginny sighed. As well as them using the absurd name, Slim and Connor were fond of betting on what Ginny and her friends would do next. But she'd never seen any money change hands, so perhaps it was only theoretical betting.

Did that make it okay?

Deciding it was safer not to answer, she joined her friends at one of the reading tables.

'There you are.' Tuppence looked up from the pile of paper tags she'd been working on. 'We've spent all morning driving around Little Shaw looking for Danny Ling, but no one has seen him. Do you think he's done a runner?'

'I hope not.' Hen shuddered. 'If he's behind the murder, I don't like the idea of him escaping from the law.'

'Let's assume Wallace has eyes on him,' JM said, taking the box from Ginny's hand. 'In the meantime, we should start. I need to be back at the theatre in an hour.'

'And I can't stay away too long,' Ginny said. 'Cleo and Andrea will be leaving soon and it's been busy all morning with the Larks and journalists.'

'Speaking of journalists, we'd better make sure they don't know what we're working on,' Tuppence said then raised her voice. 'Ah, Hen, I do love your old recipes for wart removal. It's quite a collection.'

Several nearby people shuddered and drifted away. Tuppence grinned.

'That was jolly good,' Hen said, taking one of the piles of newspaper clippings that Ginny had put out on the table. 'Now, let's get started.'

As well as newspaper articles, there were piles of old photographs, theatre programmes and ticket stubs. The articles were only positive ones, which Ginny could understand, since Andrew had planned for Monica to sign them. She skimmed through the first pile.

Larkwell delivers a performance worthy of the West End. We've found our next star.

The Queen of First Kisses *spotted in the South of France with football's latest wonder kid.*

Our favourite matriarch is crowned Queen of the Mountains.

'It's hard to believe this was only *part* of Andrew's collection,' Hen said an hour later as she smoothed out another theatre stub and added it to the pile, while Tuppence used a magnifying glass to check for any hidden clues in the numerous red-carpet shots.

'It's a fine line between collecting and hoarding.' JM discarded a used Monica Larkwell-shaped car air freshener.

'Here, I think I've got something.' Tuppence held up an old theatre programme with *Mother Goose* printed across the top. 'This is from thirty years ago. And look at the photographs. There's two of Monica on her own, but here's one of the cast. See that man next to her, that's Alan Holdsworth.'

Ginny studied the low-quality image. It was a party photograph, featuring a group of people messing around, waving their hands in the air and poking out their tongues, trying to out-goof each other. They appeared to be enjoying themselves immensely. Monica stood regally in the centre of the picture.

The man that Hen said was Alan Holdsworth had blond hair and a gold chain around his neck, but she didn't recognise anyone else in the photograph so lowered her gaze to the names of the cast.

From left to right: Beano, K-man, Sarah T, Alan 'Alfie' Holdsworth, Moni Larkwell, Big P, Jimbo Mansfield, Crunch Time, Junie Northam.

Ginny rubbed her jaw. Junie Northam? Was it possible she was related to Desiree? She checked the photograph again and found a lovely looking woman with corkscrew curls and dark skin. Before she could ask, JM made a clicking noise with her tongue.

'Beano, K-man, Big P? What's with all the names?' her friend demanded.

'They're stage names.' Cleo appeared, pushing a book trolley, with Andrea trailing in her wake holding a script in one hand and a water bottle in the other. 'I remember Alan Holdsworth once telling me that he flirted with being called Allan in the mid-nineties.'

'What's the difference?' Tuppence frowned.

'With two "l's", of course.'

'Yes, but it sounds exactly the same, so what's the point?' Tuppence continued.

'The point is that it's a stage name,' Cleo repeated, enunciating her words to help Tuppence understand. Before anyone could comment, Andrea coughed and tapped her wrist. Cleo's eyes widened. 'Hen, wouldn't your time be better spent at the theatre working on my costume? Now I've been rightfully reinstated as Queen, it's important that my costumes are glorious.'

'It's also important that we get to take a break,' JM retorted and rolled her shoulders. 'However, since I do need to be back at the theatre, I suppose we'd better finish up.'

'No time to waste.' Cleo pushed the trolley away, Andrea trotting at her heels.

'I know she's fantastic on the stage, but she's starting to wear at my patience,' JM admitted as they packed away the memorabilia. 'Hen and Tuppence, are you coming back with me?'

'Yes,' they both chorused and turned to Ginny.

'Connor's locking up this afternoon so I'm finishing at lunchtime. I have to run a few errands but will be there as soon as I can. In the meantime, I'll do more research on the internet.'

'Excellent. Last night made me realise how many people we need to interview.'

'Including Desiree,' Ginny said, recalling the name Junie. 'Is it possible her mother was in the original cast? I saw someone in the photograph with the same last name.'

'Oh yes. Junie Northam,' Tuppence agreed. 'Lovely woman. She was in many shows and also did costumes. She was Desiree's mother... well, she still is but is in a care home now with Alzheimer's.'

'I'm sorry to hear that.' Ginny shuddered at the terrible disease that took so much from people. And while they wouldn't be able to ask Junie any questions, it made it more essential to talk with Desiree. Especially because Desiree had not only fought with Monica about the TikTok dance, but as the understudy, she had a lot to gain with the actress out of the way.

Was it possible that her mother, Junie, had also clashed with Monica? Was Desiree carrying an extra grudge – the need to get revenge on behalf of a beloved parent who could no longer do it for herself?

It didn't take them long to pack up and make their goodbyes.

Ginny returned to the counter in time to prevent Cleo from telling William off for doodling on the newspapers. The rest of the morning was busy and Ginny's attempts at researching both Monica and Desiree and her mother Junie fell flat. So much for thinking she could help Wallace.

SIXTEEN

SATURDAY DECEMBER 13

'Hey, Mrs C, wait up.'

Ginny came to a halt as Connor jogged over to where she was standing outside the theatre. She'd only seen him a few hours ago when she'd left him and Slim to lock up. Since then, she'd eaten lunch, fed Edgar and done a few bits of housework as well as some casual checking out the window to see if Wallace had returned. An update on the case would be nice, but there were no signs of the white EV. Eventually, she'd driven to the theatre and parked as close as she could before walking the rest of the way.

'I didn't know you were part of the volunteer crew.' She slowed down to wait for him. He'd changed out of the black combat trousers and hoodie he had been wearing at work and was now in dark denim jeans and a beige knitted jumper peered out from under his coat. Ginny did a double take. It was the lightest colour she'd ever seen him wear.

'I'm not.' He came to a halt. 'But after you left work, I saw your search history on the computer and Monica Larkwell's name was there, so I thought I'd help out.'

'You researched Monica for us?' She winced. Despite Connor showing her and everyone in his Savvy Senior Skills course how to delete the computer's search history, she continued to forget to do it.

'Yeah.' He shrugged. 'My name isn't on the list so I couldn't get into the theatre. I was about to call when I saw you.'

Oh.

Ginny thought of the sign-in sheet that she'd had to fill in each time she came and went. Since Monica's murder, JM had doubled down on it.

'I'm pleased it wasn't a wasted trip. I was going in there now, would you like to come along?' she asked, uncertainly. Despite considering him a friend, she worried he might feel obliged to spend so much time with a group of women in their sixties and seventies. And while they loved having him around, she was very aware that he was only twenty and might want to spend time with people his own age.

'Sure.' He fell into step beside her. Since the theatre had reopened, a different person had been on the stage door, and today it was a tall man wearing a Santa hat and a homemade Christmas jumper. At twenty-nine, he was very handsome with blond hair, a chiselled jaw and sparkling green eyes. On his belt was a radio telephone that emitted beeps and buzzes.

Kaleb Shepard, the man the Prissy goose costume had been designed for.

He was on their suspect list, so was his appearance at the door because JM had already spoken with him about an alibi?

'Um, hello, my name's Ginny Cole. I should be on the list.'

'Cole. Cole. Cole,' he muttered to himself, his finger tracing up and down the list several times. 'Could you spell it for me?'

'Of course.' Ginny proceeded to do so, then leaned over and pointed to her name. 'There it is.'

Kaleb's brow furrowed. 'Oh, and that's definitely you? JM told me not to let anyone in who isn't on the list.'

'That's right, but as you can see, Ginny *is* on it.' JM strode up to the stage door and stood next to Kaleb. 'And with her is

Connor West. You can write his name down as a guest. Then let them both sign in.'

'Connor West?' Kaleb repeated then peered up, recognition flooding his handsome face. 'Alright, Con. Didn't see you there. Everything good?'

'Can't complain,' Connor answered and patted Kaleb on the arm. 'Want me to write my name down?'

'Thanks, man,' Kaleb agreed and thrust the clipboard at him. Connor scribbled his name then handed it to Ginny and soon JM was leading them through the corridors to the costume room.

'Sorry about that. He's a lovely fellow but after a quick chat, I've decided to take him off the suspect list. He hadn't even realised Monica had been murdered. Thought the media and fans were in town for some Christmas party. Plus, he left the theatre with his mother and grandfather at eight o'clock on the night of the murder and went out for a meal,' JM said.

'Kaleb really loves Christmas,' Connor confirmed. 'When he was younger, he'd wear his reindeer antlers all year round. Good call to rule him out. He might have muscles but that's from working on a farm. He's never been in any kind of trouble.'

'Glad you agree,' JM said as they reached the costume room. Hen was leaning over the cutting table, a bolt of fabric in her hands, and Tuppence was walking around Flora, a thoughtful expression in her eyes. Brandon was curled up on an old quilt, but on seeing Connor, he lumbered up and ambled over.

'Hello, boy.' Connor dropped down to pat the friendly dog. Then he looked at the dress form covered with dangling notes and masking tape. 'And Flora... you been roped in, too?'

'Connor, what a lovely surprise.' Hen beamed. 'I can see you've already met Flora.'

'My sister was in *Mary Poppins* one year, so our paths have crossed,' he said in a dry voice as he nodded at the dress form.

'Connor did some research for us,' Ginny explained, knowing how little he liked being in the spotlight. Funnily enough, neither did she, but she was always keen to make sure other people's contributions were properly acknowledged. 'So, I thought it's only right he come in.'

'It's not a big deal,' he mumbled, bowing his head over Brandon. 'It only took a few minutes. Plus, I thought you might want some help, er... interviewing people.'

Ginny's jaw loosened. That was strange. Connor had helped them numerous times before, and while his people skills had improved, especially when it came to the library, interviewing random suspects he'd never met before was something she would have thought he'd avoid, much like her cat avoided taking medicine.

'We do indeed,' Tuppence agreed, stopping in front of Flora and pointing to Andrew and Hazel's tags that now hung from the form's shoulder. 'These are the people we've officially cleared, and Kaleb is the latest one,' she added, unpinning the tag and moving it over with the others. She also made a note that his mother and grandfather had been with him.

'To be fair, Kaleb virtually removed himself,' JM retorted then narrowed her gaze on Connor, her nose twitching. 'Are you wearing aftershave?'

Colour crept up Connor's neck and he got to his feet, awkwardly shuffling from side to side. 'I took a shower, that's all.'

'Hmmm.' JM's mouth tightened as she stepped closer. 'And put on new clothing? I haven't seen either of those items. What's going on?'

Ginny's eyes widened. Her friends were right. She'd seen Connor go to the pub enough times to know this was something different. Curiosity tickled her skin, but it wasn't their place to pry. She gave him a reassuring smile. 'It's okay, you don't need to answer that.'

To her surprise he sighed. 'I heard you say you were going to interview Desiree Northam tonight. I thought you might need some help.'

'Why would we need help?' Tuppence said. 'Oh, don't tell me you like her? But she's almost twice your age.'

'Why does age have to be a barrier?' JM demanded, gaze stern. 'Connor's free to like whoever he chooses.'

His colour deepened and he quickly shook his head. 'It's not like that. I know her a bit. And her family.'

'Her family?' Hen wrinkled her nose then clapped her hands. 'Oh, Iris. Desiree's daughter. You must be the same age. She's such a lovely girl. Didn't she go to Newcastle to study?'

'I think she's home for the break,' he mumbled before realising they were staring at him. 'We used to be friends, back in the day.'

'And judging by the way you've ironed those jeans, I'd say you want to be *more* than friends.' Tuppence whooped and Ginny couldn't hide her smile. That was why he'd wanted to come into the theatre: to see Desiree's daughter, Iris.

Connor let out a long groan. 'It's no big deal. I thought since I know them it might help. Plus, I'm heading to the pub later and... er... was going to see if she wanted to come along.'

'Oh, that's so lovely.' Hen dabbed at her eyes and Connor's colour rose.

'Um, maybe we should fill Connor in on what we've discovered and then look at what he's found?' Ginny quickly said, knowing that as thrilled as his unofficial aunts were, he'd be hating the attention. She resisted the urge to smile at him too broadly, though she was smiling on the inside.

It didn't take long for the four of them to get him updated.

'We're waiting for Wallace to get back to us on what's happening with Danny Ling,' JM said. 'But we know better than to put our eggs in one basket. So, what do you have?'

'Most of it tallies up with what you've got. I did find quite a few articles about Monica's age. There were several sites that were dedicated to what plastic surgeries she'd had, but other places insisted that she'd never had any work done. A couple of years ago, Monica did an interview where she talked about the perils of being an ageing woman in an industry that only cares about youth.'

'Oh, that's so sad.' Hen's hands flew to her mouth. 'And she was so lovely looking.'

'It's a ruthless industry,' Tuppence said with a shake of her head.

Ginny closed her eyes. Poor Monica.

Getting older was something they all experienced and knew firsthand that there was only so much you could do. And even then, it was about maintaining your health, fitness and mental attitude. She could too easily imagine the stress of trying to stop wrinkles, skin tags and stray hairs from appearing, all in the face of the world's media.

'You said she never married, but what about her dating history? Or any mention of the affair with Alan Holdsworth?' Ginny asked, not wanting to dwell on Monica's battle with ageing.

Connor passed Tuppence a list of names to add to Flora. 'I couldn't find anything on Alan Holdsworth, but back in the nineties she dated several boy band members, then a football player, a newsreader and a tennis player. They were all high profile, but the dates took place around the time when she had a new show or something to launch. It reads to me like her manager set up most of them. I looked into them, but nothing lasted longer than a month and there was never any scandal attached. None of them had a bad word to say about her.'

'What about more recently?'

He shrugged. 'I guess she had a type. Because she continued to date men in their twenties, but never for long.'

'Oh, that's very sad.' Hen's large eyes misted over. 'She helped all those other couples find love but never found it for herself.'

'It does seem cruel,' JM agreed, her face softening. Was she thinking of her late wife, Rebecca? It wasn't often JM showed her vulnerable side, but Ginny did sometimes catch her staring off into the distance. It was a reminder that everyone dealt with their grief in different ways and it didn't lessen what they were feeling.

'Poor Monica.' Tuppence retrieved a pencil and sketched a slim figure standing on her own, while a nearby couple held hands. She put it up on Flora, next to the original sketch of the actress. 'Do you think it's possible someone from the show was getting revenge? Maybe they didn't find love and blamed her?'

Ginny raised an eyebrow. She hadn't considered that, but it meant they had even more research to do.

'I can look into that,' Connor quickly said and she gave him a grateful smile.

'And we still can't rule out that one of Monica's own lovers was out for revenge. Just because the relationships were short, doesn't mean it's not a motive.' JM shook away the pensive expression that had crossed her face, and began to pace the floor. '*If* we can find the lover.'

'For all we know, the murderer could be one of the trolls Andrew talked about. After all, he went from being one of Monica's biggest fans to now disliking her,' Tuppence added.

'Yeah, that's possible. There was some nasty stuff on the forums,' Connor admitted then handed them another piece of paper. 'This is Monica's manager, Stuart Mathers. She'd been with him for her entire career and she was his only client. Which means her success or failure directly affected him.'

'Manager, eh?' JM studied the paper and handed it around. Stuart Mathers was of medium height with thick grey hair and a barrel chest. 'We definitely need to speak to him.'

'His office is in Manchester, and he lives there as well,' Connor said.

'What a nuisance, considering how busy we are right now.' Tuppence frowned. 'Oh, I wonder if he will be at the memorial on Monday night?'

'I expect so, let's make sure we corner him,' JM said as Kaleb appeared in the doorway, his Santa hat sitting to one side of his head.

'Hey, boss. There's someone who reckons they're here to fix a toilet. Do you think they're legit?'

'Yes, I do.' JM pushed back her shoulders and pointed to a line on the clipboard. 'See, I've written the name of the plumber on the list. Here, I'd best come with you.'

'I can keep going through the memorabilia,' Tuppence announced.

'Sorry. I left it at home,' Ginny admitted.

'That's okay. I have scenery to paint anyway, and I can pump people for information.' Tuppence smiled.

'I've got to do a fitting with Cleo for her dress,' Hen said. 'What about you, Ginny?'

She bit back another smile as she took in Connor's outfit. 'I think we'd better go and talk to Desiree so you can get to the pub. If your offer still stands.'

'Yup.' He straightened his shoulders and smoothed down his hair, clearly torn between excitement and nerves. Brandon clambered to his feet, picked up a well-chewed teddy bear in his jaw, and nudged Connor's leg. 'No, boy, you stay here.'

'Oh dear.' Hen wrinkled her nose. 'I think Brandon must've heard me mention Cleo's name. Last time she visited she told him to stop snoring so loudly and I don't think he likes her anymore.'

'He can come with us,' Ginny said. After spending a day with Cleo and her dress obsession, she didn't want poor Brandon getting told off for anything. Then she led Connor and Brandon back down the corridor to Desiree's dressing room.

SEVENTEEN

SATURDAY DECEMBER 13

'It's lovely to see these two together again. They used to be thick as thieves but the last few years we haven't seen as much of Con.' Desiree Northam peered fondly at Connor and Iris, who were hunched over their phones laughing at something.

Iris was every bit as beautiful as her mother, with thick dark hair and ebony skin, combined with long legs and large eyes that sparkled as she spoke. Or maybe that was only when she spoke to Connor? All Ginny knew was that as soon as they'd walked into Monica's old dressing room Iris had let out a squeal and launched herself at him. He'd responded with something mumbled before they fell into a rapid-fire conversation.

Ginny was grateful he'd wanted to accompany her. Not only had it helped break the ice with Desiree, but it also distracted Ginny from the fact that she was currently standing in the exact position in the dressing room where Monica's body had been found.

And possibly talking to a killer.

Shivering, she wrapped her arms around her waist. There was no sign of any blood and apart from the faint smell of cleaning chemicals, it would be hard to know anything had happened. She peered up to where a simple light bulb was now hanging; the ceiling was smudged with faint powder from where SOCO had dusted for prints. Had the killer pressed their palm against the ceiling tiles as they cut the chandelier?

If so, they must've been wearing gloves if Wallace didn't have any suspects.

She dragged her gaze away and it landed on a blanket that was draped over the huge mirror leaning against the wall.

'Awful, isn't it?' Desiree shuddered while Brandon snuffled around the walls, tail wagging. 'As if there aren't enough mirrors in this room already. Apparently, she had this one moved in here. It gives me the creeps, which is why it's covered. It's so distracting. I have to look at myself in the mirror when I'm dancing, but I don't want to keep seeing myself as I go about my business. Though, clearly, Monica Larkwell was concerned about her appearance, which I realised after spending ten minutes in her company.'

Ginny thought of the arguments she'd seen on the stage, and then about the article Connor found, where Monica was complaining about the ageist industry she was in. Had her personality changed as she got older, trying to stay relevant in her chosen profession?

A tug of sympathy went through her. None of her own jobs required her to look a certain way, so it was hard to imagine what kind of pressure the actress might have been under. And while the concept had always seemed superficial to Ginny, she now realised that whatever decisions Monica Larkwell might have made about her appearance, probably had been born because of the industry where she made her living.

Swallowing, she turned to Desiree. 'Was it a shock to discover Monica wasn't the same as she appeared on television?'

'Not really,' Desiree admitted, drifting to the dressing table and sitting down. She gestured to a second chair. 'My mother met her here thirty years ago and told me a few stories, so when Paul suggested we bring her back, I wasn't keen.'

It fitted with what she'd seen about Junie Northam being in

the cast, but was there more to Desiree's dislike? After all, Hazel had wanted to cast Desiree in the role, and Monica was determined to block the choreography. The thoughts ran around in Ginny's mind like a train that refused to slow down.

Then there was the fact that Paul Atkins was the one who wanted to bring Monica back to Little Shaw. *Interesting*.

'Did you vote against it when Paul floated the idea?' Ginny asked.

Desiree gave a delicate sigh. 'I did, but changed my vote after speaking with Suzette and Ian. They're a lot more pragmatic than Paul... or even Hazel. They showed me the figures and after Monica's fee and the other running costs, the pantomime would still have been profitable. So, I agreed, even though I knew it would mean I'd become her understudy. I suppose I took one for the team.'

'Is it usual for members of the board to also be in the plays?' Ginny asked.

'Totally normal. It's also normal for the board members to rope in their husbands, kids, cousins and anyone else they can find to help out. My mother dragged me along to everything and I've done the same. Isn't that right, kiddo?'

Iris looked up and grinned. 'Yup. Mum's been bringing me along to this place since I was a baby. Not that I mind,' she suddenly added. 'Mum loves it here, and she's the most amazing actress. I keep telling her she needs to audition for a show in London. Or something on television.'

'Thank you, sweetheart, but I think that boat's well and truly sailed.' Desiree gave her daughter a fond smile.

'It's never too late to do what you want to do,' Iris said in a firm voice, and gave her mum a hug before returning to Connor's side.

'I didn't know you wanted to be a professional actress,' Ginny observed.

'I'll admit there was a time when I thought my future was in the West End. But then I got pregnant and life took a different direction.' Desiree let out a wistful sigh and a faraway look filled her eyes, as if she'd often thought about the path she hadn't travelled down.

Did she regret her decision?

It didn't seem likely considering the close relationship she had with her daughter.

'Is that why you joined the board? To stay connected?' Ginny asked cautiously.

'You know what they say: if you can't act, get into governance,' Desiree said, but the wistfulness had been replaced by something else. Anger.

The hairs on Ginny's arm rose. Maybe Desiree *did* have regrets. Was she angry at Monica for trying to override the dance that Desiree had suggested?

'Did you speak to Monica much before that first rehearsal?'

'Not really,' Desiree said, as a knock sounded from behind them. 'Come in, it's open.'

'Sorry to interrupt,' a familiar voice said, and Ginny looked up to see Ted Wallace appear in the doorway. Next to him, clutching a mover's trolley, was a lean man in his seventies with blue eyes and grey hair that swept across his brow. 'We're here to collect a mirror.'

Brandon barked and loped over to Ted's side to say hello. Wallace's father patted him, not put out by the friendly dog.

Desiree's eyes lit up. 'Oh yes. Sorry to be a nuisance but I find it so off-putting. Please, take it away.'

Ted gave Ginny a small nod of acknowledgement, before he and the other man loaded the mirror onto the trolley. She recognised the other man from the library but didn't know his name, and Ted didn't appear in the mood for introductions.

He really was a man of few words.

Ginny tried to hold onto Brandon to stop him from following them out, but the dog was distracted by the extra space left behind by the giant mirror. He bounced over and sniffed the scuffed wooden wainscotting. It was in need of repair, with several holes in the wood. Was that the real reason the mirror was there, despite the superstitions about them? To hide the neglect?

'Do you think it's strange that Monica asked to have the mirror in here? I know some people in the theatre think it's bad luck.'

'That applies to having them on the stage,' Desiree corrected then shivered as Brandon continued to sniff the wall. 'But... in this case I *was* surprised to see it.'

'Why?' Ginny's brow creased. Desiree had already acknowledged the mirror was in keeping with Monica's personality.

'It's okay, Mum. She won't think it's weird. I can tell by her eyes. They're kind.' Iris encouraged her mother.

Ginny flushed at the unexpected compliment then studied the other woman.

Indecision flashed across Desiree's face then she sighed. 'That particular mirror is cursed.'

'Cursed?' It was Connor who spoke first, but he exactly expressed Ginny's sentiments. This wasn't the first time she'd come across a local superstition so she shouldn't really be surprised to find another one.

'How so?' Ginny asked, not sure she really wanted to know.

'My nan told us a story about it,' Iris said defiantly. 'If you look into it for too long, it'll suck out your soul and you'll be killed within days.'

'Oh.' Connor blinked. Ginny couldn't be sure if he thought it was nonsense and didn't want to upset Iris, or if he was speechless.

'Why did your mother think this?' Ginny asked Desiree.

'Because apparently that happened to one of her friends in the eighties. She had it in her dressing room and became obsessed with it. Called it her glamour mirror, but halfway through rehersals, she died.'

Iris shivered. 'I can't believe they didn't get rid of it. Or destroy it.'

'Because no one wanted to run the risk of breaking a mirror,' Connor suggested.

'Oh, that's a good point. Still, I'm pleased it's not in here. I can't believe they made you use this dressing room,' Iris said.

'They didn't *make* me. It was easier than having to shuffle other people around. And I really don't mind. At least now the mirror's gone.' Desiree shivered.

'I guess so,' Iris conceded then wrinkled her nose. 'Speaking of gone... I know I said I'd stay and help you with your lines, but Con told me that Angie from school is about to bugger off to Thailand; she's having some going-away drinks at the pub. Would you hate it if I went? I haven't seen anyone in so long. Plus, Con and I have loads to catch up on. Like, how he finally got a haircut that lets me see his gorgeous face.' Iris playfully messed up his hair, her mood restored.

Ginny's chest expanded with joy. It was lovely to see Connor connecting with someone his own age. Especially someone as lively and bright as Iris.

'Of course not. I've already taken up far too much of your study time. And if this can make up for me dragging you here on Sunday night when a murder happened, well, it's the least I can do.' Desiree stood and gave her daughter a kiss, then grinned at Connor. 'Don't be a stranger.'

'Thanks, Mrs Northam,' he said in his usual voice, but he couldn't hide the glow in his eyes.

'Goodness, how many times have I told you to call me Desiree? I'm not old enough to be a Mrs,' the actress retorted and waved them both off. Once they were gone, she returned to her chair. 'I've always had a soft spot for that lad and was so pleased when I heard he was working in the library... I know not everyone has much time for the Wests, but Con's a good one.'

'No arguments from me,' Ginny said, pleased to hear that Iris's mother wasn't against the idea of Connor and Iris dating. *If that's what they end up doing*, she corrected herself. She considered what Desiree had said about Iris being there on Sunday night. 'I didn't realise your daughter was here when Monica was...' She trailed off, reluctant to say the final word.

Desiree sighed. 'We left not long after Monica walked off the stage. I thought it was the safest way to avoid arguing with her. And while I suppose us leaving before the murder stopped both of us from being suspects, I would've preferred if Iris hadn't been here.'

An alibi? Ginny couldn't say she was disappointed. She liked Desiree and Iris. Her lips twitched. Was that the other reason Connor had wanted to come along? Because he was worried they might accuse Iris's mother of being involved in the murder?

'It must've been a shock for her,' Ginny said.

'It was,' Desiree agreed. 'I just hope the police catch whoever did this.'

'I'm sure they will. And thank you for talking with me. I really appreciate it,' Ginny said.

'The pleasure is all mine. And, if you would like to find out more about the mirror, I could put you in touch with Jerry Niven. He's a lovely man. He was the chairperson for many years and directed Monica in the original *Mother Goose*. He and Mum were always close, so I grew up with him.'

'Thank you. That would be wonderful.' Ginny brightened. She had no interest in finding out more about the cursed mirror, but if Jerry directed Monica, he might be able to give them some insight about her.

'Excellent. I'll call him now.' Desiree picked up her phone but was cut off by the sound of a thump on the door.

'Knock, knock,' a voice said and a member of the crew Ginny didn't know appeared in the doorway. 'Desiree, Hazel wants to chat with you about the dance in act two. Are you okay to see her? She's on stage.'

'Of course.' Desiree rose, her lovely dancer's posture immediately making Ginny stand straighter. 'By the way, tell Hen that when we moved Mum out of her house last year, I found loads of old patterns, ribbons, lace and pieces of fabric. I've bagged them up and I'll bring them in. I know the budget is tight so they might help.'

'She'll be thrilled. I won't keep you any longer, but it's been lovely talking,' Ginny said and bent to scratch Brandon's head. 'Come on, boy, let's go.'

'Woof.' Brandon didn't move. 'Woof.'

Ginny wrinkled her nose and peered around, hoping for a solution. She was more of a cat person than a dog person, and while she didn't claim to understand most of Edgar's moods, she at least felt capable of meeting his needs. However, she wasn't sure what to do about an unhappy dog.

'I think it's his teddy bear.' Desiree pointed to the abandoned toy in the middle of the room.

Ginny tentatively picked up the well-chewed toy and was relieved when Brandon stood up and extracted the toy from her hand, then trotted to the door. Her phone buzzed as she walked down the corridor. She stopped to study the screen. It was a text from Connor with a photograph attached.

> This was on Danny Ling's social media page on Sunday afternoon, before Monica died. Didn't want to freak out Iris or her mum but figured you should see it.

The photograph was of Monica and Danny.

They were standing next to each other, smiling as they held up a camera. Then Ginny let out a sharp exhale and goose bumps skittered along her arms. They were looking directly into the large mirror that had been removed from the dressing room where Monica Larkwell had been murdered.

EIGHTEEN

SATURDAY DECEMBER 13

The sky was a hazy black by the time Ginny got home. The dark mornings and evenings were probably the most depressing part of winter for Ginny; she longed for spring, when she didn't have to come and go in darkness. The fact she was tired didn't help.

After Connor discovering the photograph of Monica and Danny Ling standing in front of the mirror, she and her friends had discussed it at length. The idea of the mirror being cursed was hard to take seriously, and yet... what if it was somehow important?

While Hen had finished sewing a stunning cerulean cape, Ginny had looked online for any mention of the cursed mirror, but she hadn't found anything. It was a relief. Because if the newspapers and online forums got hold of the idea that Monica Larkwell had been killed by a cursed mirror, it would be another headache that Wallace didn't need.

The only other useful piece of information she'd got from Desiree was that Paul Atkins had been the one to suggest Monica come back to Little Shaw. It was something they'd have to follow up.

After that, Ginny had spent the next hour tackling an aubergine costume, before they'd all agreed to call it a night. Hen was having dinner with her neighbour, JM was having a video call with some of her old colleagues from when she worked in London and Tuppence had wanted to do some painting in the art studio that she and her husband had once shared.

And I'm going to curl up and read my book.

Smiling, Ginny locked the car. There was no sign of Edgar as she walked up the path, which she hoped meant he was nice and warm inside. She held her key up to the lock and gasped.

Her lovely pink door—the one that had first made her fall for Middle Cottage—had a large piece of tape across where the lock barrel should be and the wood around the edge of the door was splintered.

Ice crept along Ginny's spine as Wallace's front light came on, and father and son stepped out.

'Don't be alarmed, but someone broke into your house,' Wallace said in a calm voice as they walked down the driveway and joined her. 'Ted noticed a person leaving ten minutes ago. We went inside to make sure you weren't at home and were about to call you. Singh and Bent are on their way, and I put the tape on in the meantime.'

She stared at them. The logical part of her brain could follow Wallace's words, but a more primitive part filled with fog.

'I think she's in shock,' Ted said; he was holding a toolbox. There was a builder's apron around his waist and his matter-of-fact air helped slice through the heaviness in her body and the ache in her chest.

'Thank you for that observation. And you can't fix the door until we've dusted for prints,' Wallace said, following his father out the gate and around to Ginny's side of the house. Wallace pulled gloves onto his hands and cautiously pushed open the door.

'Let me go next,' Ted advised, putting his toolbox down on the mat. 'It could be messy. Might be best if you wait next door.'

'No. I want to see,' Ginny croaked as a furry, black body darted towards her. Ginny let go of the costume bag and lowered herself down to scoop up her cat. 'Oh, sweetheart. Are you okay?'

Edgar answered by nudging his head into her chest, purring loudly. She wrapped her arms around him as a police car slid to a halt outside her gate. DC Anita Singh and PC Liam Bent got out.

Ginny peered around cautiously as she walked into her house. Her coats were hanging in their usual spot, as were her slippers and trainers. Ted led her through to the kitchen and Ginny's stomach tightened as her gaze went straight to the bookshelf. Then she let out a breath. Eric's book collection and their photo albums were there.

The relief left her dizzy as she tried to focus on the rest of the room, but, as far as she could see, everything was as she'd left it. The crossword sitting neatly on the table, the few breakfast dishes in the drying rack, and a small pile of mail waiting to be read.

Wallace came in, mouth set in a frown. 'Ginny, could you do a walk through with me? We can't see any sign of a disturbance apart from the broken lock.'

'Can I start securing it?' Ted was immediately by his side. 'I have a spare barrel I can use, then I'll add a new deadlock tomorrow.'

Wallace nodded and his father disappeared back down the hallway.

Ginny swallowed and continued to look around. 'So far, I can't see anything out of place.'

'Your house is very neat,' Wallace said.

'Thank you,' she replied, not sure if it was a compliment or not. She'd always been tidy, but now, without her husband, her clean and tidy habits had become more of an obsession, partly to keep herself busy and stop from falling back into the dark void of Eric's death, and to avoid the ongoing loneliness that tried to creep in, in the long stretches of silence. *Well, that, and talking to myself.* But Wallace didn't need to know about that.

'Would you mind checking your drawers and cupboards? And, if you have a safe or somewhere that your valuables are kept, we'll need to check that, too.' Wallace led her upstairs, where PC Bent was examining the window locks.

'Of course.' She deposited Edgar onto her bed, where he settled down, though his amber eyes followed her around the room. There was no safe and she didn't have any jewellery of note, just her mother's pearls and a couple of gold bracelets, which were nestled in her jewellery box. Her passport and documents were also safely stowed in the spare bedroom. Everything was there.

Oh. Her spine stiffened as her gaze fell to the coffee table where the box of Monica Larkwell memorabilia had been sitting. She'd left it there. Or... had she put it on the kitchen table? She went out to check, but all she found was Anita, walking back in from the garden.

'Is everything okay? If you're worried about your tools, the lock on your potting shed is untouched and your back gate is secured.' she said.

'No... it's not that.' Ginny frowned and told Wallace and DC Singh about the missing items. 'I have a spreadsheet of everything. But why would anyone take them?' she wondered then caught herself. She knew why.

Because there must have been something in those papers that was a clue to the killer's identity.

A shadow crossed Wallace's face. 'Can you give DC Singh the spreadsheet?'

'Yes, I'll email it to you,' Ginny said as Anita left the room.

Wallace raked a hand through his short hair. 'Would you consider staying with one of your friends?'

'Do you think they'll come back?' Ginny shivered, wishing she still had Edgar's warm body in her arms.

'No. And Ted will get the door secured. I just thought you might feel more comfortable not being alone here tonight,' he explained.

'In that case, I'd rather stay,' she said. While she hated the idea that someone had been in her house without her consent, Ginny didn't want to run away. She'd considered it once before in the early months after she first moved to Little Shaw. But part of accepting her new life without Eric, was also accepting that she had to face things alone. 'The memorabilia came from Andrew.'

Wallace's brows shot up. 'Another thing he forgot to mention. Is there no end to it?'

'He was still upset by everything. Have you spoken to Danny Ling?' she asked tentatively.

'Yes, though not much came from it. Ling admitted that he did argue with Monica before her death, but said it wasn't unusual during the filming process. Especially when the subject was being raw and open with him. We're going through his financial records. It seems he was exaggerating about his investment in the documentary and there is no other evidence to tie him to it.'

In other words, it was a dead lead. She let out a sigh. 'Oh dear. We haven't been much help so far.'

'On the contrary, you're getting to the truth, which allows us to properly discount certain people. Though, it wasn't my intention you should suffer a break-in while helping me out. Dad said he saw you talking with Desiree Northam this afternoon. She and her daughter have an alibi that checks out.'

'So I discovered,' Ginny agreed. She hadn't asked Desiree if she'd mentioned the cursed mirror to Wallace. If she was sensible, she wouldn't either. But what if he *didn't* know, and there was something in it?

'What is it?' Wallace demanded, as his father reappeared, clutching a screwdriver.

'Desiree said the large mirror that was in Monica's dressing room is cursed.'

'Cursed?' Wallace raised an eyebrow.

'It's true,' Ted agreed. 'Garth Shepard told me the same thing when we removed it from Desiree's dressing room. It involved having your soul sucked out if you looked into it.'

Garth Shepard? Ginny raised an eyebrow. Was he related to Kaleb?

She was tempted to ask, but Wallace's dour expression made her bite her tongue. Instead, she nodded. 'That's what Desiree said. And while I know it sounds ludicrous, Connor did find a photograph on Danny Ling's social media page of him and Monica looking into the mirror.'

Wallace's heavy-set eyes darkened as he turned to his father. 'Are you saying you want me to add a cursed mirror to my report?'

'Not my call to make.' Ted shrugged.

'Correct answer.' Wallace huffed. 'I'm heading to the station. Can you fix the door and... if you see any souls climbing out of a mirror, be sure to let me know.'

With that, Wallace, Anita and Ben left, and Ted let out an apologetic sigh.

'He's a little stressed right now. I'm sure he didn't mean it.'

Ginny was sure that he did, but couldn't blame him if cursed mirrors were all she had to offer to the investigation.

NINETEEN

SUNDAY DECEMBER 14

'You should've called us last night, not waited until this morning.' Hen was on her feet as soon as Ginny walked into the costume room. It was Sunday, but they'd all agreed to work weekends to make up for the lost days. A trail of fine orange feathers from the new Prissy 2.0 trailed in her wake as she dragged Ginny into a hug.

'Yes, it's terrible to think you slept there all night. I wouldn't have got a wink.' Tuppence joined the hug.

'Has Ted finished with your front door?' JM got up from her own seat behind a roll of fake brown fur and rubbed Ginny's arm. 'I'm appalled this has happened.'

A lump formed in Ginny's throat as the three women guided her to a badly sprung fainting couch in the corner of the room. It had been used on various productions until the springs had become too dangerous, and now it was smothered in cushions to help soften the blow. Ginny cautiously eased herself down, not sure what she'd done to deserve such fiercely wonderful friends. She'd already told them everything that had happened on the phone, but they clearly wanted more details.

'I'm okay. I promise. Ted worked on a makeshift lock for

hours until he was happy with it and was back again first thing this morning.'

'Everyone in the props department has commented on what an excellent carpenter he is,' Tuppence said. 'I bet he'll have it as good as new by the end of the day.'

'Yes,' Ginny agreed, not adding that Ted had mumbled something about there being some dry rot in the corner so he planned to fix that too, which meant it might be better than ever. She hoped he'd eat the biscuits she'd left out. She also had a sinking feeling that he and Wallace would talk her into getting a security system.

They'd already insisted she get a car alarm, and while they hadn't bullied her with words, it was surprisingly hard to argue with two men who didn't indulge in small talk. Worse, Eric would have sided with them. A knot of discomfort lodged itself in her belly as her old world and new world collided in an unsettling way. Still, that was a worry for another day.

'It's strange that the only thing they stole was the box of memorabilia.' Hen retreated to her machine and came back with three matching paisley waistcoats and a sewing box. She threaded a needle and selected a button, while Ginny and Tuppence did the same.

JM, who hated sewing, tapped her chin in thought. 'The robbery confirms we're on the right track.'

'Yes. But there were so many things in the collection. How do we know what the killer was after?' Ginny pushed the needle into the fabric. 'I have given the police the spreadsheet but unfortunately, I didn't take photographs. I feel like we've gone back to square one.'

'Who says we need the whole collection?' Hen looked up from her stitching.

'What do you mean?' Ginny's lips twitched with curiosity.

'Yes, I'd like to know, too,' JM said.

Hen stopped her sewing, colour rising on her cheeks as she realised they were staring at her. 'It's probably nothing, but aren't we mainly concerned with Monica's time at Little Shaw?'

'Why would you think that?' JM demanded. 'Who is to say it's not an ex-boyfriend or a rival from a London play years ago? Andrew's memorabilia collection was full of random articles.'

'That's true,' Hen said, voice pensive. 'But if we agree that the killer staged her death—and wore the goose costume—it might be because they were connected to the original pantomime, thirty years ago.'

The room was silent as Hen's words hung in the air. It made sense. Of course, it *also* made sense the killer wasn't connected to the play and had purposely staged the scene to divert attention. But, with so few leads to go on, it was worth exploring.

'Well done, Hen. It's a jolly good idea. I think everyone from the original cast should be considered a suspect,' Tuppence announced before wrinkling her nose. 'That is, once we figure out who they are.'

'Let's see what we can find online.' JM tapped something into her phone, then looked up, frown lines radiating around her mouth. 'Can someone please tell me why the internet is so full of waffle? I can't find any mention of it apart from the obituaries for Monica.'

'Surely some of the board members or crew might know,' Hen suggested.

'When I spoke to Desiree yesterday, she was going to put me in touch with Jerry Niven. He was the director,' Ginny admitted. 'And we know that Junie Northam was also part of the original cast, though we can't ask her, unfortunately.'

'Such a pity we don't have another copy of the programme. I wonder if Andrew had a spare?' Hen continued to sew, the colour finally fading from her cheeks.

'I could call him,' Ginny said, not relishing the idea of telling him the fate of his collection. But it was only right she did so.

'And we can ask Hazel. She must have an idea of who was involved. Plus, yesterday I heard her talking about an archive room. I'll text her.' JM retrieved her phone and Ginny did the same, but there was no answer.

'He didn't pick up,' Ginny said after leaving a message for Andrew.

'Hopefully he will call you back. And we should hear from Hazel soon,' JM said as Kaleb Shepard appeared in the doorway. His handsome face was framed by a beanie in the shape of a Christmas pudding.

'Hey, Mrs McArthur, I'm here for my headdress fitting.'

Hen got to her feet. 'Thank you for coming in. We're doing the suit in orange this time.' She pointed to the huge pile of feathers on the sewing table.

'Choice.' His green eyes lit up. 'It's going to be epic.'

'It is indeed,' Tuppence agreed warmly as she walked to the cutting table and held up an enormous headdress with green feathers around the crown that sprouted out to long orange tail feathers. It reminded Ginny of something a showgirl would wear, which made it perfect for pantomime.

Kaleb grinned. 'Man, this is so much better than the other one.'

'You'll have to remember to duck your head when you go through doorways, though,' JM warned as Hen rolled a chair over and gestured for Kaleb to sit down.

'I'll take real good care of it. Promise.' Kaleb lowered himself down and held his breath as Tuppence placed it on his head. Once it was on, she held up a mirror so he could see the full glory of it. Awe filled his face.

'Do you like it?' Tuppence asked.

'Do I *ever*.' He stood up, one arm stretching skyward. 'Good day to you, fine sirs. It is I, Prissy of the Farmyard, and it is a delight to meet you all. Have you come to inspect my golden egg? It is quite delightful.' Kaleb finished the dialogue with a flourishing bow and then peered up, eyes bright. 'That's my first line.'

Ginny blinked. It was as if the feathers and dialogue transformed him from a mild-mannered giant to a believably well-spoken goose, and it wasn't a struggle to see why he'd been cast in the role.

Hen clapped her hands together. 'Oh, aren't you clever to have remembered it already?'

'I'm off book,' he said proudly, moving his head from side to side, to test the headdress.

'Already?' JM raised an impressed eyebrow.

'Yup.' He stood and walked across to the pile of feathers to examine the rest of the costume. He appeared ludicrously tall with the headdress adding to his six-foot height. 'I've been practising at home like I promised Monica I would.'

At the mention of Monica, Ginny and her friends turned to him. His handsome face was free of conceit and he gave them a friendly smile.

JM spoke first. 'Kaleb, did you talk with Monica last Sunday?'

'I sure did, boss.' He nodded, the long feathers almost sweeping across JM's face.

'And when was this?' JM asked, taking a step back to avoid another round of feathers.

'Let's see.' He scrunched up his face. 'It was after lunch. I went to her dressing room because she wanted to meet me.'

Meet him? Ginny tried to imagine the short-tempered Monica she'd seen having a conversation with the sweet-tempered man in front of them. Did she know him already? Or was it purely because she was wanting to engage with the cast? Then she remembered the documentary. Perhaps that was why Monica had requested his presence.

'That's jolly kind of her,' Tuppence said. 'What did she talk about?'

'Just stuff. About how nice it was to be back in Little Shaw and that she'd been here years ago. I think she did *Mother Goose*, before,' he added helpfully.

'That's right,' Ginny agreed, struggling to make sense of it. 'Did she want to do some filming with you?'

'I don't know, but the camera guy wasn't there, so I guess not.'

Ginny wondered if this footage had also been on Danny Ling's hidden camera. 'Did she tell you if she knew anyone at the theatre, from her last visit?'

He shrugged and walked back to the mirror to inspect the headdress again. 'She might have.'

'Do you think you could remember?' Hen asked in a coaxing voice, but, before he could answer, an alarm on his phone went off. He studied the screen and then jogged to the door. 'Gotta go. It's time to rehearse my lines on stage.'

'Oh no. Wait, Kaleb, come back.' Hen hurried to reach him before he went crashing through the doorframe while wearing the tall-feathered creation. 'Remember you have your headdress on.'

He came to an abrupt halt, a flush colouring his cheeks. 'Sorry, Mrs McArthur. My bad.'

'It's okay, you're not in trouble,' Hen quickly assured him as he bent down so she could remove it. 'But can you remember how you knew that Monica wanted to meet you?'

'The film director told me,' he called out as he left.

Tuppence strode over to Flora and dragged the cape away as soon as Kaleb's heavy footsteps faded. 'Well, that's a plot twist if ever I've heard one.'

'Why would Monica single him out? It's very odd.' Hen put the headdress on the sewing table and joined them.

'Why does an older woman clinging to her youth want to meet a handsome younger man? Not sure Kaleb is the most riveting conversationalist, but he's friendly enough, and he's gorgeous.' Tuppence uncapped a pen and added some notes to Kaleb's tag. 'What if she wanted an affair with him?'

JM pursed her lips. 'We know she dated a variety of good-looking men in the nineties, and that she continued to date younger men.'

'It could be that Danny Ling wanted some extra footage, and

Kaleb is handsome,' Ginny suggested. It fitted if the director was the one who had passed on the message.

'So why didn't they film it, then?' JM countered.

'Perhaps Monica wanted to chat with him first and see what she thought?' Tuppence suggested, though Ginny wasn't convinced. Monica surely had other things to do besides arrange arbitrary meetings.

Brows pressed together, she turned to her friends. 'Is there another way that Monica might've known him? If he's twenty-nine, it means he wasn't born last time she visited. Could Monica be a family friend?'

Hen raised an eyebrow. 'I suppose it's possible, but I can't picture it. Kaleb's mother Trish Shepard runs Holly Farm. You might have met her when you went to visit Andrew. She's not... exactly sociable.'

'And I can't imagine her being interested in celebrities,' Tuppence added.

Oh. Ginny sucked in a breath. Kaleb was sunny and outgoing and the woman at the B&B had a tired formality to her, in stark contrast to her son. It was even harder to picture Trish being friends with Monica Larkwell. It was an ungenerous thought and she shook it away.

'I did meet her briefly,' Ginny admitted. 'She wasn't in a great mood, though it was understandable because Andrew was trying to cancel his booking.'

'She's had a tough life,' Hen said sadly. 'Kaleb's father left before the lad was born, so she's raised him singlehandedly. It's left her a little... negative.'

'Does she own the farm as well?' Ginny asked. She hadn't thought about it when she'd first visited the place, but the land appeared substantial, given her limited knowledge of agriculture.

'Trish's father, Garth, does. He's a nice fella. A bit like Kaleb, but less chatty. He sticks to himself most of the time but does help out when Kaleb's in the production.'

'I met him when he and Ted came to remove the mirror,' Ginny said, . 'That's nice he helps out.'

'Yes, he's very supportive of Kaleb. And so is Trish, though not when it comes to this place. She refuses to step foot in the playhouse,' Tuppence added.

'I forgot about that,' Hen admitted. 'But it's true. She's a lovely seamstress and I know Ants tried to get her to help with costumes one year, but she refused.'

'Why is she so against it? Kaleb's a wonderful actor,' Ginny said.

'Kaleb's father, Kyle Chambers, was into amateur dramatics,' Hen said. 'I suspect this place holds too many bad memories for her.'

'And poor Kaleb is the spitting image of his father, so I bet Trish finds it doubly hard to see her son on stage,' Tuppence added.

Ginny paused and did the maths. 'Is it possible Kyle was in the original production of *Mother Goose*? Do you remember seeing him in the programme?'

'No, but everyone had a stage name. I wish I could remember who was in it at the time. Let me think.' Hen rubbed her chin and silence filled the space as the friends stared at each other. Neither Ginny or JM had lived in the village that long, but Hen and Tuppence had. Hen finally sighed. 'Sorry, I can't recall, but I'm sure we can ask around.'

'We should do that,' JM agreed and retrieved her phone. 'We can try the internet. Please find information on Kyle Chambers and Monica Larkwell. Little Shaw. Lancashire.' She spoke into the phone then studied the screen. 'Well, well, well... will you look at that?'

They gathered around the phone. There was a grainy image of a young Monica surrounded by a group of people outside what looked like the local pub, The Lost Goat. Ginny could pick out Alan Holdsworth but didn't recognise anyone else. JM pointed her finger at a man in the far corner. Ginny squinted, catching a chiselled jaw and blond hair. A man with classical good looks, who was almost identical to Kaleb.

So, it was true. Kaleb's father, Kyle Chambers, had been involved in the production.

Which made him a suspect.

'JM, can you find anything recent on him?'

Her friend tapped away at her phone but shook her head. 'No, there's nothing here. Just a whole lot of social media profiles for all the Kyle Chambers in the world. Though none of them look like him. Let's search my ancestry software.'

'And I can get him up on Flora.' Tuppence filled in another tag and pinned it to the dress form.

'There's no one here who fits his age.' JM frowned. 'I wonder if he used a stage name, like everyone else?'

'Well, that's jolly annoying,' Tuppence said. 'So, we have no idea if he's dead or alive.'

'Nope,' JM agreed.

'We also don't know why Monica wanted to speak with Kaleb.' Hen's brow gathered. 'Was she asking after his father?'

'I've got no idea, but I would like to find out.' JM pocketed her phone and clicked her lips together. 'We need to consider Kyle Chambers a suspect. We have a photograph of him at the pub with Monica thirty years ago and she specifically wanted to speak with Kaleb... Kyle's son.'

'I could visit Trish and ask some questions. I've been out there recently so she might not think it's odd. I can also see if Danny Ling is there,' Ginny volunteered, not confident the surly woman would give her too many answers. But if there was a connection to Kyle Chambers, it was worth investigating.

'Excellent.' Tuppence updated Flora as JM's phone beeped with a text message.

'It's Hazel. The archives are kept in the boardroom, which is five doors past the storage cupboards. She's going to meet us there in five minutes.'

TWENTY

SUNDAY DECEMBER 14

The Little Shaw Playhouse's boardroom was dark and gloomy, with a long table in the middle and mismatched filing cabinets. It was a stark reminder of how underfunded they were.

'The archives are kept in those first two cabinets,' Hazel said once they crowded in. 'I take it this is about Monica's death.'

'That's correct. Do you mind that we're looking around?' JM countered.

'Considering I'm no longer a suspect, I'm agreeable to it,' Hazel said, pulling open one of the large drawers, which was crammed with drop files. 'Plus, the sooner the killer is caught, the sooner my actors will focus. I've come from the worst rehearsal. Everyone's very jumpy.'

'It's not nice knowing that someone is out there,' Hen said.

'Am I allowed to ask what you're looking for?' Hazel gave them a curious glance.

'One of the Larks gave us some of Monica's memorabilia, including a programme of the original *Mother Goose* performance. But it was stolen,' JM admitted.

'Stolen? Where from?' Hazel's mouth puckered with worry.

'They broke into Ginny's house,' Hen said.

The lines around Hazel's mouth deepened. 'This is dreadful.

I've been trying to tell myself that whoever did it, was only targeting Monica, but what if that's not true?'

'We don't know that,' JM said in a firm voice, which seemed to settle Hazel's nerves. The director gave her a grateful smile.

'And lovely Ted Wallace has already repaired her door,' Tuppence was quick to assure her. 'But the fact they stole the memorabilia made us think there must have been something important in there.'

'A murder and a robbery?' Hazel swallowed hard. 'I really hope you and the police get to the bottom of this soon. Please help yourselves to the archives. We don't have a huge amount. I was going through them for the memorial. I couldn't find any programmes, nor do I have one at home, but there's a chance some things have been misfiled. We don't keep anything locked, you see, so it's a bit of a mess. After the pantomime's finished, I'll get a volunteer to help sort it out.'

'Excellent idea. It's always good to have your archives under control,' JM said. 'Can you remember if Kaleb's father, Kyle, was in the original production of *Mother Goose*?'

'Or anyone else. We've collected several names, but it would be useful to know who the entire cast and crew were,' Tuppence added.

'Kyle Chambers?' Hazel's eyes widened. 'Goodness, I haven't thought of him in years. It's possible he was. He was a farmhand who worked for Garth Shepard but was a lovely-looking fellow and had real stage presence, though his dramatic timing was... questionable. However, it didn't stop him from getting cast in lots of roles. And yes... he was in the original production. As for other cast and crew members... there were a few. Here, let me write them down for you.'

'Thank you,' Ginny said as Hazel jotted down several names and passed it over. 'Do you know if Kyle's ever come back to the area?'

'Sorry, if he has, I haven't seen him.' Hazel shook her head.

'Can you think of anyone else involved in the original

production who might have had a vendetta against Monica?' Hen said. 'Or who played Prissy?'

'I hadn't thought of that.' Hazel widened her eyes. It was now well-known *how* the killer had committed the murder and what they were wearing. But clearly, she hadn't considered it might have been the original Prissy behind it. Then she pointed to the list in Ginny's hand. 'It was Warren Makepiece. But he's now in his eighties and even in his prime, he was only five foot seven. I don't think he could possibly have done it.'

'It was always a longshot,' JM admitted. 'Still, at least we can now rule him out.'

'Along with everyone else.' Hen sighed.

'I wish I could be of more help,' Hazel said. 'But if you come across anything useful about Monica in the archives, could you email it to Suzette so she can add it to the slideshow?'

'Absolutely.' Tuppence glanced at the long table, which was covered in thick folders with *The Glow Room* printed across the top and a photograph of a girl in a white bikini. Next to her was Paul Atkins, his dazzling white smile a sharp contrast to his deeply tanned skin. One arm was slung around the girl's shoulder and the other was high in the air, making the same V for victory sign he'd done on stage last week. Next to the folders, there were also bundles of pens as well as what looked like a paint chart of browns and oranges on the table.

'Do you mind if we move this stuff so we can use the table?' Hen asked, her gaze transfixed on the over-the-top merchandise.

'Of course. Paul has a bad habit of using the boardroom as a second office. I've asked him to pack everything away when he's finished in here.' Hazel walked over to the table and began to stack the folders up.

'It's okay.' Ginny quickly joined her. 'We can manage. You must have so much to do and we didn't mean to drag you away from it.'

'Thank you.' Hazel passed over a stack of folders and left them to carry on.

• • •

An hour later, Ginny coughed as dust caught in her throat. She opened another folder of press clippings that went back to the seventies. Most of them involved casting calls and advertisements trying to sell tickets to productions. She continued to flick through until a headline caught her eye. *A Deadly Vision or An Unlucky Accident?*

The date had been handwritten on it by whoever had made the decision to archive it, and it was from June 1984. Well before Monica's time at Little Shaw.

Bracing herself, Ginny scanned the article.

The tragic death of local resident, Meg Madison, can now be laid at the feet of a cursed theatre mirror. Chair of the Little Shaw Dramatic Society, Jerry Niven, says there has been a long history associated to the deadly mirror.

'Everyone at the theatre knows better than to stare into it for too long,' Niven reports. 'The reflection the mirror offers up is dazzling and hypnotic. But it comes at a price, as poor Meg discovered.'

A second actor, who preferred not to be named, says that they warned Meg not to fall victim to the mirror, but she was seduced by her vision of longer legs and dewy skin. The Little Shaw police department has refused to look into any claims involving the mirror, which means this is one dark mystery that might never get solved.

Ginny couldn't blame the police for not looking into it. She could almost imagine the 1984 detective version of Wallace telling the Dramatic Society not to bother him (or her) with their nonsense. But she did recognise the name Jerry Niven. He was the man Desiree had promised to put Ginny in touch with, in connection with the cursed mirror.

'Anything interesting?' JM leaned over but after catching the headline she gave a weary shake of her head. 'I should be surprised that this was published in the local newspaper, but having read far too many of their ridiculous articles, this feels very on brand.'

'Tell that to Monica Larkwell,' Tuppence said. 'We saw the photograph of her and Danny Ling looking in the mirror. I don't think we can discount it from our investigations.'

'I disagree.' JM picked up a folder. 'I haven't been able to find a programme from the original production. Though the other shows are here, with multiple copies.'

'That's annoying. I wonder what happened to them?' Hen said.

Hazel's words came into Ginny's mind.

We don't keep anything locked.

Was it possible that someone had come into the boardroom and removed all the *Mother Goose* programmes? It was a guess, but all the same, she shivered. 'Hazel's already told us she doesn't have a copy of the programme at home, but I think we should ask other people who have been connected to the theatre for a long time. I'll call Andrew again.'

'And Desiree could check Junie's collection and see what she has,' Hen added.

JM got to her feet. 'Excellent. Now, I'd better get back to the stage and make sure the only drama is coming from the script.'

'I have to finish the guard costumes,' Hen said, stacking up the files. 'Should we take some of these to the costume room so we can keep looking?'

'Definitely.' Tuppence finished tidying up and left the boardroom.

As Ginny followed, she pushed down the guilt of knowing the clue they needed had been stolen while it was under her care.

TWENTY-ONE

SUNDAY DECEMBER 14

Ginny's second visit to Holly Farm B&B didn't get off to a better start than her first. As someone who disliked visitors arriving too late at night, she'd opted to leave the theatre early to talk with Trish before the light faded. However, she hadn't accounted for the icy roads and the clouded sky, meaning it was almost dark by the time she navigated the long driveway and pulled up in front of the stone cottage. Several cars were parked outside, and a No Vacancy sign hung up on the door.

Did that mean Trish would be in a better mood? She hoped so.

Ginny let out a steamy breath and climbed out of the car. The light was on and Trish was hunched over the computer at the reception counter. The fire crackled in the lovely open-plan room and several Larks that Ginny recognised from the library were sitting on a sofa drinking red wine.

'We're full.' Trish didn't look up from the computer.

Swallowing, Ginny continued to walk to the reception desk. So much for her theory that Trish would be in a good mood.

'Hello, how are you?' she asked, in a friendly tone.

'Just marvellous,' Trish muttered and finally looked up. Her flyaway hair framed her gaunt face, while a gold necklace with the letter K hung around her neck. Her mouth tightened. 'Oh, it's you. If you're here to see that overly dramatic fellow from number three, you're too late. He checked out last week and left a terrible review for good measure.'

'I'm sorry to hear about the review. I think he was upset about Monica Larkwell's death. He was a big fan.'

'You don't say,' Trish said and then rubbed her eyes. 'Aren't you the woman from the library?'

'That's right,' Ginny agreed, pleased to find some common ground. 'Are you a member?'

'I don't have time to read,' she said as a beeping noise came from the computer.

Trish clicked the mouse several times then rolled her chair to one side, shaking her head. Clearly, she was still having computer problems.

'Is it glitching?' Ginny asked tentatively.

'I wish. The only glitch that's happened to this computer is my father. He's been messing around with it again. I told him he isn't allowed to touch it until he's passed his full digital MOT—that's why I sent him to that library course you're running.'

Ah. Ginny nodded in understanding. So that was why she recognised Garth Shepard.

Even though she didn't sit down with the attendees for each workshop, she did greet them on arrival.

'Connor's ever so good at working with people, regardless of their skills. I'm sure your dad will get better.'

'And I'm sure that pigs will fly. Now, what can I help you with? It's been a long day.'

Isn't that the truth?

Ginny let out a breath. Here went nothing. 'I want to ask you about Kaleb, and whether he knew Monica Larkwell. Or perhaps you're friends with her?'

The air went still, as something flashed across Trish's face, but then it disappeared, leaving her mouth tight and unyielding. 'Me? Friends with a celebrity?' Trish let out a bitter laugh and waved her arm around. 'What do you think? As for Kaleb, he's a good lad, but most of his time is spent out on the farm with his granddad. Why are you asking?'

Because we're floundering with a case and are desperate for a clue.

Ginny swallowed. 'It was something he mentioned. He told us that Monica called him to her dressing room and helped with his lines.'

At the mention Trish's jaw relaxed. 'Oh... *that.*'

'So, you knew about it?' Ginny asked, her pulse thundering with nerves. Talking with Trish was like walking on thin ice and waiting for a cracking sound. And yet, now she was here, she couldn't drop it.

'DC Singh let me sit in when Kaleb gave his statement. To support him. That scumbag of a human being, Danny Ling, wanted him to be part of the documentary and took it upon himself to drag my lad into it. Didn't think to ask me first.'

'Would you have been against it?' Ginny said, thinking of how eager Andrew had been to be part of the documentary.

'Of course I would. Each year during panto season Kaleb gets the acting bug and it takes months for him to settle back down into his regular life. The one that pays him money. He helps me and my dad out around the place and the last thing I wanted was someone like Ling or Larkwell turning his head. He has some... challenges... you see, and it's hard for him to know when someone's being authentic or when they're feeding him a load of crap.'

Trish's anger faded as genuine concern filled her eyes. It made so much sense. Kaleb was so sunny and trusting and she could only imagine how challenging it might be for Trish to keep him safe while letting him live a full life. She thought of what her friends had said about Trish and the challenges of being a single mother.

And here I am making things worse.

Yet, if she didn't ask the question now, she might never get another chance.

'Is it true that Kaleb's father, Kyle Chambers, also liked to act?'

Trish let out a hissing noise under her breath and pain filled her eyes. 'Why do you want to know about Kyle?'

'I'm so sorry that I've upset you. I wondered if Kyle knew Monica.'

'It wouldn't surprise me. Kyle liked to think he was a ladies' man and was full of one-liners and cheesy gifts,' Trish retorted in a scornful voice as her hand crept up to the gold necklace at her throat. Ginny had assumed the K stood for Kaleb, but had it come from Kyle? Poor Trish, was she hung up on the man who had deserted her and her son?

'Has he ever come back to Little Shaw?' Ginny asked.

The pain clouding Trish's eyes disappeared and she snorted. 'In a manner of speaking. Kyle died twenty years ago in London. So much for him making it big in the West End. He spent most of his time cleaning toilets and died with nothing. I had to pay to have him cremated. The ashes are in that jar over there. Only did it for the sake of the lad.'

So, he was dead.

Ginny walked over to the simple urn resting on a shelf. The name Bertram Julius 'Kyle' Chambers was engraved on the front. That was why they couldn't find any more information on him. Because the only time his stage name—Kyle Chambers—made the newspapers was when he'd been standing next to Monica Larkwell. It also meant he couldn't be a suspect. So why did Monica want to speak with Kaleb?

Was it a coincidence... or something else?

'It must have been quite a surprise when Kaleb mentioned what happened,' Ginny said diplomatically.

'One of the many surprises I've had this week.' Trish's angry mask reappeared.

'Do you mean when Andrew left early?'

'That was the start. Though the cherry on top was that Danny Ling. Three times I've tried to process his payment and three times it's bounced. And every time I ask him, he promises he'll fix it.'

Danny Ling?

'Is he still staying here?' Ginny perked up. Perhaps it wasn't a wasted trip after all? 'I was hoping to speak with him.'

'You and me both, but he's not come back. Been out all day.' Trish pinched her nose, as if wanting to avoid a bad smell.

'What will you do?' Ginny asked. She hated having any kind of debt, so would have felt dreadful if her payment had bounced. She recalled the argument that Andrew had overheard where Danny Ling accused Monica of costing him a fortune. Though Wallace had told her that they'd gone through his financial records and couldn't find proof of it.

'If I had my way I would've kicked him and that cameraman out days ago. But when I told Suzette and Ian about it, they promised to cover his expenses if he doesn't pay. I suppose I should be grateful, but I don't like having dishonest people under my roof.'

Pursing her lips, Ginny tried to stop the flood of questions from showing on her face. But why would Suzette and Ian Ryan be covering Ling's accommodation? And Trish spoke like she knew them. Were they friends?

'That's very kind of them. I haven't formally met them yet, but they seem lovely.'

'They're good folk. They do the books for this place and for the farm and know how tight things are. That's why they've been recommending us to everyone. Monica Larkwell was meant to stay here as well but wanted to drive from Cheshire every day. Suppose I should be grateful that she wasn't here.'

'It's nice to see them supporting you like that.'

She shrugged. 'Like I said, they're good ones... and they dote on Kaleb. It's the only reason I let him do the damned panto each year, because I know they're involved. They couldn't have kids of their own, you see, and they've always treated him like he was theirs. Or at least their nephew. Speaking of that lad... I need to chase him down to help prep for tomorrow morning's breakfast.'

Ginny thanked her and made her way back to the car. Kyle Chambers was no longer a suspect, but where did Suzette and Ian Ryan fit into it all?

TWENTY-TWO

MONDAY DECEMBER 15

Ginny swallowed the last of her tea and snipped at a thread of cotton. Despite her repaired door, she hadn't slept well and spent most of the night sitting in her front room, finishing off the last aubergine costume. Her sewing would never be as lovely as Hen's, but it was perfectly serviceable for a vegetable.

Plus, it helped appease her guilt for not getting as much work done yesterday as she'd planned. She'd returned to the theatre after her visit to Holly Farm and updated her friends with what she'd found. She winced. If she could call it a find.

They could officially take Kyle Chambers off their list, and Trish was too short to have worn the Prissy suit, not to mention that she had an alibi, along with her son and her father. Ginny wasn't sure what to make of the other piece of information. Why had Suzette and Ian Ryan decided to vouch for Ling? After all, the documentary was separate from the playhouse. Unless they were hoping for some good publicity out of the relationship?

It was possible.

They'd discussed it at length, before talking to some of the older volunteers to find out who was in the original production. They'd been given a few names, but two people had moved away from the village, and the third, like Junie Northam, was in a retirement home.

A horn honked outside her gate, and Ginny looked out of the window to where Tuppence was waiting. The parking had become progressively worse around the theatre with the influx of visitors and the cast and crew, and, since it was Ginny's day off from the library, Tuppence had offered to collect her. They planned to park at the church hall and walk the rest of the way together.

Ginny folded up the thick quilted fabric as best she could and squeezed it into her largest shopping bag. She checked Edgar's food and water bowls then bundled herself up. A blast of wind greeted her as she opened her front door, pushing her back. She braced herself and hurried out to Tuppence's car.

'Your door looks lovely. I couldn't even tell it had been damaged.' Tuppence climbed out and helped Ginny jam the aubergine costume into the back seat alongside an enormous piece of foam cut out in the shape of a cloud. But instead of leaving it white, Tuppence had painted on a stunning face, cheeks fat as it blew out a gust of wind.

'Ted did an excellent job,' Ginny agreed. He'd refused to take a payment, but she'd been pleased the biscuits were gone. He was like Santa Claus without the red nose or *ho-ho-ho*.

They drove past the theatre, in case there was a nearby parking space, but after a row of cars sat double parked in the street, Tuppence honked her horn and pulled around them, heading for the church hall.

'What a nuisance. I thought we could drop our bags off. Now we'll have to carry them,' she said as they climbed out of the car and gripped at the oversized shopping bag and giant cloud. 'At least it's good exercise.'

Ginny, who wasn't a huge fan of exercise, tightened her grip on the heavy bag, though it would take some gust to drag the costume into the air. She supposed that was a good thing. They had reached the end of the car park when Ginny's phone rang.

She gave Tuppence an apologetic look. 'I'd better answer it in case it's Wallace or Ted. I have a feeling they want to put the security system in straightaway.'

Tuppence agreed cheerfully and went to the side of the old church to shelter from the wind as Ginny extracted the phone.

Nancy's name flashed up.

Ginny's pulse quickened with guilt. She'd texted her sister-in-law last night to tell her about the break-in, so if she didn't answer now, Nancy would only worry more. Plus, with a full day of sewing ahead and the memorial tonight, there wouldn't be any chance to return a call.

She answered.

'Oh, so your phone *is* working?' Nancy said, by way of greeting. On anyone else it might have sounded snarky, but Ginny could too clearly hear the undertone of worry that disguised her sister-in-law's voice. 'Are you sure nothing else was stolen other than those papers?'

'I promise. And my neighbour fixed it for me, so you don't need to worry.'

'Don't I just? Because, the murder of a national treasure and you getting broken into isn't a concern?' Nancy retorted. 'And about your promise to sit this one out like a sensible person might... I'll believe it when I see it.'

Ginny winced, realising she hadn't updated Nancy on the latest turn of events. 'As it happens, we've agreed to help the police.'

Nancy let out a strangled groan. 'Ginny, this is getting ridiculous. And, furthermore, it's one thing to say you can't come with us for a family Christmas because of the pantomime. But now you'd rather look for clues in fields of freezing cold mud than spend time with us?'

Fields of freezing cold mud? Where had that come from?

'You know it's not like that,' Ginny said, her tone coaxing. 'There's nothing to worry about. We're helping get to the truth. I'm not sure if it's because it's panto season or because there are so many amateur actors involved, but there's been trouble getting accurate statements. All they need us to do is ask a few questions. I promise there won't be any fields of freezing cold mud.'

'You can't know that. This morning one of the headlines read: *The Lark Sings No More. An in-depth investigation of how a beloved actress met her death and why it means the end of days is almost here.* It's clear to me that no one has any idea who killed her.'

'Just because the police don't know who it is, doesn't mean they won't find out,' Ginny said hotly, then clamped down on her lower lip to stop herself from saying anything else. She'd seen the ridiculous headline along with numerous others, but they were no reflection of what Wallace and his team were doing. It was even more reason to help them, if it was so required.

'Oh, hell. Gin, I know it's not my place to tell you what to do,' Nancy capitulated. 'I *am* happy you have your new life, but that doesn't mean I don't miss you. We all do.'

Ginny's throat tightened, her anger forgotten. When she'd first decided to move to Little Shaw and start the life that she and Eric had planned together, a small part of her had also wanted to get away from the things that reminded her of what she no longer had. Her husband. Her best friend. Her future.

And, while she'd never voiced it out loud, she knew that Nancy had been left hurt by the move. She'd been even more hurt when Ginny refused to join them last year for Christmas, but the grief had been too raw for Ginny to explain why the idea of being around Eric's family on their favourite day of the year had been unbearable.

But it had hardly been fair on Nancy, who had loved her older brother and had taken his death as badly as Ginny had. And while she'd visited her sister-in-law since Eric's death, she'd also avoided discussing him at length, scared of the pain that might come from poking at the wound that still hadn't healed.

Was that what she was doing now? Avoiding Eric's family, because it still made her too sad?

She pushed her shoulders back, pain catching in her throat. 'I miss you all as well, and I promise I'll come down to Bristol in the New Year. Who knows? Maybe next year you might want to spend Christmas with me.'

'In Little Shaw?' Nancy made a sharp noise that sounded scarily similar to something JM might utter. 'No offence to Lancashire, but I'm not sure it compares to the Northern Lights. Next year we're thinking of the Christmas markets in Austria.'

'I understand,' Ginny sighed. They'd already had this argument several times, and, while her home was charming, she couldn't deny that with the grey weather and the long stretches of moors, the dramatic landscape wasn't for everyone. 'The Christmas markets sound lovely.'

'Does that mean I can count you in? Who knew that the day would come when I'd have to book you in a whole year in advance?' Nancy grumbled, but her mood improved.

'Oh... well, I suppose so,' Ginny said, not quite ready to face this Christmas, never mind next year. She dragged a small paper calendar from her sensible black handbag and was about to jot it down when a familiar figure walked past on the other side of the street. He was Asian with bleached blond hair and a phone glued to his ear.

Danny Ling, and trailing him, with camera gear on his back, was Nolan Archer.

Tuppence let out a little squeal and pointed, while Ginny's eyes widened.

'What's that noise? Is something wrong?' Nancy demanded.

'Nothing. The noise was the wind.' Ginny quickly shook her head as Tuppence wrinkled her nose by way of an apology as Danny and Nolan disappeared past the church hall in the direction of the cemetery. 'But... er, I've realised I'm running late. I'm due at the theatre... to help with the costumes. I've finished sewing an aubergine.'

'Do I want to know why *Mother Goose* has an aubergine in it?'

'Probably not,' Ginny admitted, pleased Nancy seemed to have forgiven her. 'I'm sure it's essential to the storyline. Give my love to Ian, Em and the girls. And Nancy... I appreciate everything you've done for me. You know that, don't you?'

'Of course I do,' Nancy said gruffly. 'Now, go and do whatever it is that's so urgent.'

Ginny's mouth twitched with a smile as she dropped her phone into her bag and picked up the aubergine. Next to her, Tuppence clutched at the giant cloud.

'Was that your sister-in-law? I hope she didn't think I was rude to make that noise,' Tuppence said. 'But we've been looking for Danny Ling everywhere. Especially now he's been captured in the cursed mirror. I wonder if he knows about it?'

'I'm not sure about the mirror, but Nancy was fine. She's started to accept that I won't be spending Christmas with them, but she was already trying to book me for the following year.'

'I'm pleased you spoke to her. It's not nice being at odds with your family,' Tuppence said earnestly and Ginny swallowed, knowing how right her friend was. She might have built a new life in Little Shaw but that didn't mean she wanted to forget about the people from her old life.

Tuppence stepped out of the shelter of the church and began marching towards the hall. 'Let's follow them. It looks like they're heading to the cemetery.'

A knot of worry formed in Ginny's stomach. What was Ling doing in the cemetery? Then she shrugged and followed her friend. They would find out soon enough.

TWENTY-THREE

MONDAY DECEMBER 15

This wasn't Ginny's first on-foot suspect chase, and the inclement weather stung at her cheeks as she and Tuppence climbed the steep path, dragging along an oversized aubergine costume and a hand-painted cloud.

Little Shaw Cemetery was tucked behind a set of freshly painted wrought iron gates, shadowed by two oak trees. Catching her breath, Ginny pushed open the gate, which no longer squeaked, thanks to regular maintenance. She and her friends volunteered to keep the cemetery tidy, and the gravestones were well-tended, no longer surrounded by weeds and litter. The fact that the gate had been regularly painted and oiled also meant that Danny hadn't heard them enter.

'There they are.' Tuppence pointed to two men hovering around a grave in the part of the cemetery known as the West Wing. 'Gosh, will you look at Nolan's equipment? So many people on YouTube use their phone, but he has tripods and everything. How exciting.'

'It's a lot to carry,' Ginny said, arms already hurting from lugging around the aubergine.

Danny beckoned to Nolan and pointed to a gravestone. The

man immediately began to film it, while Danny marched in circles, as if deep in thought. What was going on?

'Should we go over?' Tuppence whispered, dragging Ginny from her musings.

'Yes, I suppose we should,' Ginny agreed, wishing she felt braver than she did. Her pulse thundered in her ears as they threaded their way through the many plots until they were close enough to catch Danny's voice.

'Don't worry about the name, we'll photoshop it out and put in Monica's. No one's going to care if it's not the real thing. And I want some sky. It looks like it's going to storm, which is much better, atmospherically speaking.'

'You're the boss.' Nolan shrugged, then nodded at Ginny and Tuppence. 'We got company.'

'Give me strength. If I have to listen to one more Lark telling me we've lost a legend, I'll throw up my breakfast.' Danny shuddered. 'What are you doing here?'

His dark eyes were shrewd as he studied them. Ginny patted down her wool hat and pushed back her shoulders. Her interviewing techniques varied from dumb luck through to hugely embarrassing and she didn't feel confident enough to predict where this might land.

'Er, hello.' She plastered on a bright smile that felt at odds with the grey sky and the empty cemetery. 'My name's Ginny Cole.'

'And I'm Tuppence.' She secured the cloud between her knees and held out a hand. Danny shook it then frowned, as if annoyed at his own response.

Ginny followed suit, forcing him to do the same. It didn't improve his mood. She took a deep breath. 'We'd like to ask you a few questions.'

'About what?' Danny asked, a bored expression covering his features.

'We have all the interviews we need,' Nolan elaborated. It earned him a dark glare from his boss.

'Go get the footage,' Danny snapped, his eyes never leaving Ginny and Tuppence. 'Unless this is important, I don't have time. We're only staying for the memorial then we're out of here.'

Leaving? Ginny's mind whirled. Had Wallace given him permission to go home? It made sense based on her conversation with the detective. And Hen was right—what killer would forget about their own hidden camera?

Bridging the gap in conversation, Tuppence stepped forward and smiled. 'We have some questions about Monica Larkwell.'

He snorted. 'Shocker. You and half this village. You wouldn't believe the things people have done to get in the documentary.'

'I can assure you we don't want to be part of it,' Ginny said as the wind continued to blow, stinging her eyes. 'Let's get out of the breeze. There's a shed nearby.'

He opened his mouth and then shut it again as Nolan crawled along the ground on his belly to get a shot. Then he shrugged. 'Fine. You have five minutes.'

'Thank you.' Ginny led him to the open shed, which was really a glorified potting bench with an overhanging roof. Tuppence dragged over three metal buckets that they used to collect weeds in and flipped them upside down.

'There, this is much better,' her friend said, gesturing for Danny to sit. He ignored it.

Oh dear. Ginny forced her brain into action. 'How are you? It would've been horrible to hear about Monica's death.'

'That's an excellent question.' Tuppence enthusiastically gave Ginny a thumbs-up then turned to Danny, her face taking on a solemn air. 'You must have been quite a fan.'

Danny let out a bark of laughter and sat down. 'A fan? Hardly. I could have happily spent my life not knowing her.'

'Huh. I didn't expect you to say that,' Tuppence confessed.

Ginny sat down on the second bucket, realising too late that they were eye level with the shopping bag, from which the aubergine costume was trying to escape. It wasn't adding to her credibility.

Ignoring it, she fixed Danny with what she hoped was a serious expression. 'How did you end up working with her?'

'Because I'm a fool,' he muttered then leaned forward, his arms resting on his knees. 'Truth is that she came to me and said she was launching a comeback and wanted to make a documentary about it. She told me all sorts of crap about how the networks would be falling over themselves to buy it. She promised to give me exclusive stories that would really blow up.'

'Oh.' Ginny mouthed. She wasn't quite sure what *blow up* meant, but assumed it would be good for sales. And this tied in with the argument Andrew had overheard.

'I was in between projects,' Danny continued. 'And needed a win after my last two documentaries tanked... so I foolishly took her at her word. After all, she's been around the block a few times and was sure to have some juicy adventures to tell.'

'Foolishly?' Tuppence frowned.

'You mean you bankrolled it?' Ginny gasped. Was that why his credit card kept bouncing at the B&B? Because he was broke?

He shrugged. 'Ish. I used a lot of my own funds but did bring in some investors as well. But it wasn't until we got here that I realised how much she'd played me.'

'How so?' Ginny asked uneasily.

Danny took a deep breath. 'For a start, she'd already pitched the damn show to every network and production company in the United Kingdom before she got to me, and they'd all turned her down. But even worse, it wasn't until I got her in front of the camera that I realised she had no intention of spilling the beans on anything interesting. Which meant I was buggered. The bigger the scandal, the bigger the price tag. And the converse is true. All because Monica freaking Larkwell wouldn't play ball.'

'That doesn't make sense.' Tuppence frowned.

Ginny agreed. She studied his face for signs he was lying, but his gaze met hers and his breathing was steady. 'If this was part of her comeback, wouldn't she want the documentary to do well? After all, she was the one who approached you.'

'Who knows what was going through her mind?' Danny said, flashing his white teeth for the first time.

'She must've said something?' Ginny pushed, remembering too late that she needed to tread gently, because he hadn't wanted to speak with them.

His reserve fell away and he let out a cynical snort. 'Oh, she said something. Told me that since we'd made our deal, she'd got some huge book contract and promised the publisher she'd give *them* exclusive stories. Things that no one else knew.'

The wind picked up around them as Danny's words hung in the air.

'Monica was writing a book?' Tuppence's eyes went wide.

'Yeah,' he spat, two burning balls of colour rising in his cheeks. 'Apparently, she'd finished it, but would she tell me a single thing that was in it? No, she would not.'

A book deal? Ginny's pulse hammered in her ears. If Monica had a book deal and was holding out on Danny Ling as far as the documentary went, was he angry enough to kill her? She looked at the silver flecks in his flashing eyes and sucked in a breath.

It was entirely possible.

'So, she lied to you. Is that why you put the camera in her dressing room, to get some extra footage?' Tuppence asked, dragging Ginny back into the conversation. She really must stay focused.

'Of course not. Monica knew the camera was there. I might've been pissed at her, but I'd hardly invade her privacy like that. Not that I had much hope of getting anything. She's pretty tight-lipped, as I've discovered.'

'Were their other hidden cameras?' Ginny pushed.

'I told you, they weren't hidden,' Danny growled. 'They weren't visible if people didn't know they were there.'

Ginny wasn't quite sure how that differed. 'Did you tell the police about the other cameras?'

'Yes, Miss Marple, I did. And I showed them the footage as

well as gave them my alibi.' He folded his arms in front of his chest.

'You had an alibi?' Ginny said in what she hoped was a casual voice, though she wasn't sure how casual she could be while sitting on a bucket in the middle of a cemetery. Irritation flashed across Danny's face, which made her wonder if he was even going to answer her.

'My cameraman and I were interviewing Suzette and Ian Ryan about what it meant for them to have Monica in the pantomime. It was after Monica left the stage. They were called in because of the argument, and we left the theatre together at nine pm and filmed in their house. We weren't finished until after eleven.'

So that meant not only were Danny Ling and Nolan Archer in the clear, but so were Suzette and Ian Ryan, from the board. And while from a safety point of view, she was pleased he wasn't the killer, it also meant they were no closer to the truth.

She remembered the Ryans' assurance to Trish about Ling's bouncing credit card. Was there more to the joint alibi than he was letting on?

'Were Suzette and Ian Ryan investors in your documentary?' Ginny asked. 'I know they've agreed to cover your accommodation.'

'How the hell did you find out about that?' His eyes clouded with rage. 'Wait, don't tell me. It was the miserable witch at Holly Farm. Well, tell her with *my* compliments that the funds cleared this morning. I pay my own way. And no, the Ryans aren't investors, but, unlike some people in this town, they understand the bigger picture. We have a golden opportunity to turn this documentary into something positive.'

Something positive?

Bile rose in Ginny's throat. 'You and the Ryans want to benefit from her murder?'

He snorted. 'What rock did you crawl out of? I'd be a fool not to make the most of this chance. And I'm not the only one.

The newspapers are going to town. You know the old saying. If it bleeds, it leads.'

'That's terrible.' Tuppence gasped.

'What's terrible is being stuck with hours of footage that no one wants to buy,' he retorted. 'I'm just trying to recoup my losses. I say it's resilient. Get knocked down seven times, get up eight. That's me.' He rolled his neck. Was he getting ready to leave?

Ginny's brow throbbed. She wasn't sure what Danny Ling would be like, but to hear him only talk about Monica's murder as a business opportunity was sickening.

'Do you know why Monica would want to see Kaleb Shepard?' Tuppence asked in a casual voice, as if she wanted Danny to pass the salt and pepper.

It caught him off guard and instead of snapping, he laughed. 'The good-looking kid who was playing the goose? I thought that was obvious. He doesn't have much going on top... but I caught the way she was eyeballing him and since she hadn't given me any decent content, I suggested we shoot some footage.'

Ginny and Tuppence exchanged a silent look. So, it was true that Monica had been contemplating an affair with the likeable young man. What would Trish Shepard have said about that? Somehow, she couldn't imagine it going down well.

'And she agreed?' Tuppence asked.

'She agreed to talk to him before making a decision.' He shrugged. 'What's this about, anyway?'

'N-nothing,' Ginny quickly said, not feeling up to explaining their role as unofficial detectives. Also, the fact that it was Danny who had instigated the meeting between Monica and Kaleb answered the question of why the young actor had been there. She sucked in a breath. 'What about the book contract? Did you tell the police about that?'

'They never asked.'

'And you didn't think it was important enough to offer up?' she said, again in awe of how differently people could act around the police. For her it was with terror and an overwhelming urge to tell them everything she knew. Yet Cleo, Arnold, Andrew and now Danny seemed happy to omit vital parts of their story.

'How can I say?' He shrugged. 'I'm not here to do their job.'

'They can't do that job if you don't tell them the truth.' Tuppence took over, giving him a stern look.

'If I have to stay here too long, it will mess with my production timeline.'

'If you don't tell him, I will, and then see where you'll be,' Ginny said, with more bravado than she felt.

'Fine,' he snapped. 'Whatever.'

Nolan rolled onto his back so he was filming the dull grey sky. Neither man seemed upset that the subject of the documentary was dead. Ginny shivered.

'That's called a worm's eye view.' Tuppence nudged Ginny.

'Save me from amateurs.' Danny huffed and stood up, stopping only to stick out his foot and knock over the bucket he'd been sitting on. He fixed them with a penetrating glare. 'The best thing Monica Larkwell did for me was get herself murdered. This documentary is now worth a fortune and I'm eager to get it to market as quickly as possible.'

'That's all well and good. But what are you going to do about the cursed mirror?' Tuppence frowned. 'You took a selfie of you and Monica in front of it and now she's dead. You need to take care.'

'Are you threatening me?' His brow rose.

'Goodness, no. I'm making sure you're aware of it. We don't know the exact details, but it appears to be a soul sucking situation. It's a pity you felt the need to take that photograph,' Tuppence added.

Danny's mouth opened, then he clamped it shut and stalked away, checking his phone and barking orders as he went. Ginny's stomach tightened as the bucket rolled around on its side. He definitely had a temper.

A chill went through her.

Danny Ling had enough of a motive to kill Monica. Not only had she cost him money, but her death also meant his documentary had more value.

'Wow,' Tuppence whispered as she returned the three buckets to their space under the potting bench. 'I'm not sure he understood the curse. Then again, if he *did* kill Monica, then he's part of it. Like a self-fulfilling prophecy.'

Ginny closed her eyes to consider. Danny wasn't tall enough to wear the Prissy costume, but Nolan was.

And where did the Ryans fit in? Or Trish Shepard, for that matter?

Ginny tapped a text message to Wallace, telling him what they'd discovered, aware that Danny was planning to leave town tomorrow. Then she picked up the heavy costume bag and shivered.

It had nothing to do with the weather.

TWENTY-FOUR

MONDAY DECEMBER 15

'Have you heard from Wallace yet?' Tuppence looked over from the large golden egg she'd been painting onto the bottom of a rainbow, which would be lowered down onto the stage before the show started. It was five o'clock in the afternoon and they'd spent most of the day working on props, helping Hen with the sewing and fitting in some sleuthing between tasks. Their list of people who had worked on the original production, had both grown and shrunk and they'd been quickly discounted, mainly because of age and lack of mobility.

'Nothing.' Ginny put down her paintbrush and peeled off a glove so she could check her phone yet again. She was starting to feel like one of the people she saw walking down the street with their nose glued to their screens. Was this how it started?

She was tempted to send him another message but fought the urge. Wallace wouldn't thank her for it. He'd answered her original text with a thumbs-up emoji, but there had been nothing since.

'It's rude that he doesn't reply when we found the breakout clue.' Tuppence rolled her shoulders and stepped back from the large sign. 'I think that's enough. Shall we go to the costume room? Connor should be there by now.'

Ginny readily agreed and cleared away her paintbrushes. Connor had promised to come over after the library closed to help search for any information about the memoir. They'd tried to look on their own but hadn't discovered any mention of a book deal.

Did that mean that Danny had been lying?

She hoped not. So far, they hadn't been able to help Wallace much and she hated the idea of sending him on a wild goose chase when the real goose-clad killer was at bay.

And now I'm making bad puns to myself.

Following Tuppence's lead, Ginny washed her brushes and put the props on a shelf to dry, while Tuppence moved the sign to a table. Any spare time they'd had during the day was spent researching Danny Ling and his previous productions. One had been on the lifecycle of gnats and the other had been on the history of shoemakers in Northampton. Neither had done well and it was clear he needed a win.

A win at Monica's expense?

The best thing Monica Larkwell did for me was get herself murdered. This documentary is now worth a fortune and I'm eager to get it to market as quickly as possible.

It niggled at Ginny that Danny had admitted his dislike of Monica to her, and said how much better off he was now she was dead. But none of that made him guilty.

The twisting corridors were filled with buckets, random pieces of scaffolding and other props: Ginny and Tuppence navigated the obstacles until they reached the costume room. Hen was at the far end, draping a neon-green jacket over Connor's shoulders. He looked alarmed, though Ginny wasn't sure if it was because he was worried about being stabbed with a pin, or because the fabric was so bright.

There was no sign of JM, which wasn't a surprise considering rehearsals were in full swing and her skills were needed on the stage supporting Hazel and the whole production team.

'Sorry, I thought I'd steal him for a few minutes.' Hen

straightened. 'He has the same measurements as the second guardsman.'

'Lucky me,' Connor said, but remained still as Hen carefully took the jacket off him.

'There you go.' Hen patted his arm, releasing him from duty. 'And thank you.'

'Working backstage is about multitasking.' Tuppence made her way to Flora and swept off the crushed velvet cape. They'd already added their notes about the Ryans' alibis and their possible relationship with Ling.

'Connor, how did you go with digging up information about Monica's memoir?'

'I didn't have any luck,' he admitted, joining Ginny at the cutting table and un-pocketing his phone. Brandon, who had been asleep in the corner, trotted over to Connor and nudged his leg. 'I found a place where publishing deals are announced but there was no mention of Monica.'

Ginny was pleased it wasn't their bad search skills, but it didn't help them move forward. She picked up the theatre's archives and spread out some of the press clippings. They'd discovered several that mentioned Monica, but none that mentioned the rest of the cast and crew.

She'd also heard back from Andrew and he didn't have an extra copy of the original *Mother Goose* programme, but said he would ask on the Live, Lark, Love message boards. Ginny and her friends didn't fare any better with any of the older members of the theatre.

'What about any scandals that we've missed?' Ginny wondered. 'If she was writing a memoir, we have to assume that she'd be sharing some secrets.'

'Oh yes. Skeletons from the past,' Hen agreed.

'No skeletons.' Connor shook his head. 'The worst I could find was that one ex-boyfriend complained she put her career before her personal life. But that's hardly front-page news.'

'Which only makes her secrets juicier,' Tuppence said. 'After all, if everyone knew what the skeletons were, it wouldn't be very exciting. Maybe that's why Monica and the publisher were keeping it under wraps. So that it would be more sensational when it came out.'

'*If* it comes out. What if the publisher decides not to print it now she's dead?' Hen wondered.

Ginny shivered, thinking of Danny's quote. *If it bleeds, it leads.* It was hard to imagine her publisher not releasing the book—*if* it had been written.

'What about Stuart Mathers, the manager?' Ginny nodded to the dangling paper tag hanging off Flora. 'Did JM get in touch with him?'

'No.' Hen shook her head. 'She's left messages but there has been no reply. We don't know if he will be at the memorial tonight.'

'According to his social media profile he'll be there.' Connor looked up from his phone and showed them the screen. There were several posts filled with photographs of Monica at red-carpet events and the words RIP across the screen along with broken heart emojis. The final post had a photograph of a bright floral suit and underneath it said: *Honouring the Grand Dame of television tonight. Her legacy will live on.*

'Well, if he is, we need to corner him. If anyone knows about the memoir, he will.' Tuppence jotted some notes down on the tag and then stepped back to study Flora. 'We need to talk with the rest of the board as well.'

'Knock, knock,' a voice said from the doorway and they turned to where Iris Northam was standing. Brandon, clearly remembering her from the other day, barked at her in greeting.

'Hey.' Connor put down his phone and straightened up, while Tuppence stepped in front of Flora and stretched her arms out wide as Hen covered the mannequin with the cape.

'Con... I didn't know you were going to be here.' Iris's face brightened at the sight of him. 'I thought we were meeting later at the pub.'

'Yeah,' he agreed, colour staining his cheeks. 'I had to swing by and give Mrs Cole something.'

'Library related,' Tuppence quickly added as she swept the cape back around Flora's shoulders, hiding away the makeshift murder board. 'Something *very* library related.'

'Er... okay. Sure.' Iris blinked and put the bag onto the cutting table. 'I didn't mean to intrude but my mum wanted to give you these. It's from Nan's sewing room.'

'Oh, how lovely. I'll use some of it on her dress.' Hen moved to the bag, eager to see the contents.

'She'd love that,' Iris said and peered down at the press clippings of Monica that they'd taken from the board room. 'Gosh, she was so photogenic.'

'Yes, absolutely stunning.' Tuppence glanced at the *Mother Goose* poster on the wall. 'I don't understand why she tried so hard to stop herself from ageing. It's very sad.'

Iris wrinkled her nose. 'I get that it's dangerous because it gives a false perspective of ageing rather than normalising it, but from a branding perspective I can see the appeal. And even if actresses lose micro-movements in their face, from having work done, it does make them familiar and recognisable, which might help with their career, and in turn their identity. Perhaps she found comfort in being able to control at least something in a ruthless industry?'

Silence filled the space, and Iris shifted from foot to foot, as if uncertain. Ginny opened her mouth to say how impressed she was at Iris's bravery in speaking up and sharing a different perspective, but before she could Connor stepped closer to her.

'I hadn't thought of it like that. Then again, I haven't thought much about the topic,' Connor said.

'That's because you avoided social media when you were younger and weren't influenced by how we're meant to look,' Iris said and then turned to Ginny and her friends. 'Sorry for the rant... but it's such a complex topic and we studied it last term.'

'Goodness, don't be sorry,' Hen said warmly. 'It's a reminder that we shouldn't judge what someone else chooses to do. Especially if you're right and if it gave Monica comfort.'

'I guess we'll never know about that.' Iris glanced at her phone. 'I'd better go help Mum with her lines.'

'Need a hand?' Connor asked.

'No,' Iris said in a solemn voice then grinned and planted a kiss on his cheek. 'But I do need someone to sit in the corner looking all dark, broody and mysterious. Think you're up to the task?'

'See what I can do.' He gave a nonchalant shrug though his eyes locked with Iris's. Then he seemed to remember they weren't alone in the room. Wincing, he turned to Ginny. 'I'll head off, unless you need anything else.'

'No, but thank you for bringing over that... library thing,' she said, biting back on a smile. It would only embarrass him if he knew how delighted they were for him.

Connor patted Brandon between the ears and led Iris out the door. Ginny watched them go, so proud of the man he was becoming. Tuppence and Hen were both wearing matching smiles, equally proud.

'How quickly they grow up.' Hen dabbed at her eyes.

'Oh, I do like her a lot. What a perfect match for our Connor,' Tuppence said as JM appeared in the doorway.

She stared at them all. 'What have I missed? Why are you looking like that? Is it to do with Connor and Iris? I saw them leaving together. Delightful couple. Very well-matched.'

'Aren't they just?' Ginny agreed, her face warm from smiling. There was something very special about first loves, and it was clear that Connor was smitten. 'They're heading to the pub, which I'm pleased about. I don't think a memorial service is the best place for young love to flourish.'

'Definitely not.' Hen lifted rolls of delicate lace ribbon, piles of vintage fabric and handmade patterns from the bag that Iris had given her.

Ginny gave JM a hopeful look. 'Did you hear back from Stuart Mathers?'

'No, which was disappointing,' JM said. 'We need to talk to him about the memoir.'

'He's going to the memorial,' Hen said.

JM brightened. 'Excellent. Which reminds me, we need to get ready if we don't want to be late.'

'I was planning to go as I am.' Tuppence peered down at herself. Her overalls were covered in flecks of gold paint and there were smudges of oil on her fingers. Ginny was in much the same state while Hen had threads hanging off her. 'Okay, maybe you're right.'

'I'm not often wrong,' JM said dryly. 'The rest of the cast and crew have already left. And don't forget the dress code is floral.'

Ginny nodded and followed her friends out of the theatre to get ready for Monica Larkwell's memorial.

TWENTY-FIVE

MONDAY DECEMBER 15

Suzette and Ian Ryan lived in a modern free-standing house in one of the newer estates that flanked Little Shaw. It wasn't the kind of house Ginny liked, but it was clear by the winter garden and leaf-free driveway that the Ryans were proud of it.

'It's very neat,' Hen said, her nose wrinkling as she peered around.

'Not to mention expensive. I remember when these first came up for sale. They cost a bomb,' Tuppence said. 'But it's the kind of house I'd expect a couple of accountants to own.'

'That's a stereotype,' JM corrected. 'I've known some wild and wonderful accountants who have lived in buses, had tattoos and liked drinking tequila on a Wednesday night. Though... in this case, I accept that you might be correct. The few times I've spoken to Ian and Suzette they have been very well-groomed. And sensible.'

Ginny bit back a smile. JM's description was spot on. The house *was* very well-groomed, and while the other houses on the street were glowing with mismatched Christmas lights and inflatables, the Ryans' only decorations were tasteful hanging glass lanterns.

Ginny smoothed down her navy skirt and floral jacket. It was more designed for spring weather than the frigid temperatures, but she hadn't wanted to ignore the dress code. JM had on a magnificent floral coat that hung down to her knees, and underneath was a plain black jumper and wide-legged trousers. Hen had on a lovely Laura Ashley number and Tuppence had woven delicate buds of daphne into her curls, which cloaked her in a delicious scent.

At least they were dressed the part.

'What's the plan?' Hen asked as they reached the threshold.

'We need to find Stuart Mathers and speak to the board members. Plus, anyone else who might be able to give us insight,' Tuppence announced. 'I suggest we look for the weepers. They're sure to spill secrets.'

'Weepers *and* cold-hearted statues,' JM corrected. 'There's a good chance that our killer is emotionally numb.'

'In other words, it could be anyone,' Hen whispered and knocked on the door. 'I wonder who will turn up?'

'This is Little Shaw, which means everyone will be here,' Tuppence said.

Her confidence was rewarded. As they stepped through the front door, they were greeted with an explosion of noise as people milled around the large open-plan room, dressed in all kinds of floral fabrics. Ginny nodded to Cleo, Arnold and Andrea, who were having an animated conversation with Hazel, while most of the cast and crew were dotted around, clutching martini glasses.

On the far wall, a digital projector was showing photographs of Monica through her years in showbiz, while candles covered every surface along with numerous vases of snow-white flowers and framed photographs of the late actress.

Food was spread out on the kitchen counter, and a bar was set up by the window. It was more like a well-orchestrated movie set than a house. Was it for the sake of Danny Ling, who had said he'd be attending to get footage? He'd denied that the Ryans were investors in his documentary, but Ginny wasn't sure she trusted his word.

And where was Danny, anyway?

She searched the room but couldn't see him. Could it be that Wallace had him in for questioning?

'Oh, you're here.' Suzette Ryan descended on them. Her long blonde hair hung down her back in a curtain, stunning against a navy dress with large magnolias printed across it. Despite never meeting Suzette in person before, Ginny found herself swept up in a hug. 'To think that Ian was worried no one would turn up. But I said to him, honey, if we build it... they *will* come.'

'He was right.' Tuppence peered around, eyes wide like saucers as she took in the Instagram-ready interior.

'It's a lovely tribute to Monica,' Hen said.

'Bottoms up,' a voice suddenly boomed out, and they turned to where a well-tanned man was holding a martini glass, sprawled out on a long white leather sofa, wearing a pink floral shirt.

Paul Atkins, the charismatic board member.

At the sound of his voice, Suzette stiffened and glanced over to where her husband, Ian, was sitting. His dull brown eyes were downcast and he had one arm on Paul's sleeve.

Ian gave his wife a hapless shrug, as if to say, 'I'm trying my best.'

Suzette flinched but then collected herself and smiled at Hen. 'Thank you. It's the least we can do. It's hard not to feel responsible since it was the board's decision to hire Monica.'

'Was it a joint decision? We heard that Hazel was against the appointment,' JM said. Her voice was calm and Ginny could only admire how skilful her friend was when it came to questioning.

Suzette nodded. 'That's true. And Hazel's a sweetheart, so don't think I'm saying this out of malice, but she's also hot-blooded and passionate. And while we encourage boldness, there has to be a balance. When Ian and I first joined the board, it was only made up of actors, which made for brilliant productions, but the books were... to be blunt, a big mess. They were very close to going under and hadn't applied for any grants in a long time. I suppose you could say that we bring the level-headedness to the team. But while I'd like to claim it was our idea to bring Monica onboard, that honour goes to Paul.'

Ginny nodded. This confirmed what Desiree had told them. She looked behind her again. Paul was struggling to get to his feet from the sofa, and, in the process, dragging a hapless Ian Ryan up with him. Ian was almost as tall as Paul, but that was where the similarity ended: he appeared like a ghost against the tanning salon owner's mahogany hue.

'Did Paul and Monica know each other beforehand?' Ginny asked, dragging her attention back to Suzette.

'Oh.' The chairperson considered it with a delicate wrinkle of her nose. 'I'm not actually sure. Paul is so, well... *over the top* at times, it's hard to know if he's meeting someone for the first time or if he's known them his entire life. Why do you ask?'

'No reason,' Ginny quickly answered, hoping she hadn't been too obvious. 'I'm just interested at how many different skills you have on the board. They are lucky to have you all.'

Suzette flushed at the compliment. 'Thank you, that's very sweet. Though I must admit it was Ian's doing. He was the one who wanted us to join the board, you see. He doesn't look it now, but he once had dreams of stardom himself.'

He did? Ginny turned to study Suzette's mild-mannered husband, but it was hard to imagine him taking centre stage. He looked more like he wanted to burrow into the ground. Ginny, who wasn't fond of parties where she didn't know anyone, could sympathise.

'More drinks.' This time Paul held up his empty glass and staggered to his feet, shaking off Ian Ryan, who was attempting to steady him. Suzette flinched, but her face softened as Kaleb, wearing a bright smile and an elf hat, walked over to Ian and helped him guide Paul in the direction of the garden.

'Kaleb's very kind-hearted,' Ginny said, thinking of what Trish had told her about Suzette and Ian's relationship with the younger man.

'An absolute sweetheart,' Suzette agreed, her face softening for the first time. 'Ian and I both adore him. Though if you will excuse me, I'd better go and check on Paul. He's taken the news of Monica's death badly. Maybe the martinis were a mistake?'

'I think he'll be the first of many casualties,' JM said as a waitress floated past with a tray of drinks. 'We should stick to the soft stuff.'

Ginny, who didn't drink often, heartily agreed and took a soda water. If they had any chance of getting answers, they'd need their wits about them.

'That's interesting that Paul might have already had a relationship with Monica. I wonder what kind of relationship it was?' Tuppence pondered.

'You think they were lovers?' JM raised an eyebrow. 'I suppose it's possible. In fact, it's an excellent question.'

'Paul's name is on Flora,' Hen agreed. 'But it's been so busy we haven't had a chance to interview him.'

'Well... there's no time like the present.' JM peeled off in the direction of the garden, where the figure of Paul Atkins was facing the dark sky, a trail of vape steam haloing out around him.

'I'll see what I can get out of Ian.' Tuppence drained her glass then darted off through the throng of mourners to where Ian was standing behind the bar, a bewildered expression on his face.

'I keep thinking I'll get braver as I get older,' Hen said as a large photograph of Monica wearing a sequin gown flashed up on the screen. 'But the idea of talking to strangers scares me.'

'And me,' Ginny admitted. 'When I'm at work I don't mind because I'm helping people... so I've been trying to tell myself that's all I'm doing now.'

'Oh, that's a lovely way of looking at it,' Hen said as she peered around. 'I suppose we'd better look for Stuart Mathers.'

He wasn't hard to spot. Connor had shown them several photographs from the internet; Ginny spied him having an animated conversation with Desiree. He was wearing the same floral suit that he had been on his social media account, and judging by the unsteady way he raised his hand in the air, it appeared that he'd also imbibed in one too many martinis.

'There he is,' she whispered to Hen as Desiree detached herself from Monica's manager and hurried away. They threaded their way through the crowd and reached him as he swayed into the table and knocked Hen's arm.

'Schorry,' he slurred, and tried to right himself. 'Where's the bar?'

'Why don't we help you find a chair and get you a glass of water?' Ginny said, taking his arm to stop him falling.

'Yes, let's sit down. It's ever so crowded here.' Hen took his other arm and they steered him to the white leather sofa, which was now deserted.

'And you'll get me a drink?' He slumped down on the couch, like a puppet whose strings had been cut. 'It's been a ghastly day. I can't believe she's gone.'

Ginny settled herself down as close to him as she dared. 'We're both very sorry for your loss. Am I right in thinking you were Monica's manager?'

'I am... I mean, I *was*.' He shifted his weight and peered at Ginny and then Hen, and some of the drunken air fell away. 'I've been looking after her for over thirty years, and the one time she needs me...' He paused to hiccup. 'It's a terrible business.'

'I'm sure your appearance will give so many people comfort,' Hen told him warmly.

'That's what Paul Atkins said. He's been messaging me all day to come.' Stuart let out a sigh and slumped back on the sofa as more photos appeared on the wall, all of Monica. 'The things Monica and I achieved were amazing.'

'She had quite the career,' Ginny agreed, deciding it wasn't worth beating around the bush with their questions. 'We heard from Danny Ling that Monica was writing a memoir and it was going to be explosive.'

Stuart snorted. 'Danny Ling is a twat. He had the cheek to tell me how great it is that Monica's dead because now he can sell his documentary. Insensitive prick.'

'How dreadful of him,' Hen said.

'Yeah, though in fairness Monica did bring some of it on herself. She never should have bluffed him about the memoir.'

'Bluffed him?' Ginny's brow furrowed. 'What do you mean? Are you saying she didn't write one?'

'Oh, she wrote it all right. I've got no idea what Ling thinks is going to be in it, but I doubt it's as exciting as he expects.'

Ginny's mind whirled. 'How could you not know what's in it?'

His face darkened. 'Because she cut me out of the deal, didn't she?'

She had? Ginny didn't know a lot about how managers and agents worked but she'd heard the magic number of fifteen percent, and had to assume that if Monica sold a book, it would've made a fair bit of money. Was Stuart Mathers bitter that she'd bypassed him?

'Why would she do that?' Hen asked, eyes bright with curiosity.

'Because when she first mentioned writing one, I advised her against it. It's one thing to do a comeback but it's another thing to air your dirty laundry.'

'What kind of dirty laundry?' Ginny gently pushed.

'Just your regular celebrity kiss and tell stuff.' He shrugged. 'Here's the thing—everything she's ever done is already out there. There's no big, exciting revelation. But I couldn't convince her that no one would care what it was like to date a D-list popstar who has now gone to seed.'

'That's a bit harsh,' Hen protested.

'It's called being realistic. This industry is brutal and it's my job to help my clients navigate it. That's what I did with Monica. There's only one way to stay relevant in this industry. And that's to look hot and keep your mouth shut.'

'You don't really believe that, do you?' Ginny shivered, thinking of the many articles that discussed the plastic surgery Monica had allegedly had. Was it because of her manager's views on the world? Had he been whispering this kind of misogynist rhetoric into the actress's ear? A wave of sadness ran through her. It didn't seem like Monica had much of a support system to navigate her life in show business, or to check on her mental health.

'Believe it? This isn't an opinion, it's a fact and I told her what would happen if she tried to age disgracefully. No one would care. Or worse, they'd take the piss out of her. But would she listen?'

'You mean about doing the memoir?' Hen asked.

'Sure... and the pantomime. I'd got her a nice little guest stint on *Coronation Street*, but she turned it down for a two-bit panto in the middle of nowhere.'

'Wasn't it to tie in with the thirty-year anniversary of when she was first here?' Hen asked, though her mouth was tight, no doubt from the disparaging way he'd spoken of Little Shaw.

'I'd hardly call it an anniversary.' He snorted. 'But that was Monica all over. One part talent, two parts stubborn cow.' He shrugged then looked at his hands. 'Hey, where's my martini?'

Hen scrunched up her face. 'I'm not sure you should drink any more.'

'Who are you? My mum?' He lumbered to his feet and staggered into the crowd.

'Oh dear,' Hen said, clutching at a cushion and tugging the corners. 'I know I should feel sad for him because he's grieving, but I didn't warm to him.'

'Nor did I,' Ginny admitted, going over everything he'd said. Was it true that he didn't know what was in the memoir, and that

Monica had cut him out of the deal? Stuart had tried to convince them there was nothing of interest in Monica's history. But if that was so, why had Danny Ling been so eager to get her to share the information on camera?

And where *was* the manuscript? Had Monica handed it in to the publisher yet? Would Wallace be able to get access to it? Had she written it on her own, or hired a ghost writer?

Then there was the pantomime. If Monica was making a comeback, then why turn down a role in a national soap opera to do a two-week stint at a small regional theatre?

The questions crowded Ginny's mind, stacking on top of each other, without an answer in sight. What she needed was some fresh air and peace and quiet. But before she could stand, Suzette appeared in the middle of the room and rang a bell.

'On behalf of Little Shaw Playhouse, I would like to thank you all for coming here tonight. And now it's time for us to listen to a few speeches from those people who knew Monica best. Ian and I hope that by sharing our collective pain it will help us heal. With that in mind, I'd like to call Stuart Mathers to say a few words, then our board will speak. After that, we'll hand it to the floor. We expect it will last for two hours so grab yourself a martini and get comfortable.'

There were some murmurs as people clustered onto the long sofa, locking Ginny and Hen firmly in place, leaving them trapped. Ginny closed her eyes as Stuart Mathers stepped to the centre of the room and told three inappropriate stories about Monica then burst into tears. The speech lurched on before Suzette stepped in and took over, telling her own collection of recent anecdotes.

'Is it strange that none of Monica's other friends are here to speak for her?' Hen peered around, scanning the room.

'Maybe they're mourning her in their own way?' Ginny closed her eyes. She'd been to several funerals and memorials since Eric's death and while the pain wasn't as intense, it was still there lurking below the surface.

'I hope so.' Hen squeezed Ginny's hand. 'I feel bad that we only came here to get information, when we should be thinking about Monica and the fact her life is over.'

Ginny swallowed and returned the pressure of Hen's hand. Her friend was right. They'd all been too caught up in trying to solve Monica's murder and get justice for her death, that they'd forgotten to take time to commemorate her life.

TWENTY-SIX

TUESDAY DECEMBER 16

Edgar hissed and his black fur stood on end the next morning. His annoyance was focused on Flora, who was in the corner of Ginny's front living room, the numerous tags dangling from the unmoving torso, while the crushed velvet cape lay resting over the arm of Ginny's favourite reading chair. They'd brought her along so they could add the updates of what they'd learned the previous night.

'I've never seen him so angry,' Hen said in alarm as she bent forward and patted Brandon, who was curled up at her feet. 'Why do you think he dislikes Flora so much?'

'Because Flora's an inanimate object that has invaded his space?' JM suggested.

'Maybe he's upset that we've almost solved the mystery without his help. You know he likes to get involved,' Tuppence offered.

By way of answering, Edgar jumped onto the coffee table and gave Ginny's library book several nudges until it fell onto the carpet, landing spine up. The cat peered down, his amber eyes blank, as if confused how it had got there. Then he curled up on the coffee table and purred.

'I'm not sure that's the answer. And we haven't solved the

mystery yet.' Ginny retrieved the book and put it up on the shelf. She'd hoped his book-attacking days were behind him, but clearly not.

'That's because Wallace is terrible at staying in touch. Ginny found out about the memoir yesterday morning and we haven't heard a sausage from him. For all we know Danny Ling has killed Wallace as well and we're none the wiser,' Tuppence retorted.

Ginny was certain that Wallace wouldn't interview a murder suspect without taking the necessary precautions, but agreed the waiting was difficult to endure. It was why they'd decided to catch him before he left for work.

Unfortunately, when JM, Tuppence, Hen and Flora had arrived, there was no sign of Wallace's car, and the only noise from next door was the incessant whirr of Ted's power tools as he did goodness knows what.

'We can at least update Flora.' Tuppence studied the dress form-cum-murder board. The cardboard tags on the shoulder were growing. Along with Hazel Holdsworth, there was Kaleb, Andrew, Danny Ling, Nolan Archer and Suzette and Ian Ryan. 'But we don't have alibis for Paul Atkins and Stuart Mathers.'

'I didn't get anything from Atkins, though he did try to sell me ten vouchers to his tanning salon,' JM said.

'We know he likes martinis and vaping.' Tuppence filled in his tag. 'How did you get on with Stuart Mathers? He also seemed to like martinis.'

'All we discovered was that he was drunk and mean-spirited,' Hen said.

Ginny sighed as they stared at each other. The whole evening at the memorial had been a waste of time, in terms of the investigation—although Ginny was glad they'd attended to pay their respects. In the past they'd found that alcohol made people talkative, but the night before had the opposite effect. Maybe that was why Monica liked to drink martinis—because it stopped her from spilling secrets to strangers?

'Let's hope Wallace had better luck.' JM looked up at the sound of a car door shutting from outside. She brightened and marched to the window. 'It's him.'

'Excellent. It's about time he showed up.' Tuppence was across the room in a flash, nose pressed to the glass. 'He's on his phone talking to someone.'

'How exciting.' Hen patted Brandon then slipped next to Tuppence. 'JM, I don't think he can see you gesturing.'

Ginny stood as JM knocked on the glass, trying to attract Wallace's attention. Edgar looked up with interest and perched himself on the windowsill to see what the fuss was about.

'Maybe we should wait until he's ready to give us an update?' Ginny joined her friends as Wallace finally turned to see them staring through the glass at him. Despite the early morning gloom, it was clear he wasn't pleased. Still, whatever he thought about the matter, he was soon pushing open Ginny's gate and walking up the path. She met him at the front door and ushered him inside before he could knock.

'Sorry,' she mouthed at him. He shrugged and walked into the room, with Ginny following behind.

Edgar had repositioned himself on the sofa and someone had put Flora's crushed velvet cape back on, as Tuppence valiantly stood in front of the dress form casually spreading out her arms, as if yawning.

Wallace stared at it then shook his head. 'I'm not going to ask.'

'Good to see you're in a sensible mood.' JM ushered him into the reading chair. 'What news do you have for us on Danny Ling? Did you squeeze him?'

'Did he sing?' Tuppence added.

'Is he under arrest?' Hen said hopefully.

'There was no squeezing, singing or arresting,' Wallace told them bluntly.

'Why not? You can officially hold him for twenty-four hours,' JM reminded him.

He grimaced and rolled his shoulders. 'No one has seen Danny Ling since Monday evening when he left Holly Farm Bed and Breakfast.'

The blood rushed from Ginny's head and her mouth dropped open.

'No.' Hen's hands flew to her mouth.

'When we didn't see him at the memorial, we thought it was because he was being questioned down at the station.' Tuppence's face drained of colour.

'What do you think happened to him?' JM said in a softer voice and they all leaned forward.

Wallace returned their gaze. 'This stays between us, but it's possible he's gone on the run. Archer admitted he and Ling doctored the footage that they originally handed into us.'

'You mean they removed part of it?'

Wallace nodded. 'They did.'

'Scumbags,' Tuppence said, eyes bright. 'To think I felt sorry for Danny living under the shadow of the cursed mirror. But now...'

'What was on the footage?' Ginny asked. She might not believe in cursed mirrors, but it was becoming clear that Danny Ling had lied to them all. 'Did it involve the memoir?'

Wallace acknowledged her guess with a nod of his head. 'It was from Monica's dressing room and showed her dictating her thoughts. She recorded them, then listened back to handwrite it. The part he caught on the recording was that when she was at Little Shaw thirty years ago... she fell pregnant.'

Silence settled around the room, broken only by Edgar's purring and Brandon's snuffling.

Pregnant?

So that was the skeleton.

Had Stuart Mathers known about it? Last night he'd downplayed the memoir, suggesting there was nothing in it that the public would care about. Yet, it was hard to imagine he *hadn't* known. Had it been bitterness at being cut out of the deal that caused him to lie? Or was there another reason?

'I take it you don't know who the father was,' JM said.

'Correct. The cameraman showed us the footage, and Monica is interrupted by one of the crew. We have contacted her publisher and Mathers but neither have the manuscript. The publisher only has a proposal but no chapter outlines.'

'We spoke to Stuart last night and he told us Monica cut him out of the deal and went directly to the publisher,' Ginny said.

'He told Anita the same thing,' Wallace confirmed.

'So that's why she was murdered? To stop the news coming out?' JM frowned. 'It seems extreme.'

'I agree.' Wallace gave her a curt nod. 'However, in lieu of more evidence, that's our current theory. This isn't public knowledge, but her apartment was ransacked, and so was her car. We are working on prints and nearby CCTV footage but haven't got a hit yet.'

'Were they looking for the manuscript?' Ginny continued to sort everything out in her mind. The pregnancy angle finally gave them a motive for Monica being murdered.

JM was right about it being extreme. Who would it affect if the news came out? Especially for something that happened thirty years ago. Was it because she wasn't married? That kind of attitude was from an older generation, but there seemed to be a shift back to 'traditional values' by some sectors of society.

'I can only guess.' Wallace folded his arms, clearly not happy that he didn't have the answers.

'But why?' JM made a clicking noise with her tongue. 'It's incredible in this day and age that there's no digital copy of the book. Have you checked her devices?'

'Strangely enough, we have.' Wallace gave her a sour look, as if he was being taught to suck lemons. 'Before you ask, yes, forensics have gone through her phone and cloud storage to search for recordings and documents. There were none. All we have is the snippet from the hidden camera in her dressing room.'

'Don't get testy with me. You're the one who hasn't been telling us things,' JM retorted.

'I was very clear at the beginning what I could and couldn't share with you,' Wallace replied then rolled his shoulders. 'Sorry... I'm grateful for the help. But it would all be for nothing if I take any shortcuts that might be challenged.'

JM returned his gaze then gave a slow nod. 'Legal loopholes. You are right. I withdraw my objection.'

A faint smile twitched around Wallace's mouth. 'Thank you.'

'What did Stuart Mathers say when you told him about the pregnancy?' Ginny asked, going back to the manager's behaviour the previous evening.

'He swore he didn't know about it.'

Hen wrinkled her nose and leaned forward to scratch Brandon's ears. 'I don't understand where Danny Ling fits into it. Why has he disappeared? Is it because of the argument he had with Monica?'

Wallace rubbed his chin. 'According to Archer, Ling blackmailed Monica about the pregnancy. He wanted her to confess it on film, and said if she didn't, he'd release the footage that he already had.'

'Blackmail? That's all this case needs,' JM retorted.

'I couldn't agree more.' Wallace gave a bitter laugh. 'We believe that's what Ling and Monica were arguing about when Andrew overheard them outside the theatre. Our strongest theory is that Ling discovered who the killer was and tried to blackmail them as well.'

'Playing both sides. Risky.' Tuppence whistled.

'That's a lot more leverage than simply having a confession of a pregnancy that happened thirty years ago,' Ginny admitted. 'I take it you've double-checked the footage the cameraman gave you to make sure it hasn't been doctored any further.'

'Oh, we've checked. There's nothing on there that gives away the identity of the killer. But the cameraman is being held until we've found Ling.' Wallace got to his feet, face pale. 'I need to get a shower and prepare for a press conference.'

'Press conference? Is that wise?' JM frowned. 'Sounds like you're starting to get somewhere. That might send the killer underground.'

'If you want to explain that to my DCI, please be my guest. Though... if you happen to find Ling, I don't want you going anywhere near him. No squeezing, no singing, no nothing. Are we clear?'

JM flinched but gave him a slight nod. 'Clear.'

'Thank you.' Wallace bent and patted Brandon on the head, tickled Edgar under the chin and disappeared back outside.

Once he was gone, Tuppence turned to Flora and folded her arms. 'I think it's obvious what we have to do next.'

'It is?' Hen blinked.

'Absolutely,' JM agreed. 'We might not be able to go searching for Danny Ling, but that doesn't mean we can't find out who the father of Monica's baby was.'

'And what happened with the pregnancy?' Hen asked in a quiet voice. She was the only one of them who had a child. And while her daughter was now an adult, it was clear Hen was thinking of her own pregnancy and delivering. 'Did she carry it to term and was the child born?'

Ginny frowned, remembering what Stuart Mathers had said. Everything about Monica was online, in black and white. Did that mean if they searched hard enough, they'd find the answers they needed?

She certainly hoped so. Because if Monica had been killed by an ex-lover, the murder was very personal and it was impossible to know how far the killer would go to keep their secrets. She closed her eyes. A missing manuscript... a secret pregnancy from thirty years ago, and now blackmail? It was as over the top as the pantomime itself.

TWENTY-SEVEN

TUESDAY DECEMBER 16

'Sounds like everyone had a booze-up.' Slim turned on the library lights as they prepared for the day. 'So, what's the difference between a memorial and a funeral?'

'A body,' Connor said in a dry voice as he started up the self-issue machines. But despite his deadpan answer, a smile hovered around his mouth. Ginny longed to ask how his date with Iris had gone.

'Funny lad,' Slim retorted with a frown. 'I still don't get why the board had their own memorial when there's sure to be a big fancy funeral.'

'It was to support the cast and crew,' Ginny said. It had also given them some insight into Monica's manager.

Ginny closed her eyes trying to tease out the tangled puzzle. Who was the father of Monica's baby? And was that person the killer? It made sense. It would also explain the missing manuscript. To prevent the truth coming out, the father of Monica's baby had silenced her and destroyed the manuscript—only to find out that Danny Ling had recorded something that gave away their identity.

And while Danny might not have committed the murder,

not being honest with the police, and possibly blackmailing the killer for his own gain, surely made him as bad.

No wonder Danny had gone on the run: he must have panicked after she and Tuppence had spoken to him at the cemetery.

A fissure of guilt ripped through her. It was the double-edged sword of getting involved in an investigation, because every clue they discovered had the capacity to create a new ripple of events. And Ginny and her friends were responsible for those ripples...

Then she caught herself. If Danny Ling *was* guilty of trying to profit from someone's murder, that was his decision, not hers. Still...

'William's asking when the new books are coming out.' Connor appeared in her office door an hour later. *Oh dear*. She'd been so preoccupied with the pantomime and the case that she'd been neglecting her duties at the library.

Ginny squared her shoulders and composed herself. It wasn't fair on the patrons for her to not be present while she was at work. 'They need to be scanned into the system, if you'd like to finish them?'

'Sure.' He stacked up the book trolley then paused in the doorway. 'Sorry I skipped the memorial yesterday. I hope you didn't mind.'

'Of course not,' Ginny said, relieved that he hadn't come to what had been a very depressing evening. Then she remembered his date and her mood improved. 'Iris is lovely, by the way, and very smart.'

'Super brainy, right? He grinned, pride filling his words. 'She always killed it at school. How did you go with the research?'

'We spoke with Wallace this morning and he's going to give a press conference.'

'That explains where everybody is.' Connor nodded at the empty library. 'Are you allowed to say what he told you?'

'Yes, it will be out there soon enough.' Ginny filled him in on the memorial service, Monica Larkwell's pregnancy, the missing manuscript and Danny Ling's disappearance.

'Sounds messy.' He shook his head and tapped his fingers against the trolley. 'I wonder if Stuart Mathers was the father? He's been her manager her for long enough.'

'I wondered that as well, though he swore to Wallace he didn't know about the pregnancy. I suppose that still doesn't rule him out. It's a tangle, and, thanks to the late night, my mind isn't at its best.'

'The speeches sound like a nightmare. I reckon me and Iris dodged a bullet.'

'Several,' Ginny admitted, then gave him a curious smile. 'Did you have a nice time at the pub?'

'Yeah,' he said then dipped his head, not quite making eye contact. 'Iris is... well... she'd already been thinking of transferring to Liverpool University. It's not confirmed yet.'

'Oh... well, Liverpool's a lot closer than Newcastle,' Ginny said diplomatically, not wanting to pry too much in case he retreated. 'I imagine that if you did want to see more of each other... you could.'

'Yeah,' he said with a shy smile. 'That's what I was thinking.'

'Goodness, Connor, why are you standing there doing nothing when I'm rushed off my feet?' Cleo burst into the office to complain that some of the patrons were breathing too close to her while she was issuing books, and she couldn't risk getting sick before the upcoming dress rehearsals. Ginny left the books to Connor, smiling to herself at his confidences. They might not seem like much to someone else, but Ginny knew him well enough to know that even sharing that much information showed he trusted her. Her heart warmed. If anyone deserved happiness, Connor did.

Then she went out onto the floor to smooth the ruffled feathers. The library had emptied out while the press conference was on, but people drifted back in the afternoon, all talking about

Monica Larkwell's pregnancy, Danny Ling's disappearance and the police's inability to solve the crime.

'Setting up a helpline... you know what that means,' a man at the counter had moaned.

'That they don't have a clue,' his friend had replied.

All the comments had caused Ginny's brow to pound with the start of a headache. Or perhaps it was because she'd become peopled out from a busy day? All she knew was that by closing time, she longed for her house. She couldn't remember when she'd last stayed in and read a book with a cup of tea and Edgar curled on her lap.

However, she had promised to help Wallace find out the truth, so she wrapped herself up in her coat, scarf and hat, and walked through the village to the theatre.

'Ah, perfect timing,' Tuppence said as Ginny reached the costume room. 'We're trying to work out who the father of Monica's baby might be.'

'Us and everyone else,' Connor said, looking up from his phone. He'd finished work earlier but had clearly decided to continue helping. 'Since the press conference this afternoon, the newspapers and online commentators have already linked it to fifteen different singers and ten footballers. Though half of these photos look like they've been made by AI.'

'They do?' Hen said as Connor showed her a photograph of a younger Monica Larkwell leaving a well-known London nightclub holding hands with a popstar. There was a small bulge in her stomach. 'How can you tell?'

'See how perfect it looks? And there's a beer brand in the background that didn't exist back then.' He pointed to the image. 'I double-checked and Monica was in Mexico on holiday when this photo was allegedly taken.'

'That's dreadful. The poor police are going to have a nightmare sifting through everything.' Hen's eyes were filled with worry.

'Which is where we come in,' JM reminded her in a stern

voice. 'Let's start at the beginning. We know Monica was pregnant when she was in Little Shaw, but we don't know who the father is. However, we do know who the father *isn't*. Ginny, while you were at work we spoke with Hazel Holdsworth. She confirmed that Alan was infertile.'

'So he couldn't have been the father?' Tuppence added then wrinkled her nose. 'Oh, right. That's what infertile means.'

'And what about the pregnancy itself? Did it go to term?' Hen asked in a cautious voice. 'If the baby was put up for adoption, then perhaps her own child is the killer, out for revenge?'

'That would make them twenty-nine years old,' Tuppence mused.

'I don't think she could have carried the baby to term,' Connor piped up again. 'I'm going through her press releases and photographs after she was announced as the *First Kiss* host. There's no hint of any pregnancy, which makes sense if it's just after the pantomime finished. But there are more, at four months, six months and eight months.'

'Maybe it just didn't show,' Ginny said. She'd never had children of her own, but she'd seen her fair share of pregnant women at the surgery, and knew how much it varied.

'Which means it's possible Stuart really didn't know about the pregnancy,' Hen wondered.

Ginny agreed. It also meant they were right back at the start. Anyone could have been the father of Monica's baby. Then she stiffened. The killer *couldn't* have been anyone. It had to be someone who had access to the theatre on the night that Monica was killed. She walked over to Flora and unclipped the list of people who signed in and out. How silly that they'd forgotten.

'Pregnancy aside, whoever murdered Monica has to be here.' She held it up and one by one her friends groaned, as they, too, realised their mistake.

'What were we thinking?' Tuppence pushed aside the press clippings she had been flicking through. 'Though, according to Wallace, everyone on the list has an alibi.'

'And nearly everyone on the list has held back at least something from him.' JM shut her MacBook and paced the room.

It was true. Ginny frowned as she continued to stare at Flora, trying to work out how everything connected.

'If only solving mysteries was as easy as sewing.' Hen sighed and returned to the pile of fabric and lace that Iris had brought in from Junie. She picked up a calico toile of a long coat. 'Oh, isn't this lovely?'

She shook it out to examine it properly, which dislodged a piece of paper that fluttered to the floor. Hen frowned and retrieved it. Then she let out a little gasp.

'What is it? Don't tell me it's someone's old script?' Tuppence said, eyes bright with curiosity.

'No.' Hen shook her head and beckoned them over. 'It's the original *Mother Goose* programme. How extraordinary. The actor must have slipped it into the pocket while Junie was measuring them for the coat. To think it's been here since yesterday, waiting for us to find it.'

'Which we never would have done without you,' Tuppence said with a grin. 'Now, let's see what we've got.'

Ginny's heart pounded as they leaned over the original cast photograph.

This time she ignored the stage names and studied the faces, though the photograph was such poor quality that it was hard to distinguish many features. She squinted, noticing that the young man on the other side of Monica was holding an arm up in the air, making a V for victory sign with his fingers.

Oh. The hairs on Ginny's arm prickled as she scanned down the list of names.

Big P.

Was it possible that Big P was Paul Atkins? The youth in the photograph didn't look anything like the tanning salon mogul, though. He was skinny and had long hair half covering his face.

She thought of their conversation with Iris yesterday and the point the young woman had made about the familiarity of someone's face. Was that why they'd overlooked him? Because the man in his fifties in no way resembled the youth in the photograph?

Suzette had told them that Paul was taking her death badly. How well did he know her?

Enough to have slept with her?

To have murdered her over a pregnancy?

Her stomach knotted, leaving her heavy.

It all fitted together, and he was certainly tall enough to have donned the Prissy costume. The only part that didn't add up was that he wasn't on the sign-in sheet.

Ginny went through it again, in case they'd missed it. Or had he used a different name? She searched for anything that might indicate he'd been there that night.

'What is it?' Tuppence joined Ginny, mouth puckered in concern. 'You've gone very still.'

'It's quite hot in here,' Hen fretted.

'Nonsense, she's clearly figured something out. Care to tell us what it is?' JM joined them.

It snapped Ginny out of her thoughts and she showed them the photograph, explaining her theory.

'But how did he get inside the building to murder her?' Tuppence wondered.

'I've got no idea, but this is the only suspect we've had that makes sense,' JM said. 'I suggest we speak with Hazel. She wasn't in the original production, but her husband was, and we need to know what type of man Atkins is.'

Ginny shivered, recalling his performance on the stage last week. She'd thought he was somewhere between a motivational speaker and a cult leader, but did that mean he was capable of murder?

TWENTY-EIGHT

TUESDAY DECEMBER 16

'You want to know if Paul Atkins and Monica Larkwell had an affair thirty years ago?' Hazel Holdsworth put down the cup of tea she'd been nursing and pushed the sea-green glasses into her hair. They'd found her in the theatre kitchen, surrounded by scripts and jotting down notes in a small book. The kitchen itself was as dilapidated as the rest of the backstage, with old posters, cracked plaster and well-worn carpet on the floor.

'That's correct.' Tuppence slid into one of the mismatched chairs at the table. 'You said she was sleeping with someone, and that Alan never confirmed that he was the one having the affair.'

'And did you know Paul was in the original production?' JM asked.

'Was he?' Hazel's eyebrow shot up. 'I don't remember... though he could have been an understudy. As for whether he and Monica met and had an affair, you would have to ask him.'

Ginny exchanged a glance with her friends. That's exactly what they intended to do, once they found out more about him.

Swallowing hard, she faced the director. 'Could you tell us what Paul was like back then?'

'For a start, he looked different. He was tall and skinny but quite attractive, though not my type. *Clearly.* He was also very ambitious. If I recall he was in a local boyband and had dreams of becoming the next Take That.'

'Oh, I always wanted to see them perform,' Tuppence said then winced. 'Sorry, I didn't mean to get distracted. But it does explain the name in the programme. Big P.'

'Yes, he fancied himself a pop rapper,' Hazel confirmed with a bemused smile. 'I shouldn't judge but the few times I heard him sing at karaoke... well, I don't think the pop-rap world lost out too much.'

'Even if he did have the talent, I believe it's difficult to break into the music industry,' JM said. 'I wonder if Atkins became friendly with Monica to help him and his band get a record deal?'

Hazel nodded. 'I never thought of it at the time, but that's exactly the kind of thing he would do.'

'Except we know that didn't happen. Monica left Little Shaw and went on to fame and fortune,' JM said.

'Exactly, and not long after that, Paul bought his first tanning salon. He puts on a good show of being a successful local businessman, but I've always suspected that underneath it he's bitter that he was never famous,' Hazel said.

Ginny shuddered as she thought of the way the dressing room had been staged with the fallen chandelier, crushing Monica's body. It seemed they were right. It was a clear message saying her time in the spotlight was over.

'Yet he's stayed on the theatre board this whole time?' Hen said.

'It's good for his business because he gets a lot of free advertising for his salons, and while he's not in this panto, he often gets cast in great roles. It suits him very well.' Hazel glanced at the clock on the wall and stood up. 'I need to cut this short. Suzette and Ian are coming in for a budget meeting.'

'Thank you for your time. Before you go, could you tell us one final thing?' Ginny said, the words catching in her throat. 'Do you think Paul Atkins is capable of murder?'

The room went silent as Hazel chewed on her lower lip then she let out a long sigh and nodded her head. 'Yes. Yes, I do.'

'What do you mean, he's not here?' JM leaned over the sleek white counter that shimmered blue thanks to the strip of neon lighting running across it. The Glow Room tanning salon was tucked a block behind the high street, and, between the bright lights and the malty scent of chemicals, Ginny wasn't sure it was a place where she could spend much time. Framed photographs of bikini-clad girls in a variety of poses hung on the walls, all accompanied by Paul Atkins and his V for victory sign.

They'd called Wallace but there was no answer. It wasn't a surprise considering the press conference's appeal for help. He was probably dealing with leads, and his focus would be on finding Danny Ling. So they had decided to speak with him directly.

'Just what I said.' The girl behind the counter had poker-straight hair, an espresso tan and dazzling white teeth peering out from behind puffy lips. 'He owns the place... doesn't mean he works here. Try the pub.'

'How about *you* try the pub?' JM retorted, eyes flashing. The girl, who had been looking at something on her phone, finally put it down and took JM in. She must have realised she'd met her match and she sighed.

'Look, I really don't know where he is and it's more than my job's worth to call him. He's got a nasty temper.'

Nasty temper? Ginny's stomach tightened. The more she was learning about Atkins, the less she liked him.

'Okay, so what if you "*hypothetically*" tell us where he is?' Tuppence joined JM at the counter, using air quotes to punctuate the sentence.

'I would "*hypothetically*" tell you the same thing,' the girl retorted, also using air quotes, though Ginny sensed that there was a dash of mockery in there.

'Are you sure that's your final answer?' JM folded her arms, not interested in making tiny shapes with her fingers.

'We'd appreciate it,' Hen added in a motherly voice.

'You're really not going to leave, are you?' the girl said as the doors opened and a group of teenagers walked in, laughing and giggling.

'We don't want to get you into trouble,' Ginny explained. 'And we do understand you need to protect his privacy, but it's important that we speak with him.'

The girl let out a pained groan. 'You didn't hear it from me but he's on the board of the Little Shaw Dramatic Society. They've got some kind of panto going on. He's been spending time there. Now, will you please leave? And if you see him, don't tell him you were here. He loses it when I don't sell a bundle to everyone who walks through the door. Don't suppose I could interest you in a wax, tint and tan combo? I could give you an OAP discount.'

'Not if you know what's good for you,' JM growled.

'We never saw you.' Tuppence made a lip-zipping motion and Ginny gave the girl a reassuring smile.

'I didn't like the sound of his temper,' Hen said as they climbed into her car, where Brandon was waiting for them.

'No, which is even more reason to get back as fast as we can,' Tuppence said as Hen started the engine and drove towards the theatre. 'Since this is an emergency, I suggest we risk double parking. What do you all think?'

Ginny swallowed at the idea of getting a parking ticket. It came in a firm second, below her fear of the police, but Tuppence was right. If Paul Atkins was at the theatre, they had to find him as quickly as possible.

'Do it,' she said, closely endorsed by JM.

'Besides,' Hen added as she came to a squealing halt directly outside the theatre and parked on the double yellow lines, 'if we catch the killer, then surely the police would have to waive the fine.'

They ran down the side of the theatre and signed in with Kaleb before separating out to search for Paul.

JM and Tuppence headed to the stage in case he was watching the rehearsals, and Ginny and Hen went to the boardroom. They had their phones out to contact each other once they found him. Not to mention Wallace, if they found proof that it was Paul.

Her heart pounded as they navigated the corridors until they reached the boardroom. The door was closed and Ginny turned the handle and stepped in.

Empty.

'Oh,' Hen said. 'I'm not sure whether I'm relieved or disappointed.'

'I know what you mean,' Ginny agreed, her gaze sweeping the room before settling on the long table. There were still stacks of The Glow Room merchandise but no sign of the owner.

Hen shivered and rubbed her hands together. 'I'm really starting to wish we'd stuck with the original plan to sit this one out. It's giving me the creeps.'

'Let's go and find JM and Tuppence and tell them that we need to hand this over to Wallace. Then it'll be his problem.' Ginny gave her friend a hug.

'I'd like that.' Hen sniffed as Brandon led the way before coming to a halt and running back to the side of Hen's leg, whimpering. 'What is it, boy?'

Ginny looked to the far end of the corridor as a figure stepped out of the storage room where the Prissy costume had been stolen from. His mahogany tan glowed in the dull lighting as he hurried in the other direction.

Paul Atkins.

'Oh my.' Hen gasped and fumbled with her phone. 'I'll call JM. Should we follow him?'

Yes. No. Uncertain.

Ginny's mind whirled as she recalled their promise to

Wallace not to take any risks. But they didn't know for sure if Paul *was* the killer.

She nodded. 'Let's see where he goes.'

'Okay.' Hen held the phone up to her ear and had a whispered conversation as they hurried after him. 'I think he's going outside.'

Ginny was about to agree when Paul came to a halt at Monica Larkwell's old dressing room. He knocked once then twisted the handle to step inside. Adrenaline flooded her system as her brows furrowed together. Was Desiree in there? Why was he going to speak with her, if so?

Was it possible that Iris's lovely mother was somehow involved in this?

Please don't let it be so.

'No,' Hen gasped, clearly reaching the same conclusion. 'This is terrible.'

'What's terrible?' Tuppence demanded, as she and JM reached them. 'Where did he go?'

'He's inside the dressing room with Desiree,' Hen whispered. 'I can't believe she's mixed up in this.'

'It might be about something else. They're both board members,' Ginny reminded them, hoping that was the answer.

'Desiree isn't in there. We've just seen her on the stage,' JM said, waving her clipboard. 'And she should've been there all evening if she's stuck to the schedule.'

'Thank goodness.' Ginny closed her eyes.

Why would Paul go into Desiree's dressing room if she wasn't there? Was he looking for something? Had he left something behind? Or was it the missing manuscript?

'I think we should face him,' Tuppence said, stepping forward.

'Okay.' Ginny swallowed her distaste as JM strode forward and turned the door handle. The last time the four of them had gone into the dressing room together, they'd discovered a dead body.

Monica crushed under a chandelier, her body limp and broken.

And now they might face her killer.

The door swung open and Brandon rushed in, barking as he went.

'No, wait,' Hen cried and darted after him. It broke the icy paralysis that had been creeping up Ginny's legs and she followed them inside.

Like the boardroom, it was empty.

'But how?' Hen gasped.

'It's not possible,' Ginny agreed, searching the room for a hiding place. 'We saw him come in here and there are no windows.'

'Well, something happened.' Tuppence peered around, as if hoping to discover a six-foot wardrobe where Paul Atkins might be hiding. But there was only a cluttered dressing table, two chairs and a free-standing coat rack that was filled with clothing.

'Woof.' Brandon barked again and pressed his nose up to the scuffed wainscotting that had been hidden behind the mirror.

'What's up with him, Hen?' Tuppence frowned.

'I don't know.' Hen dropped down to her knees and comforted the shivering dog. 'Do you think he's sensing Monica's ghost?'

'He was like this the other day,' Ginny said, remembering his behaviour when she and Connor had been there. 'As soon as Ted and Garth moved the mirror away, he kept barking..'

'Maybe he sensed the mirror was cursed? Or he's upset that this place is falling apart?' Tuppence said as she ran a hand along the damaged skirting. 'This entire wall needs replacing. Look at all the cracks. Let's hope the money they raise includes doing the dressing rooms,' she said. Then, as the panel gave way and Tuppence made a spluttering sound, they stared into the darkness.

It was a hidden passage.

TWENTY-NINE

TUESDAY DECEMBER 16

It was the final piece of the puzzle.

Was this passageway the way that someone—Paul Atkins?—had entered the theatre to kill Monica without signing in through the stage door? But why had no one mentioned the tunnels? Had they simply been forgotten over time? Ginny thought of how much knowledge got lost with every change of the guards. It was entirely possible.

She held up her phone torch to better examine the darkness. The space was narrow and the wall was built of old stone, visible beneath the faded white plaster. The air inside the passage was cool and damp. Her hands shook as she turned her phone up to the passage ceiling, which was comprised of exposed brick, layers of dust and far too many spider webs.

'What is this place? Why's it here?' Hen whispered, her hand tightly gripping Brandon's collar. He had refused to wait on the other side of the room, and since it had been his discovery, they didn't have the heart to stop him from joining in.

'I imagine it was probably a servants' passage before it was turned into flats.' Ginny lowered the light to study the walls more closely. There were deep grooves and chips of plaster missing.

Heart ringing in her ears, she took a step forward. This wasn't the first time they'd discovered a secret room, but this was much larger than the small priest hole they'd recently come across in another investigation, and they had no idea where it would end. She swept her light across the dusty floor. There were footprints leading south. Was it the direction Atkins had taken?

'Do you think it's connected to the outside of the building?' Tuppence wondered.

'It has to be, if Atkins is using it,' JM said from behind, using her own torch to study the space. Its shadows were a blur of black shapes that danced on the dusty walls. 'Surely this is how he got in to murder Monica on Sunday night. It explains why he wasn't on the sign-in sheet.'

'Should we call Wallace?' Hen wondered.

'Absolutely.' Tuppence swung her torch back around and they shielded their eyes. 'But shouldn't we try to find where it comes out first? Just to make sure?'

Ginny swayed as indecision gnawed at her. If they called Wallace, he'd tell them to wait outside, which would mean they'd miss out on seeing where the tunnel ended up. And what would they tell him? That Paul Atkins was a suspect, even though they had no real proof?

'Okay, let's see where it leads.' She shone her light further down the tunnel. 'Then we can call him.'

'Agreed,' JM said and stepped inside. They all followed, their footsteps echoing around the narrow passage. Ginny's nerves rattled as they moved further away from Monica's dressing room.

'Imagine having to do this every day,' Tuppence whispered. 'I'm glad I wasn't born a Georgian servant.'

'That makes two of us,' JM agreed. 'I'm not made for taking orders.'

Ginny glanced around. How many maids had run up and down this passage with food or laundry, scared of the dark? Did they carry candles with them?

She hoped so, and made her own torch do an arc, giving her more visibility.

Dust motes danced in the beam as they descended further into the unknown. The wind whistled, slipping through cracked plaster and chilling the air. Were they getting close to the exit?

'Look, there it is.' JM increased her pace, until they reached a plain door.

So, it was true.

There was a secret way into the theatre. A dusty curve on the floor by the door suggested that it swung inwards, and that it had been recently used. JM twisted the door's plain handle, and shafts of dull moonlight flooded in.

'This is on the other side of the theatre.' JM used her torch to show the lane that ran between the theatre and the tall brick wall of the neighbouring terrace houses. 'There's no sign of Atkins.'

'How annoying that he escaped.' Tuppence folded her arms, which sent her own torch light shining back through the tunnel. Ginny, who was still standing in the threshold, turned to avoid the brightness, when her gaze landed on a tiny purple feather wedged in part of the wall.

Ice crept through her bones as she stepped back into the tunnel to inspect it. Like breadcrumbs, a second feather appeared, also trapped in the wall.

Except instead of crumbling white plaster, there was another wooden door behind her, in the tunnel.

She gasped and her friends hurried back to her side.

'Not another one?' Hen yelped and Brandon barked, glaring at the wood.

'It can't be an external entrance,' JM said.

'The question is, what's behind the door?' Tuppence whispered, her voice sounding as shaky as Ginny felt. 'Should we open it?'

'What if he's in there?' Ginny pointed out.

'Then he would've heard us coming down the passage and is probably listening to this conversation right now. In which case, we're in danger either way.' JM located the handle and pulled it open.

The room was tiny with no windows, but the dank air of the passage was gone and the scent of burned chemicals and charcoal filled the air, along with something putrid.

Coughing, Ginny held up her phone to throw light into the room. In the centre was the charred remains of what she could only guess was a goose costume. She stepped back and saw a slumped body.

The bleached blond hair and nose ring told her immediately who it was.

Danny Ling.

Dread settled like ice in Ginny's veins as she stared at the unmoving figure. Congealed blood covered half of his head and surrounded him in a river of red.

He was dead.

'The cursed mirror got him,' Tuppence gasped. Hen began to cry and JM closed her eyes and bowed her head.

Ginny swallowed and fumbled for her phone to call the police.

Wallace answered on the first ring, and for once it was Ginny who was terse with her words.

'Danny Ling is dead. We know who did it.'

THIRTY

WEDNESDAY DECEMBER 17

Little Shaw police station was less crowded than their last visit. Then again, it was only eight o'clock in the morning, and perhaps it was quieter than before because the police were on a manhunt for Paul Atkins.

Ginny and her friends had given statements the previous evening when DC Singh and PC Bent had arrived at the theatre and set up yet another crime scene. But there had been no sign of Wallace and only a fleeting glimpse of Imogen as she hurried down the tunnel to inspect the body.

They'd been allowed to leave an hour after that, but Wallace had messaged Ginny asking them to come into the station in the morning.

And here we are.

Sweat prickled her palms and her heart beat out a rapid rhythm as they walked up to the reception desk where Wallace was waiting. Stubble grazed his chin and his shirt was crushed, as if he'd slept in it. Considering there was another dead body, it was highly likely that he had—and probably not for very long, judging by the way he clutched at a coffee cup.

'This way.' He gestured for them to follow. It wasn't the first time they'd been to his office, and while the cases he was working on might have changed, the piles of folders, books and notepads hadn't, and covered every surface. Four chairs were set up on the other side of the desk and they settled into them. 'Thank you for coming in this morning.'

'Any updates on Atkins?' JM asked, in her blunt way.

'He's gone to ground, but we got the warrant in the early hours and have searched his house and business premises. We found a handwritten copy of Monica's manuscript... and a bronze-plated television award. Monica donated it to the theatre years ago, and, according to Hazel, it was kept in the boardroom with the other archives. There's blood on it and it's consistent with both murders, though we're waiting for forensics to confirm it.'

Killed with her own award? Ginny was pleased she hadn't had breakfast: her stomach churned.

So, Atkins arranged for Monica to come back to Little Shaw. Was it to rekindle something? Or to prove how well he'd done? He clearly knew about the tunnels. Had he overheard her dictating the memoir and become enraged? Then what? He used the boardroom all the time and would have seen the award sitting there. Had he picked it up with the intention to use it, the same way he'd staged the scene by cutting the chandelier?

But that didn't explain Danny Ling's murder.

'Do you think Ling was blackmailing the killer?' Ginny asked, not sure she wanted the answer. Considering where they'd found him, hidden in the tunnels along with the Prissy costume, it was difficult to believe the murders weren't connected. But there was something so dreadful about the idea Atkins hadn't struck once, but twice.

'It makes sense,' JM agreed. 'Ling has footage that proves Atkins was wearing the goose costume, so he blackmailed him.'

'Atkins agrees to pay the price and lured Ling into the tunnel, where he killed him,' Tuppence finished with a shiver.

'But why leave him there?' Hen frowned. 'Isn't that risky?'

'It would be difficult to move a body with so much activity.

Perhaps he was waiting until the pantomime was over and things quieted down?' JM suggested.

'It's possible.' Wallace leaned back in his chair. 'Take me through how you found the passage again.'

Ginny exchanged a look with her friends. Then, she told him the story as concisely as possible about how they'd followed Atkins into the dressing room and then seen the tiny purple feather while they were in the tunnel. She studied Wallace's drained face. 'I feel you have more to tell us.'

He managed a faint smile. 'We're going through the handwritten manuscript, but there's several pages missing.'

'Could Monica have thrown it away? I've done that with my paintings before. I think they're great and the following day they look like they were done by a drunk squirrel,' Tuppence said.

'It's possible,' he agreed.

Ginny pinched the bridge of her nose, her thoughts scattering like dandelion clocks in the wind as she tried to grasp onto them. 'So, what happens now?'

Wallace got to his feet. 'Now we find Paul Atkins and bring him in. I'm grateful for your help *but...*' He paused, gaze slowly sweeping across the four of them, with a dramatic pause that would have had Hazel Holdsworth clapping in appreciation. 'This is where it stops. No more side quests.'

Ginny nodded, and her friends followed. Then they got to their feet, leaving the detective to his work.

MONDAY DECEMBER 22

Ginny ironed out the last crease from the crimson pantaloons and hung them up with the rest of the costumes she'd been working on. It had been hectic since the theatre had reopened for the second time in as many weeks. It was also the second time the board—minus Paul Atkins—had decided the show should go on.

In a way, she could see their point.

Everyone was on edge, and working on the pantomime helped distract them while the police continued to hunt for Atkins. The tanning salon owner hadn't been seen since Tuesday evening when Ginny and her friends had followed him through the dressing room door.

True to their word, they'd stayed out of it and had left the crushed velvet cape firmly covering Flora. Their updates had come via the newspapers and online outlets, but with a range of sightings that included everywhere from Alaska through to Estonia, the police weren't any closer to finding him.

She turned off the iron and peered out the window. Wallace's car wasn't there, and she supposed he was either at the station or following more leads. Part of her wished she could help, knowing the small velvet ring box in his jacket pocket was probably weighing down on him. But a promise was a promise.

The next ten minutes were spent loading up the costumes for the first dress rehearsal. They'd stayed there late last night and Ginny had decided to take everything home, determined to finish them.

Her phone rang as she climbed into the car. It was Nancy.

'Morning. Are you packed for tomorrow?' Ginny put on her seatbelt, even though she wouldn't drive while she was on the phone. Some habits were hard to break.

'Yes, and this is your last chance to join us. I checked the flights and there are seats available. Now that you're off the case, surely you can be spared.'

'Sorry, Nancy, but everyone's working hard to make up for lost time. I couldn't abandon them. I'm heading over now and they're doing a dress rehearsal this afternoon. It's been stressful but I think it'll be good for everyone here. It's keeping them focused.'

'You mean distracted from the fact a killer's still on the loose. There was another newspaper article saying that Paul Atkins had been spotted in Manchester. It's not safe there.'

'Wallace and his team have been working non-stop,' Ginny reminded her. 'I'm sure it won't be long until they find him.'

'In the meantime, you have a target on your back. You and your friends were the ones who cracked the case, so think about it. If he's evil enough to kill two people, who's to say he won't come after you?'

'I hope the fact that I live next door to a detective might put him off,' Ginny said in a light voice, and while it was true–she didn't feel in danger–the thought had crossed her mind that Atkins might be aware of who was behind the manhunt. Her heart thumped, and the car felt warm despite the weather.

'Hmmm,' Nancy said in a noncommittal tone as a high-pitched scream rang out from the other end of the phone. 'I'd better go. Ian's meant to be looking after the girls while Em finishes her Christmas shopping. But last time he did, I found them standing on the dining room table eating cereal straight out of the box.'

Ginny stifled a smile at the idea of the two young girls getting up to mischief, and she suspected that despite what Nancy said, Ian was taking good care of them. 'Go and rescue them and text me tomorrow from the airport. Don't forget we can video call on Christmas Day.'

'Video call?' Nancy muttered before sending her love and hanging up.

The drive to the theatre didn't take long and for once she managed to park close by. She carried everything into the costume room where a bleary-eyed Hen was hard at work.

'Oh, aren't you an angel? You must have stayed up all night.'

'Not at all.' Ginny took in the full rack of stunning costumes, including the new Prissy suit, with the extravagant headdress. It was clear which one of them had stayed up late. She hugged Hen. 'I hope you and Brandon went home.'

'Yes. I promise we did. Even though the tunnels are secured, I'm not ready to spend an entire night here.'

'There you both are.' Tuppence walked in, paint speckling

her face and her oversized shirt. 'We're moving the sets onto the stage. How are the costumes going?'

'Almost finished. I do hope it goes okay.' Hen wiped a hand across her tired eyes.

'Hope is *not* a strategy,' JM corrected, marching in with her clipboard, closely followed by Kaleb, who was holding an armful of balloons, which kept escaping. 'Ginny, I thought you were working today?'

'I am, but I'll be back for the rehearsal,' she promised.

'She was delivering the rest of the costumes.' Hen walked over to the rack and lovingly patted the sleeve of a pink raincoat.

'Marvellous.' JM smiled and gestured for Kaleb to deposit the balloons in the corner, then she lowered her voice. 'Any news from Wallace?'

'No.' Ginny shook her head, and her friends all sighed.

'I do hope they find him before Christmas. It will be so much more comfortable for everyone once he's caught,' Hen said.

'Then Wallace and Imogen will be able to come along to opening night,' Tuppence agreed then coughed as Kaleb rejoined them.

Ginny walked to the stage door. One of the sound technicians was based there, clutching at the sign-in sheet. She checked the time and wrote it down next to her name as Desiree appeared, buried in a long white puffer coat that reached her ankles. Her hair was concealed under a beanie, but her eyes sparkled.

'Oh, just the person I was looking for. Are you leaving?'

'I'm on my way to the library,' Ginny said. 'But if you're worried about the costumes being ready, they're almost finished. Hen needs to make some last-minute tweaks.'

'What a superstar she is. I bet Ants Mancini will be shaking in his boots once he gets back.'

'I'm not sure Hen wants the stress of doing it a second time. She'd much rather be in the background helping, than being the boss.'

'Which is what makes her so fabulous,' Desiree said then extracted a piece of paper from her pocket. 'By the way, I finally heard back from Jerry Niven.'

'You did?' Ginny swallowed. At best it had been a long shot meeting with the ex-chairperson of the playhouse's governance board, but now that the police had their main suspect and were hunting for him, it wasn't necessary.

'Yes, poor fella's been in hospital with a bad bug, but he's out now and would love a visitor. I told him how interested you were in the mirror.' Desiree held up the piece of paper then wrinkled her nose. 'I did explain you might not have time to go around... so don't feel obliged.'

Ginny winced.

She knew all too well how lonely some of the older residents of Little Shaw were. Not just from her recent investigations, but from how they turned up to the library at regular times each week, looking for books, newspapers and a sense of community. She mentally readjusted her timetable. She would visit Jerry Niven after work.

'Thank you. I'll look forward to meeting him.' She took the address and drove to the library to start the day.

THIRTY-ONE

MONDAY DECEMBER 22

Jerry Niven lived in a row of small bungalows, which looked out onto a green park with several benches dotted around. There was a huddle of older residents walking along a gentle path, and Ginny nodded and made her way through a grim concrete entrance to an inner court. She checked the door number and knocked. The dress rehearsal started in half an hour and while her friends didn't need her to be there, she wanted to show her support.

She also wanted to eat some dinner, since the library had been busy and she'd only managed half a sandwich.

'Who is it?' a deep booming voice rang out.

'It's Ginny Cole. I'm a friend of Desiree's,' she said, hoping the actress hadn't made a mistake about Jerry welcoming a visit.

'Ah. The librarian. Come in, come in,' the same voice boomed. 'It's open.'

She stepped in, wondering what Wallace would think of people leaving the front door unlocked. It wasn't the first time it had happened in her investigations and while she could appreciate how trusting people were... it also made her worry.

A short hall led through to a sitting room where a burly man with bright red cheeks and a shock of dark silver hair was sitting in an armchair. Despite his recent stay in hospital, he was dressed smartly in a tweed jacket with a duck egg blue silk cravat which perfectly matched his shirt. He was somewhere between seventy and ninety, though it was difficult to tell. A dangling pearl earring hung from one ear and his eyes twinkled.

Ginny had no problems believing that Jerry Niven had once been involved in the theatre. Next to his chair was a stack of photo albums, and she sensed they had been hauled out for her visit.

'Thank you so much for agreeing to see me,' she said, holding up a plate of biscuits. She'd made them last night and had detoured home, not wanting to turn up empty-handed. 'Would you like a cup of tea?'

He shook his head and nodded to a cut glass tumbler on the coffee table. 'Cocktail hour. Though Dr Brewster only lets me have one a day so I need to take it slowly.'

'Doctor knows best,' Ginny said, putting the biscuits down and taking a seat. She'd met the local doctor several times and he was sensible. And skilled, if he managed to convince his older patients to reduce their daytime drinking.

'So he keeps telling me.' Jerry shrugged then leaned forward, his voice conspiratorial. 'Desi said you're interested in *the* mirror.'

'I was surprised when she told me it was cursed,' Ginny admitted, not wanting to offend him. Especially since he had mentioned it in a newspaper article. 'Do you really believe that?'

He straightened up and burst out laughing. 'Of course not. It's a pile of nonsense, but I'm amused the story's still floating around. I suppose it means we did an excellent job.'

Her jaw loosened and she glanced at the glass of brandy at his side. Had he really stuck to his doctor's orders and only had one? It was hard to tell. She swallowed. 'I'm sorry, I don't follow. Didn't you speak to a journalist about it back in the eighties?'

He winked. 'I sure did. Which is why I know it's rubbish. I made it up, you see. It was a ham.'

A ham? Why was she even surprised? Everything about this case had been over the top and dramatic. It made sense that would include a forty-year-old superstition about a cursed mirror.

'But why?'

'Because we needed to sell tickets. We were doing *The Picture of Dorian Gray* and thought it would be a good way to drum up some interest.'

A publicity stunt? It wasn't difficult to believe. Ginny had often seen how gossip had changed and grown as it was passed around. And that was clearly what had happened.

'But what about Meg Madison? In the newspaper article you were quoted as saying she died.'

'Well, in a way she did. She moved to London, you see. Left us halfway through rehearsal without so much as a word. She *became* dead to us. Though, between you and me, I never expected the newspaper to run the story. Perhaps I should have, though, considering the journalist was drunk when we met.'

'So, none of it was true?'

'Nope. Not a word.' He slapped his leg and grinned. 'But it did mean the show sold out and we charged extra for backstage tours as well. You wouldn't believe the number of people who wanted to stare into the cursed mirror. There's nowt so queer as folk.'

'It would seem so,' Ginny agreed. 'Were you surprised to hear about the secret tunnels?'

'I was aware of them, but hadn't realised not everyone else was. Not until I read it in the newspapers,' he admitted with a sigh. 'Maybe if I wasn't in hospital at the time I would've thought to go forward to the police and tell them about them.'

'You weren't to know,' Ginny assured him.

'Kind of you to say so. It's a terrible business about Paul Aitkens.'

'Did you know they were having an affair back then?'

Jerry shook his head. 'We all thought she'd been sleeping

with Alan, but I'm not really surprised... back then everyone was... a bit randy.'

'I see.' Ginny nodded, not sure what else to say.

'But let's try and not think about that.' Jerry reached for one of the photo albums next to his chair. 'Here, would you like to see some of the behind-the-scenes snaps?'

Ginny checked the time. She was due to leave if she wanted to catch the start of the rehearsal, but she didn't have the heart to cut short her visit. 'That would be lovely.'

She took the album and flicked through it, as Jerry gave her a commentary on who everyone was. Now she knew what Paul Atkins and Kyle Chambers looked like back then, she found them in several of the snaps, as well as Alan Holdsworth. There were also numerous photographs of a tall man with dark brown hair swept across his brow and a movie-star smile. He was older than the rest of the cast, possibly in his early forties. She frowned, turning the photograph over to look for a name. Why was he familiar?

'That's Garth Shepard,' Jerry said.

'Oh.' Ginny blinked and peered closer, trying to search for features, but like with Paul Atkins, she couldn't see much of the man the farmer had become.

'I know. It's hard to pick but back in the day the ladies—and the fellas—used to be mad on him. Called him the Errol Flynn of Farming. These days he's a bit of a recluse. Look, here's one of us together.' Jerry pointed to a snap where Garth and a younger Jerry were talking about something in the centre of the stage. 'Youth is wasted on the young.' He drained his glass and closed his eyes.

Ginny quickly shut the photo album and got to her feet. She had stayed too long.

'I'd better get going, but thank you so much for letting me visit and answering my questions.'

'I should be thanking you. It's nice having a trip down memory lane.' He got to his feet and shook her hand. Then he chuckled. 'Sorry for scaring everyone with the nonsense about the mirror. I never expected it to still be doing the rounds.'

'I'll do my best to let people know the truth,' Ginny assured him, then frowned as one last question occurred to her. 'Is there a reason Monica would have requested the mirror to be moved to her dressing room? Do you think she knew about the tunnel?'

His lips twitched. 'Far be it from me to speak for her, but if I had to guess I'd say it was to hide her drugs.'

'What?' Ginny's jaw went slack. There had never been any mention of Monica having a drug problem. Her shock must have shown on her face.

Jerry held up his hands. 'Well, maybe not drugs. But if she had something to hide, the mirror is the place to put it. There's a secret compartment in the back of it in the corner. There's a small button that you need to push. We used to stash our weed in there. That's why I said everyone looked better when they looked into it... but that it came at a price. Addiction is a nasty thing.'

A hidden compartment?

Ginny thought of the missing page of Monica's memoir. Was it possible that's where it was?

Her heart hammered as she made her farewells and headed to the theatre.

THIRTY-TWO

MONDAY DECEMBER 22

Ginny signed the attendance sheet and hurried inside the theatre, her breath burning in her throat. She'd toyed with calling Wallace, but what was there to tell? That there was a secret compartment in the mirror? She already knew what he thought of the curse. Besides, even if Monica had hidden the missing pages of the memoir, it didn't mean the case would change. If anything, it might go further to prove that Atkins and Monica had an affair.

It was quiet as she made her way through to the props room, where she supposed Ted had taken the mirror. Her friends would be watching the dress rehearsal, which is where she should be.

'And I will be. As soon as I've looked at the mirror. And just because no one is around, doesn't mean I should be talking to myself,' She hurried down the winding corridor. The props room was dark and she fumbled for a light switch. The scenery was gone, as were all the volunteers.

'Hello?' Ginny called out, footsteps echoing as she made her way through the large workshop. Sawdust covered the floor and tools were lying deserted on the benches. It was clear the team had been working hard until the last minute. She frowned and peered around. Where would Ted have put the mirror? Was it possible he'd taken it back to Wallace's house to work on it?

Should she call him?

But before she could retrieve her phone, she spied a hint of a gold frame leaning against the wall. Ah. There it was. She crossed the room and angled the mirror forward. Jerry said there was a button in one corner, though it was impossible to know which way the mirror was meant to hang. She ran her hand along the back and was rewarded as her fingers brushed over a raised lump.

With a click, it loosened and Ginny peered into a narrow compartment. Inside, there were several pieces of paper and a tarnished gold-plated necklace. The chain was rough against her palm as she held it up in the air. There was a charm attached to it, in the shape of a K.

Ginny's skin prickled as she studied the cheap imitation necklace. She'd seen it before, around the neck of Trish Shepard. A gift from the man who had walked out on her and Kaleb.

Kyle liked to think he was a ladies' man and was full of one-liners and cheesy gifts.

Except it didn't mean Monica had put it there.

What if it belonged to someone else? Adrenaline fizzed through her veins as she put the chain down and smoothed out the first page and studied the neat writing.

> *Part of telling my story was to get across how intrusive the press can be. The price of fame is something I've always struggled with. I caught the documentary maker going through my rubbish bin, looking for any secrets I might've thrown away. But he'll have to wake up a lot earlier in the day to get the better of me. No one will know the truth until I decide they can...*

A lump formed in her throat. It was clearly Monica's memoir. Or, in this case, a stream of consciousness about controlling the narrative and being the mistress of her own destiny.

The next page was about an incident in a night club in New York when Monica had been there in the early noughties. Putting it aside, Ginny focused on the third page.

There was only one time I thought I was in love. That was thirty years ago when I was in a regional pantomime and where I met Garth.

Oh. Ginny let out a strangled gasp. Garth Shepard? She thought of the photograph Jerry had shown her. Garth was handsome but he must have been at least forty, and Monica had only been twenty-five with a history of dating young men. Was it possible? But why the necklace from Kyle Chambers?

She continued reading.

It was the first time I'd experienced an affair while on set and suddenly I understood why so many actors succumbed to the allure. It was mind-blowing, and when I found out I was pregnant... I knew I would keep it. Garth was so happy, and despite our differences, so was I.

I know. I know. On paper it made no sense. Before then I'd only dated men my own age, or younger, because Stuart thought it would be good for my image. And even if I had dated someone older, I could never imagine them being a gruff widowed farmer from the middle of nowhere... who had a twenty-year-old daughter into the bargain.

Yet... when he looked at me with those deep blue eyes and charming smile I felt like I was home.

Stuart was furious, and I couldn't blame him, but for once I refused to listen. Besides, it wasn't like my career was doing anything. The best panto he could get me was Little Shaw, and with no promise of anything more than the occasional TV episode, I really started to believe this was my future.

A farmer's wife. A mother. A private life.

But nature had other ideas and I miscarried two weeks later... then I got the call for First Kiss and it was like waking up from a fever dream. Me? Living in the country surrounded by sheep? What a fool I'd been, so I broke it off.

Garth was devastated and begged me to change my mind. I didn't need to give up my career. We could make it work.

It was lies, of course. We both knew it, and so I took the coward's way out. I can see that now, but at the time the fog of pain from the miscarriage, and the grief of losing the child—and Garth—made it easier to do. It was like nothing mattered anymore. The universe was clearly showing me that happiness wasn't a path open for me. So, what did it matter?

I had an affair with Garth's farmhand. To be clear, it was one relationship that was never going to last. Kyle Chambers was a gorgeous, but self-centred narcissist. But he was the distraction I needed and when he followed me to London, I let the affair continue until it ran its course. We stayed in touch for a couple of years. He told me his ex-girlfriend also had a child, but he never went back to Little Shaw to see them. I often thought of Garth's poor daughter Kyle had abandoned, and the child he left behind. Then I spoke with Kaleb. So like his father, but without any of the conceit. Is he what my own child would have been like? Sweet, kind, caring?

As for Garth... In thirty years, I've never met anyone else who has touched my heart. Do I regret the decision I made? Most days I try not to think about it, because if I do, the pain is too much. Which is why I agreed to return to Little Shaw. Not to relaunch my career, but to relaunch my life. And the first step is to talk with Garth...

The writing stopped and Ginny dropped her hand to her side as she pieced everything together. It was Garth Shepard who Monica had an affair with and fallen pregnant to. But when she lost the baby and was offered the job of a lifetime, she'd had an affair with Kyle, which perhaps resulted in him abandoning Trish and Kaleb. Had he loved Monica? Or was he simply hoping to use her connections to make it big in show business?

It was a lot to take in. A wave of sadness went through her.

Poor Trish and Kaleb. And how had Garth handled the news? Was that what turned him into a recluse who spent most of his time on the farm?

Oh no.

Ginny stiffened. If both Garth and Kyle had had affairs with Monica, then why had Paul Atkins killed her? The answer was that he hadn't. Horror caught in her throat as the truth slammed into her chest.

Wallace was looking for the wrong person. Kyle Chambers was long dead, but his father-in-law, Garth Shepard, was very much alive. He was the right height, but was he capable of killing a person? Two people?

The air stilled and Ginny's fingers shook as she fumbled for her phone. Yet, before she could make a call, a rough hand grabbed her shoulder and her mouth and nose were covered with a rag.

The faint stench of chemicals filled her nostrils and the room spun.

No.

She tried to scream but it tore at her throat as everything blurred and the world went dark.

THIRTY-THREE

MONDAY DECEMBER 22

Everything hurt. Ginny's mouth was dry and the bitter taste of medicine filled her mouth as she forced her eyelids open. It was dark, but small shafts of light came in and out of focus. Where was she? What had happened? Panic thrummed through her and she tried to move, but her arms wouldn't work. Her head spun and she leaned back, catching her breath.

'You're tied to a chair,' the familiar voice of Paul Atkins said. 'We both are.'

A chair? Ginny forced open her eyes. The spinning receded and she turned to face Paul. His tan was faded and his white shirt was covered with dirt and grime. He was next to her, feet and hands bound with zip ties. She peered down to discover she was also bound up. It was why she couldn't move.

Paul's wrists were chafed and red, as if he had been trying to break free. Ginny, who had been about to try the same thing, resisted the urge, knowing that getting infected skin wouldn't help the situation. Her heart thundered in her ears as the room seemed to shrink in on itself.

'How long have I been here?' she croaked.

'Not sure. Maybe a couple of hours.'

Two hours? Was the dress rehearsal finished? Would her

friends be looking for her? She hoped so. But how would they know where to look? Unless she had dropped the necklace and the pages of manuscript on the floor. Because as soon as they saw Garth's name, they would know where to find her.

Her hope was extinguished as she spotted them near the chair leg. Had they been left there on purpose to mock her?

Panic surged but Ginny pushed it back down inside her and surveyed the space instead. Damp straw lined the floor and the walls were made of dull grey stone. A musky scent of wet wool filled the air, making her think of the sheep she'd seen grazing at Holly Farm.

'Paul, tell me everything you know,' she said, as steadily as she could.

'I wish I could. Whoever kidnapped me never speaks and always wears a mask. I have no idea what's going on. They bring in food and water... but I think something is in it because I keep passing out,' he said, none of the usual charisma in his voice. He sounded scared and tired.

She couldn't blame him. How long had he been here? Was it since he'd gone missing last Tuesday evening? Almost a week.

'We're at Holly Farm.'

'Holly Farm?' Paul spluttered. 'Why the hell would we be there? Are you saying Kaleb's behind this?'

'Not Kaleb... his grandfather.'

'That's impossible. I've known Garth my whole life. He would never hurt me. Why would he? And I've been here for days... If he was behind it, I would know,' Paul spluttered, though as he looked around the filthy shed, some of the confidence seemed to falter.

Ginny swallowed, guilt rising in her chest.

Was it her and her friends' fault that Paul had been kidnapped? After all, if they hadn't followed him into the tunnels and discovered Danny Ling's dead body, he might not have been considered a suspect. What happened then? Did

Garth decide to use their discovery to his advantage and plant evidence, pointing the finger at Paul?

Or did he already blame Paul for inviting Monica back to Little Shaw?

Either way, he kidnapped him to stop Paul denying the story, and for whatever reason, had kept him alive. Thank goodness. Then she stiffened. It didn't explain what Paul had been doing in the tunnel.

'Why were you using the secret passage from Monica's dressing room?'

'Because it let me get a better parking spot. Every time we have a production it's a nightmare to park close by. And I'd just had my hair cut. I didn't want to get it wet.'

Ginny's jaw slackened. So it really had been a case of Paul being in the wrong place at the very wrong time. And all for a parking spot. The guilt hammering in her chest increased.

This was her fault. By following Paul and assuming he was the killer, he had spent almost a week tied to a chair, in fear of his life. She opened her mouth but before any words could come out, the door creaked open and a masked figure walked in.

They were tall, at least six foot and were holding a tray with two bowls of food and two spoons.

Garth Sheperd.

Ginny's pulse pounded and fear caught in her throat. So it was true.

Without speaking, Garth put it down and walked slowly over to them. He withdrew a penknife and cut the ties before returning with the bowls. Paul stiffened as he seemed to take in the large figure, and Ginny could almost see the pieces of information shift in Paul's mind as he accepted what she'd told him.

'Garth, what the hell are you doing? You have to let me go.' Paul reached for the bowl, but his gaze was fixed on the masked man.

Ginny winced, noticing he didn't say 'let *us* go.'

There was no reply, and Ginny stared at her own bowl. Her

mouth was thick with whatever drug he had used to knock her out and her throat ached. She needed to think.

'Please, could I have some water?' she managed to say, her pulse thundering. Garth grunted and produced a water bottle from the pocket of his coat. He threw it at her and she gratefully uncapped it. 'Thank you.'

'Garth, I'm serious, man. You've got the wrong person. If this is about Monica, I had nothing to do with it.'

'He knows that.' Ginny took a long drink, and it helped push down her rising panic. 'Because he's the one who killed her.'

'What?' Paul choked. 'Of course he didn't. Why would he?'

'Because thirty years ago they had an affair and he wanted to marry her,' Ginny said. Garth froze, his hand clenching and unclenching at the memory. It sent a fresh wave of fear through her, but she had to get him talking. 'She was pregnant with his child.'

'Bullshit,' Paul spluttered. 'Why, he's almost old enough to have been her father.'

'Shut your mouth,' Garth suddenly spoke, his voice tight with fury.

'It's true,' Ginny pressed. 'But then Monica had a miscarriage and got offered the part in *First Kiss*, and she wanted out. I believe she was in a lot of emotional turmoil and felt she had no option but to break it off in a way that Garth would accept. So, she had an affair with Kyle Chambers to make Garth see that it was over between them.'

'I said, shut it,' Garth growled. Despite the mask, his anger was palpable and Ginny shuddered.

'Kyle Chambers?' Paul twisted to face Ginny. 'That doesn't make any sense. He was hooking up with Trish and she was pregnant with Kaleb. Then he buggered off and broke her heart.'

'He didn't just leave. He followed Monica to London,' Ginny continued as Garth began to stride around the shed. 'It was her way of making sure Garth knew the affair was over.'

'Enough.' Garth came to a halt and dragged the mask from

his face. His eyes flashed with rage and his jaw was set in a tight line. 'Stop saying her name. She got what was coming to her.'

'You killed her because she slept with Kyle thirty years ago?' Paul demanded. 'That's a long time to hold a grudge.'

The silence smothered the room until Garth spun back around. 'A grudge? You think this was a grudge? I was protecting the lad. She was trying to do the same to Kaleb that she did to Kyle. That two-bit hussy lured him into her dressing room and used her honeyed words. Asking him about acting and moving to London. Would've broken my girl's heart all over again.'

No.

Ginny twisted in her chair and peered down at the crumpled pages on the ground and the discarded necklace. The one that had been hidden in the mirror. Had Garth read them and simply not believed her?

'Monica wasn't trying to seduce Kaleb. She was thinking of the miscarriage she'd had and wondering what it would have been like if her own baby had lived.'

'Lies. She was seducing him. I heard it.' Garth's voice rose.

Despite his fury, Ginny was filled with sympathy at how it had played out, and how differently things might have been for Monica and for Garth. 'You were in the tunnels? Why? Was it to spy on Monica and Kaleb?'

He stiffened, as if he'd been slapped. 'I was in there to listen to her. She was dictating her memoir. I wanted to know what she was going to say about me... *then* I heard Kaleb's voice and I knew she hadn't changed. She was going to seduce the son... just like she'd seduced the father.'

Ginny's sympathy turned to sorrow.

It was easy to understand that if he took Monica's affair with Kyle at face value. But he must've known she was grieving from the miscarriage and the loss of life. Or had Monica fooled him with her acting? It was dreadful to think what a mess it had become. And all from a misunderstanding.

'Is that why you took the manuscript after you killed her? To see if she mentioned you?'

Silence flooded the space and she half-expected Garth to stalk towards the door, but finally he spoke. 'It was private. She should never have talked about me like that.'

'Except when you opened it up, you discovered part of it was missing.' Ginny glanced down at the scattered pages, recalling the pain that came through from Monica's confession. 'Did you read what she said?'

'It's all lies. I didn't believe a word of it.'

'Not even that she regretted what she did? That she was coming back to see you? To explore a future? It's all right there. That she was grieving for the loss of a child? For the life that she thought she couldn't have?'

Garth stopped his frenetic pacing. Pain rippled across his face as he stared at the pages. He moved forward but then stopped himself, as if not able to face the truth of what Ginny had told him.

He swung away. 'I have no regrets. I've done my research. Looked her up on the computer and spoke to people who knew her. It proved she hadn't changed. Self-centred, shallow, and full of crap.'

'You researched her?' Ginny frowned, thinking of all the tokenistic articles they'd read that only focused on Monica's appearance rather than who she was as a person. And of all the trolls who lived on the message boards spreading vile. 'You shouldn't believe everything you read online.'

'Would you stop pissing him off?' Paul hissed, but Ginny ignored him. If Garth left the shed, there was no saying when he might come back. She needed to keep him talking.

'So, you killed her, but you didn't know that Danny Ling had camera footage. Did he recognise you and try to blackmail you?' she guessed.

'Scumbag. He'd caught me using the tunnel the day before and pieced it together. Said if I gave him one hundred grand he'd lose the footage. Do you think I'd be working seven days a week if I had that kind of money?' Garth spun back, face turning red with rage. 'Plus, he was the one to tell our lad to go visit that harlot woman.'

'I have money,' Paul piped up. 'You could let me go and I'll pay you. Won't say a word about any of this. You can trust me. My word is my bond.'

Garth ignored him and glared at Ginny. She pressed herself back in the chair. His fury was so visceral that her skin crawled. 'You should've stayed out of it. I did the world a favour by killing her.'

'Why go to so much trouble of using the award and cutting the chandelier cord?'

His face twisted. '*That* part was a grudge... I wanted her to know the price of her precious fame.'

'How did you manage it?' Ginny pushed. 'Did you convince Trish and Kaleb to lie for you? Pretend you were together?'

'It wasn't a lie. We went to the pub for dinner and I said that I needed to go make a bet on the horses. It didn't take long and then I was back before they knew it.'

'Is that why you felt safe to wear Kaleb's goose costume?' Ginny asked. It had been the one thing niggling her. If Garth really had wanted to protect Kaleb, why make him a suspect in a murder investigation? 'Because you thought he had an alibi?'

Garth gave her a look of loathing. 'That was an accident. The lad had told me all about his costume and there was no mention of purple feathers. Or a face mask.'

'You didn't know?' Ginny sucked in a breath. It was possible he was telling the truth. Hen had decided at the last minute to make a new Prissy costume, so perhaps she hadn't told Kaleb about the change of plan?

'Of course I didn't know. You think I would've put the boy in harm's way? Still, once he told me about his new costume, and I realised my mistake, I figured it would be okay. No copper in their right mind would think Kaleb murdered anyone. He's a soft lad. Wouldn't hurt a fly.'

'And what about me?' Paul suddenly spoke up. 'Glad to hear you're so worried about Kaleb, but what the hell did I ever do to you?'

'Nothing personal,' Garth shrugged. 'As soon as I heard the police were looking for you as a suspect, it became clear what I needed to do.'

'So you kidnapped me?'

'And he planted the memoir and the murder weapon at your house,' Ginny added.

Garth didn't deny it as he glared at them. 'The pair of you need to shut the hell up. Monica Larkwell deserved to—'

Garth was cut off by a blast of cold air as the door swung open, revealing Trish standing on the threshold. Her face was pale and the gold necklace was no longer around her neck. Kaleb stood next to her, clad in the brand-new orange Prissy suit, the headdress carefully tucked under one arm.

'Dad? What's going on?' Trish said, her voice barely above a whisper.

'Grandad, why are they tied up?' Kaleb frowned, confusion dancing across his handsome face.

A vein popped in Garth's neck as he stared at his daughter and grandson. He shook his head and pointed to the door. 'You shouldn't be here. I have this under control.'

'Under control?' A sob broke in Trish's throat as she stared at Ginny and Paul. 'I didn't believe them when they said you were holding people up here. I told them it wasn't true.'

'Who said that?' Garth's voice was Arctic as he marched to the door, fury flashing in his eyes.

'The people staying at the cottage. They thought they saw you carry a body in here... but I told them it would've been the goat—' Trish broke off, her gaze fixed on Ginny and Paul.

'Is Betty okay?' Kaleb frantically looked around the shed.

'Betty's fine, lad. She's in the field. Go and see for yourself.'

'No... don't go anywhere,' Paul suddenly yelled, trying to stand from the chair, his feet still tied. 'He killed Monica Larkwell and Danny Ling and now he's trying to kill me. Kaleb, you need to help.'

'Mum, what's he talking about?' Kaleb's eyes filled with confusion as a police siren rang out. Ginny's chest expanded as she slumped back in the chair.

'It's okay,' Trish said in a firm voice, taking her son's hand. 'Granddad was right. You should go check on Betty. But first put your headdress back in the car. I'll be there soon, okay?'

Kaleb looked around, uncertainly, then disappeared outside. Trish swallowed and turned to her father, who was a rigid statue. 'I should have guessed sooner... when you left the pub that night. But I tried to tell myself it was a coincidence. Then I finally got the computer technician in and the reason it was so slow was because of a virus that came from one of the websites you'd been visiting. All about Monica Larkwell. The guy showed me your search history. Ever since it was announced she was coming back to Little Shaw, you've been on the computer reading about her.'

'I did it for you. And the boy,' he said, but the anger had left his face and his shoulders lowered.

'I know you did. But you should've left it. Monica and Kyle weren't worth it,' she said as Wallace, Anita Singh and Liam Bent strode in.

Wallace scanned the room before barking out orders. From there it was a blur as someone cut the ties around Ginny's ankles and led her outside to where an ambulance was waiting.

'I'm fine,' Ginny croaked, throat raw from the medicine. 'They need to look after Paul. He's been held here for days.'

'Don't worry about Atkins, he's in good hands.' Wallace joined her. His voice was tight, and he held an evidence bag containing the tarnished gold necklace and the missing pages of Monica's memoir.

'Garth was in the tunnel and overheard Monica speaking to Kaleb. He knew about Kyle's affair with her, and thought she was trying to lure Kaleb away, too. History repeating itself. He blamed her for Kyle leaving Trish and Kaleb, you see. And we were right about Ling trying to blackmail him,' Ginny explained.

'So it seems.' He gave her a curt nod while behind him, Anita led a handcuffed Garth Shepard into the police vehicle.

'How did you know where I was? Was it Trish?'

'And Ted. He got sick of watching the dress rehearsal and went back to the props room to do some work with Shepard. But there was no sign of him, and apparently the old man is now a sniffer dog because he thought he could smell your perfume. Neither you or Shepard had signed out, and there were signs the tunnel had been used again. Something wasn't right. We were on our way out here when we got Trish's phone call.'

'Oh.' Ginny swallowed, a lump forming in her throat. So Trish had called them before she and Kaleb had come up to the shed. 'But I don't—'

'No more questions until you've been fully cleared by the paramedics.' He shook his head. 'And please don't leave your house until I've come to collect a statement. Is that understood?'

'Absolutely,' Ginny managed to say before succumbing to the ministrations of the paramedics.

THIRTY-FOUR

FRIDAY DECEMBER 26

'I don't know about you lot... but I could use a drink. So, it's good night from me,' Desiree said, her voice crystal clear as it rang out through the theatre. The spotlight zoomed in and her hooped dress shimmered as she lowered down into a curtsey. Then, she took a slow step forward before going back on her heel. Her grin widened and she repeated the action several times then swayed from side to side, her arms swinging in a bouncing dance movement, which Ginny now knew was the griddy.

Desiree repeated the dance three times, much to the delight of the ecstatic audience who were on their feet clapping and hollering, phones high in the air to record it.

Desiree gave a final curtsey and the spotlight bounced over to Cleo.

'As Queen of Gooseland, I'm afraid that I must also take my leave of you,' Cleo announced, her silver dress magnificent with frothing lace at the neckline and sleeves.

As the applause thundered on, Cleo took a step forward, as if to replicate the dance move, but then she stopped and waggled her finger at the audience, eyebrow raised. This earned another round of laughter. Cleo gave a regal twist of her wrist to acknowledge the applause then nodded to the lighting crew to signal that she was satisfied.

The spotlight swung to Kaleb, who stood to attention and saluted, orange feathers bouncing around him. His handsome face was bright with excitement, despite his personal sadness. 'That's my cue to say goodbye, but if you've had fun here tonight, don't forget to tell your friends to come along. We're here for two weeks.'

'Yeah, and next time we'll remember our lines,' Bert and Reggie chorused together from under their cactus costumes, as the heavy curtains finally fell across the stage. The audience erupted into another round of applause before slowly making their way to the exit.

Ginny continued to clap but didn't attempt to move. Her friends were backstage. It was JM's job to make sure the entire thing had run smoothly, while Hen had hovered over the actors with her needle and thread at the ready, with Tuppence helping Ted Wallace move the scenery on and off. From tomorrow night, Ginny would be back there, too, but she'd wanted to sit in the audience for the opening night, since she had some unexpected guests.

Smiling, she turned to the tall woman in the neighbouring seat. She had warm brown eyes and a smile that she shared with her late brother, Eric.

'Nancy, what do you think? Did you like it?' Ginny asked.

Her sister-in-law, who was tapping her foot, even though the music no longer played, broke into a smile. 'It was utterly brilliant. And who was I to question the aubergines? The whole story would've fallen apart without them.'

'It was excellent.' Nancy's husband leaned across his wife. 'Just what we needed to make us forget our trip was cancelled.'

'Well... I know it's not the Northern Lights,' Ginny said. 'But everyone worked very hard on it.'

'It was fantastic, Aunty Gin. And very sweet that they did a tribute to Monica Larkwell in the middle,' Nancy and Ian's daughter, Emily, said from Ginny's other side. Next to her was her husband, along with their two young daughters who were still clapping and giggling over the performance. 'What do you reckon, Mum? Better than trying to sludge through frozen fields of mud?'

'I wouldn't go that far.' Nancy gave her daughter a stern look then sighed. 'I'm hopeful we can go there next year. But I have to admit that coming to Little Shaw for Christmas has been rather lovely.'

'And it's not over yet.' Ginny got to her feet as her friends appeared from the wings. 'There's a big cast and crew party and there's a few people I'd like you to meet.'

'Will Connor and Iris be there?' one of Emily's young daughters asked.

'And Kaleb?' the second demanded. 'He promised to read more stories to us and I want to pat the goose feathers.'

'They'll be there.' Ginny grinned and led them through to the foyer where the party was being held.

Yesterday, she and her friends had hosted a Christmas Day dinner at JM's lovely house on the banks of the canal, and not only had Nancy and her family joined them, but so had Connor, Iris, Desiree, Slim, and perhaps the biggest surprise, Trish and Kaleb. There had been an air of solemnity to the day because of what had happened, but there was also some joy, thanks to Kaleb's love of Christmas and Em's two young daughters who had been in raptures over the snow that had fallen.

And today had been about preparing for opening night.

Ginny let out a breath and looked around.

Some of the actors were in the mezzanine bar, clutching at champagne flutes. Nancy and Ian headed up there while Emily and her husband were half-dragged by their daughters to where Connor and Iris were standing. Ginny caught his eye and gave him an apologetic smile, but he just grinned and put an arm around Iris, as they both talked to the excited girls.

Ginny was about to join them when Wallace appeared next to her, holding a tray of drinks. He was followed by his father and Imogen, her lovely red hair hanging down her shoulders.

'I was hoping to catch you,' Wallace said as Imogen plucked a champagne flute from the tray and handed it to Ginny. As she did, a diamond glittered on her ring finger.

'Oh.' Ginny gasped and took the drink. 'James, you proposed.'

'He did indeed.' Imogen handed a glass to Ted then kissed Wallace's cheek. 'I had no idea he would, but let's say it's a Christmas I'll never forget.'

'I'm so happy for you both.' Ginny held up her drink and they toasted before Imogen slipped a hand onto Ted's arm.

'I can see my parents over there, they've only just arrived. Ted, let me introduce you. And James, come over once you've finished talking to Ginny.'

'Will do.' Wallace gave his fiancée a loving smile then turned his attention back to Ginny, who was delighted to see him soften from his usual terse expression at the sight of the woman he loved. 'I wanted to say thank you for the help.'

'Nonsense, we didn't do much at all. But tell me, how is the case going?'

'It's with the Crown Prosecution Service now, so it's off my desk,' he said, though his jaw had tightened again. Did he find it as disturbing as she did, that Garth and Monica's story might have ended so differently, if other choices had been made? 'I heard Trish and Kaleb spent Christmas with you all.'

Ginny nodded. 'They had lunch with us and then went over to Suzette and Ian's house. Poor Trish is still shell-shocked.'

'It's to be expected. Though I suppose it's better than her finding out further down the line.' Wallace raked a hand through his short hair and finished his drink. 'I'd better go save the old man from Imogen's parents. They *are* wonderful... but they're huggers.'

Ginny's lips twitched as she peered over to where Ted was

pressed against a wall, surrounded by Imogen's good-natured parents. She grinned and made her way to where her friends were keeping Nancy and Ian entertained. Her heart expanded to know that her old world and her new world had finally come together. It helped lessen the pain of Eric's death and she hoped it boded well for the new year.

A LETTER FROM THE AUTHOR

Thank you for reading *The Widows' Guide to Foul Play,* and to all the readers who continue to enjoy Ginny, Hen, Tuppence and JM as they navigate their lives in Little Shaw, balancing friendship, ageing and a healthy dose of murder. I hadn't intended to write a story set in the theatre but as soon as I came up with the title, I knew what was required—which was of course a giant purple goose costume. And from there the plot began to take shape. If you want to join other readers in hearing all about my new releases and bonus content, you can sign up for my newsletter.

www.stormpublishing.co/amanda-ashby

If you enjoyed this book and could spare a few moments to leave a review that would be hugely appreciated. Even a short review can make all the difference in encouraging a reader to discover my books for the first time. Thank you so much.

www.amandaashby.com

ACKNOWLEDGMENTS

I'm grateful to my family and friends who continue to put up with vague looks, unbrushed hair and random conversations about how to kill people. Clearly, I'm a delight to be around, but all the same I feel I should say thank you!

A big shout out to Emily Gowers for continuing to support Ginny and Co. the way you do. I'm so lucky! And to Anna McKerrow for going the extra mile—I'm so grateful for all the care and attention you have put into this story. I'll definitely be buying the next round at The Lost Goat.

Thank you to Oliver Rhodes, Kathryn Taussig, Alexandra Begley, Amanda Raybould, Emily Courdelle, Versha Jones, Dushi Horti, Amanda Rutter and the entire Storm team for all their hard work, and to Audio Factory Productions and Diana Croft for the wonderful narration that brings Ginny and her friends to life.

Finally, thanks to everyone who has ever read any of my books and enjoyed them. It means so much.

www.ingramcontent.com/pod-product-compliance
Lightning Source LLC
LaVergne TN
LVHW031336150826
845673LV00012B/2916

* 9 7 8 1 8 3 7 0 0 4 4 6 1 *